SUCK·I·NESS [SUHK-EE-NIS]
–noun

WATCHING your parents pay exorbitant real estate prices so that you can live in a school district with deaf programs

LEARNING that educational budget cuts include shutting down said deaf programs at your high school

DISCOVERING that your equally deaf BFF Marissa's parents have chosen to protest the decision by moving to San Francisco

LISTENING to your recently laid-off father complain about the aforementioned exorbitant real estate prices, and hypocritically criticizing his daughter for moping about Marissa leaving, when he's constantly moping about losing his job

REALIZING you're completely alone . . . even in a crowd

OTHER BOOKS YOU MAY ENJOY

Blindsided	Priscilla Cummings
Fat Kid Rules the World	K. L. Going
Guitar Girl	Sarra Manning
Jerk, California	Jonathan Friesen
Just Listen	Sarah Dessen
Looking for Alaska	John Green
My Most Excellent Year	Steve Kluger
Somebody Everybody Listens To	Suzanne Supplee
The Vast Fields of Ordinary	Nick Burd
Will Grayson, Will Grayson	John Green and David Levithan

FIVE FLAVORS OF

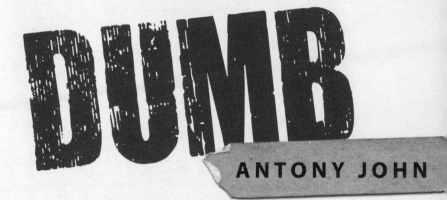

DUMB

ANTONY JOHN

speak

An Imprint of Penguin Group (USA) Inc.

SPEAK
Published by the Penguin Group
Penguin Group (USA) Inc., 345 Hudson Street, New York, New York 10014, U.S.A.
Penguin Group (Canada), 90 Eglinton Avenue East, Suite 700, Toronto, Ontario, Canada M4P 2Y3
(a division of Pearson Penguin Canada Inc.)
Penguin Books Ltd, 80 Strand, London WC2R 0RL, England
Penguin Ireland, 25 St Stephen's Green, Dublin 2, Ireland (a division of Penguin Books Ltd)
Penguin Group (Australia), 250 Camberwell Road, Camberwell, Victoria 3124, Australia
(a division of Pearson Australia Group Pty Ltd)
Penguin Books India Pvt Ltd, 11 Community Centre, Panchsheel Park, New Delhi - 110 017, India
Penguin Group (NZ), 67 Apollo Drive, Rosedale, Auckland 0632, New Zealand
(a division of Pearson New Zealand Ltd)
Penguin Books (South Africa) (Pty) Ltd, 24 Sturdee Avenue,
Rosebank, Johannesburg 2196, South Africa

Registered Offices: Penguin Books Ltd, 80 Strand, London WC2R 0RL, England

First published in the United States of America by Dial Books,
an imprint of Penguin Group (USA) Inc., 2010

Published by Speak, an imprint of Penguin Group (USA) Inc., 2011

5 7 9 10 8 6 4

THE LIBRARY OF CONGRESS HAS CATALOGED THE DIAL BOOKS EDITION AS FOLLOWS:
John, Antony.
Five flavors of Dumb / Antony John.
p.   cm.
Summary: Eighteen-year-old Piper becomes the manager for her classmates' popular rock band,
called Dumb, giving her the chance to prove her capabilities to her parents and others,
if only she can get the band members to get along.
ISBN: 978-0-8037-3433-3 (hc)
[1. Rock groups—Fiction. 2. Bands (Music)—Fiction. 3. Deaf—Fiction.
4. People with disabilities—Fiction. 5. Family life—Washington (State)—Fiction.
6. High schools—Fiction. 7. Schools—Fiction. 8. Seattle (Wash.)—Fiction.]
I. Title
PZ7.J6216Fiv 2010
[Fic]—dc22 2009044449

Speak ISBN 978-0-14-241943-4

Book design by Jasmin Rubero
Text set in Minion

Printed in the United States of America

To MY PARENTS, ROY AND ANGELA JOHN,
WHO DIDN'T MISS A BEAT WHEN
I SAID I WANTED TO BE A MUSICIAN . . .
THEN A WRITER.

And TO TAMSIN: DANCING QUEEN AND
INDISPENSABLE RESEARCH ASSISTANT.

Please don't put your life in the hands
Of a rock 'n' roll band
Who'll throw it all away

"Don't Look Back in Anger"
— Oasis

FIVE FLAVORS OF DUMB

CHAPTER 1

For the record, I wasn't around the day they decided to become Dumb. If I'd been their manager back then I'd have pointed out that the name, while accurate, was not exactly smart. It just encouraged people to question the band's intelligence, maybe even their sanity. And the way I saw it, Dumb didn't have much of either.

But they weren't in the mood to be reasoned with. They'd just won Seattle's annual Teen Battle of the Bands, and they were milking their fifteen minutes for all it was worth. Never mind that no one else at school even knew the contest existed, the fact is they *won*. The Battle organizers had even hired Baz Firkin— lead singer of defunct band The Workin' Firkins—to mentor their inevitable ascent toward rock stardom during three all-expenses-paid recording sessions. Baz hadn't heard them yet, of course—he wasn't up for parole for another week—but he was a man with experience and connections, both of which were sure to come in handy as soon as he was released.

Meanwhile, Dumb celebrated their victory by giving an unscheduled performance on the school steps first thing Monday morning. It would have been the most audacious breach of school rules ever if the teachers hadn't been attending their weekly staff meeting; instead, the band cranked up their amps, to the delight of their numerous groupies. I wanted to ignore them, but they were strategically blocking the school entrance, and hustling past would have marked me out as anal-retentive ("Doesn't want to be late for homeroom!") and indirectly critical ("Didn't even look at the band!").

Or maybe not, but that's how it seemed to me.

Anyway, I stuck around for a few minutes and watched the threesome thrashing their poor defenseless instruments with sadistic abandon: swoony Josh Cooke on vocals, his mouth moving preternaturally fast and hips gyrating as if a gerbil had gained unauthorized access to his crotch; Will Cooke, Josh's non-identical twin brother, on bass guitar, his lank hair obscuring most of his pale, gaunt face, hands moving so sluggishly you would think they'd been sedated; Tash Hartley on lead guitar, her left hand flying along the neck of the guitar while she stared down her audience like a boxer sizing up her opponent before a fight. Not that anyone—male or female—would be stupid enough to take on Tash.

I was going to slide past them as soon as they finished a song, but as far as I could tell that never actually happened, so I just held back. Anyway, the scene on the steps was oddly compelling, even aesthetically pleasing. The bright, late September sun glinted off the teen-proof tempered windows. Beside me, Kallie Sims, supermodel wannabe, was a vision of flawless dark skin and meticulously flat-ironed hair. Even Dumb's instruments looked shiny and cared for. And all the while I could feel the music pounding in my hands, my feet, my chest. For a moment, I understood how Dumb might have won the Battle of the Bands on pure energy alone. I could even believe they were set to conquer the world—if the world were a small public high school in a predominantly white, middle-class suburb of Seattle.

There must have been a hundred of us out there when I first noticed someone staring at me. I didn't even know her, but when I smiled she looked away guiltily. Then someone else glanced over. She tried to look nonchalant, but was clearly confused to see me with a group of mostly popular kids, listening to *music* of all things.

Suddenly I couldn't watch the band, couldn't enjoy the scene. As I scanned the crowd I saw more pairs of eyes trained on me, each of them wondering what I was doing there. And there was whispering too, which should have seemed comical—why go to the trouble of whispering around *me*, right?—but instead made me feel even more self-conscious. I just wanted to make it to the end of the song, but I was beginning to wonder if that would ever happen.

Finally Dumb relaxed, like they were pausing to draw breath. I couldn't bear to move, however; couldn't face drawing even more attention to myself. I watched as the performers knelt down before their amplifiers and turned a few knobs. Then, smiling at each other, they attacked their instruments with renewed vigor, spewing out noise that replicated a small earthquake, while Josh gave us an unparalleled view of his tonsils. Satisfied at having initiated seismic activity on school grounds, they played on even when smoke started rising from Will's amp—maybe they figured it was only appropriate that they should provide their own pyrotechnics as well. They didn't even seem to mind when the small black box, clearly fed up with this particular brand of thrash-scream cacophony, began sparking, then flaming gently.

Kallie's supermodel posse was first to evacuate, presumably afraid that the chemicals in their hair might spontaneously combust, although Kallie herself stuck around. This surprised me. Gradually everyone else shuffled off as well. They knew things were about to turn seriously ugly and didn't want to be at the crime scene when punishments were being doled out. Eventually only Kallie and I remained. Together we watched Dumb's unofficial concert end in a literal blaze of glory. Even as I struggled to avoid inhaling the noxious smoke, I couldn't help but admire the showmanship.

I can't say when Will's amplifier stopped producing sound altogether and threatened to ignite the school's electricity supply. But I remember *exactly* how I felt as I raised my arms and screamed at the top of my lungs—the kind of obnoxious, over-the-top response I normally reserved for our sports teams' own goals and air-balled free throws. I remember my shock as Kallie raised her arms too, like she thought I was seriously impressed with the band. And I can still picture Josh and Will and Tash smiling and pumping their fists in the air. But most of all I remember how great it felt to vent, whatever my motives, to share an animal scream with four other people who gave even less of a crap than I did. For a moment I even allowed myself to believe that the blackened air was nothing less than the whole damn school disintegrating into beautiful, blissful oblivion . . . right until the principal burst through the main door, drowning everything and everyone in foam from a gratuitously large fire extinguisher.

By the time the fire truck arrived, the amps were nothing but an electrical dog pile on our school's formerly pristine steps, and Dumb had been hit with a week-long in-school suspension for committing unforgivable acts of "noise pollution"—the principal's words, but no one seemed to disagree. It should have been the end of the group really, considering their punishment, and the inescapable fact that their amps were ruined. But in one of those crazy rock music situations I came to know firsthand, the moment of their untimely demise became the moment Dumb was truly born.

For the rest of the day, freshmen reenacted the moment when the amp *actually caught fire.* Even the band's staunchest critics began scrawling eulogies on bathroom stalls. Suddenly the world of North Seattle High revolved around Dumb—the only topic anyone discussed anymore. At least, that's how it seemed to me. I *think* that's what everyone was talking about. But in the interests of accuracy, I should admit that it's kind of hard for me to tell because, well, you know.

I'm deaf.

SUCK·I·NESS [SUHK-EE-NIS]
–noun

WATCHING your parents pay exorbitant real estate prices so that you can live in a school district with deaf programs

LEARNING that educational budget cuts include shutting down said deaf programs at your high school

DISCOVERING that your equally deaf BFF Marissa's parents have chosen to protest the decision by moving to San Francisco

LISTENING to your recently laid-off father complain about the aforementioned exorbitant real estate prices, and hypocritically criticizing his daughter for moping about Marissa leaving, when he's constantly moping about losing his job

REALIZING you're completely alone . . . even in a crowd

CHAPTER 2

As usual, my brother Finn (he's a freshman) wasn't waiting by the car (aka USS *Immovable*, a 1987 Chevy Caprice Classic Brougham that consumed fuel in legendary quantities) when school ended. What was *un*usual was that it didn't bother me. For once I wasn't in a hurry to get home, so I sprawled across the massive hood and basked in what remained of the sunshine.

I watched my fellow seniors tumble out of school, engaging in ritualistic chest-bumping, conspicuous air kissing, and flagrant butt-groping. When all socially accepted forms of physical contact had been exhausted, they ambled to their cars like they were reluctant to leave the school grounds. Some even pretended to have trouble unlocking their car doors, just in case the opportunity for further socializing might present itself. I waved to a couple of girls from Calc, but I guess they didn't see me.

I closed my eyes and concentrated on feeling the sun against my face—so warm, so relaxing, so *rare* in the Seattle fall. I must have dozed off, because the next thing I knew, Finn was shaking my arm pretty hard, which scared the crap out of me.

If anyone asks, I've been with you here the last ten minutes, okay? he signed feverishly.

I narrowed my eyes, but nodded anyway. Whatever he was about to be accused of, he was clearly guilty—otherwise he wouldn't have willingly signed. True, sign language is my preferred mode of communication, but when there's just the two of us in an empty parking lot, my hearing aids plus lip-reading are perfectly adequate.

See, deafness is complicated. I used to hear perfectly, but when I was six my hearing began to fail. It was a gradual process, but undeniable; and not completely unexpected, as my mom's parents were both deaf. When I could only follow conversations by lip-reading, my parents shelled out a few thousand dollars for hearing aids, but they work best when I'm talking to one person in a quiet place. The constant noise of school is not conducive to hearing aid use, which is why I still prefer to sign whenever I can. Finn knew this, of course, but that didn't stop him from speaking to me most of the time. Which is how I knew he was sucking up to me. Which meant that, yes . . . he'd screwed up *again.*

Barely ten seconds later, Mr. Belson—reluctant math teacher yet enthusiastic mascot of the school chess club—waddled through the door and made a beeline for my car. He came to an abrupt halt a few feet from Finn, but his enormous stomach continued to wobble. I could tell by his heightened color and incensed expression that the words were going to be shouted.

"I saw you in that room, Vaughan!"

Beside me, Finn shrank lower on the trunk.

"Admit it. You were there."

I have to say, someone who breaks as many rules as Finn really ought to work on perfecting a look of innocence, or defiance, or something. All he seems to have mastered is the deer-in-the-headlights look.

I conjured a broad smile. "Hello, Mr. Belson," I said.

He did a double take. "Oh, hello, Ms. Vaughan. What are you doing here?"

"Finn is my brother."

"*Him?*" Belson shuffled uncomfortably on the spot. "Surely not. It can't be true."

"Believe me, Mr. Belson, it still takes me by surprise sometimes."

Belson looked genuinely sympathetic. "Well, I'm sorry to say your brother was engaging in nefarious after-school activities."

Of course he was, I wanted to say, but if I did, then we'd be here another hour while my parents were summoned to appear before the principal.

"Finn and I have been here ever since school ended, Mr. Belson," I said innocently.

"That's patently untrue. I saw him in that room."

"It, uh . . . must have been someone else." Despite years of covering for Finn's misdeeds, I still felt my heartbeat quicken as the lie dribbled out.

Belson wiped the sweat off his forehead with a carefully folded paper napkin. "Don't do this, Ms. Vaughan. You're an excellent student. And an exceptional chess club captain, I might add. Don't jeopardize your own reputation to cover for him."

I shrugged, allowed the silence to linger. After all, if there was one area that I was extremely experienced in, it was prolonged silences.

Belson remained frozen to the spot, pondering his next move. Eventually he replaced the napkin in his pocket with a measured gesture and stared directly at Finn.

"You've only been here a month, Vaughan. The fact that I'm already onto you is an ominous sign for your future at our school. Your next transgression will result in suspension, you understand? There's no three-strike rule here."

He didn't wait for a response, just spun around with the grace of the Marshmallow Man and hurried back to resume patrolling the school hallways.

I'll make it up to you, signed Finn, his movements slower now, calmer.

What were you doing? I shot back.

Nothing. Just hanging out.

With all your new friends, I assume.

He looked away and refused to take the bait. Or maybe he was just trying to spare my feelings, refusing to confirm that one month into high school he was already more popular than me.

I got into the car and shoved the key in the ignition. I wanted to believe that I was pissed about having to lie to Belson, but really, that wasn't it at all. I was just pissed at Finn . . . for serially screwing up and always living to tell the tale; for knowing he could always count on me to bail him out. It was all so predictable.

But it was more than that, even. I knew he only reverted to sign language as a way to soften me up—it meant nothing to him; he had no personal investment in it—and I hated myself for being secretly grateful to him anyway. Sure, it was an improvement on Dad's complete unwillingness to sign at all, but I felt manipulated. Finn had no idea what my life was like, and I guess I had no idea what his was like either. I just knew that when he met a girl for the first time, he didn't have to worry about how his voice sounded or whether she was freaked out by the way he stared at her lips the whole time.

I honestly think I could have kept up the silent treatment all day, but when USS *Immovable*'s decrepit engine turned over and over without starting, Finn began to laugh. Thirty seconds later we still hadn't moved, and I cracked up too—restrained at first, then an all-out belly laugh. Suddenly we were shaking so hard that Finn couldn't sit still and I couldn't turn the keys.

Predictability has its upside.

CHAPTER 3

"I swear, she's like a clone of you when you were a baby." Instinctively, Mom had said and signed the words simultaneously, but she was gazing at my eleven-month-old sister, Grace, not me.

I stared at Grace's cochlear implant, a black contraption surgically attached to her right ear. She'd had it a month, but it had only just been turned on.

"Not anymore," I said truthfully.

"Don't go there, Piper. Not today," warned Dad.

Yes, my name is Piper. And no, I don't see the funny side. Seriously, what family with a history of hereditary deafness names their child after the player of a musical instrument?

"It's amazing," said Mom.

"A miracle," gushed Dad.

They took turns whispering sweet nothings to Grace, who obediently tilted her head from side to side, seeking out the source of this new world of sound. I hadn't expected the implant to work so quickly.

"Shame it wasn't around when I was younger," I said.

"Don't be silly, Piper," said Mom. She turned her mouth toward me as she stopped signing, so that I could see her lips. She still wouldn't make eye contact, though. "You didn't lose your hearing until you were six. And you know that Grace's deafness was far more severe. Besides, your hearing aids work fine."

Easy for her to say. The reason everyone assumes my hearing aids work fine is because I can lip-read with Olympic precision, and the combination of the two helps me get by. But it's still hard work, and my hearing aids are old behind-the-ear models in Barbie pink that stopped feeling cool about a week after I got them, seven years ago. I was supposed to get a new in-the-ear pair for my birthday. Mom and Dad even promised me the Bluetooth iCom hookup, so I could hear my computer and cell phone through the aids, but then Dad lost his job and there wasn't enough money. In a reckless moment I considered buying them with money from the college fund my grandparents had set aside for me, but I knew my parents would have a fit. Anyway, the fund was too important for that.

At that moment, Grace turned to me and smiled, as if to remind me that none of this was her doing. She was still the same Grace—the one whose face lit up each time I returned from school, who slept with the snuggle blanket *I* knitted, who made me feel like an inspired comedian just by sticking out my tongue. I still mattered to her, I realized.

Then Dad spoke and she looked away, breaking the spell.

I'll never hear the way she does, I signed, adding a little oomph as I smacked my chest (to indicate myself), and a lot of oomph as I flicked my hand toward Grace.

"You know this wasn't an easy decision," sighed Mom, refusing to sign back to me. "But let's not forget, the implant works best on very young children, and with your residual hearing you wouldn't have been a good candidate. Besides, it wasn't covered by insurance back then."

"It's not fully covered now either," said Dad, no doubt relieved that we were speaking, not signing. "The co-pay is monstrous. We talked about it, remember?"

Mom hushed him, then glanced at me and turned scarlet.

I felt my pulse quicken. "What are you talking about? I thought it was going to be covered."

"Well, partially," said Mom reassuringly, "but it turns out my insurance isn't as comprehensive as your dad's used to be. It's complicated."

"Try me."

"There's no need to get all worked up about this, Piper," said Dad. "We'll make up the shortfall somehow."

"Shortfall? What shortfall? Where did you get the money?"

Mom glared at Dad briefly, then turned on the charm for me. "You've just started senior year, Piper, honey. We'll return the money to your fund before you need it for college."

"And if we can't, you're even more likely to qualify for financial aid," added Dad helpfully.

I felt like throwing up. "You raided my . . . college fund for this?"

"Being part of a family entails making sacrifices, you know."

"But shouldn't that be my decision? Oma and Poppy left that money to *me*."

"What about your hearing aids? They cost money too, you know," Dad pointed out.

"A few thousand bucks, yes. But that was years ago. You said the implant was going to be over eighty thousand."

Dad raised a finger menacingly. "This is your sister we're talking about, Piper. You want what's best for her, right?"

Silence. My father—master of the rhetorical question. Of course I wanted the best for Grace, but not at my expense. The college fund my grandparents had set up for me was my ticket to another world. I'd dreamed of heading to Gallaudet University in Washington, DC, ever since they told me about it: the finest liberal arts college in the world for deaf and hard-of-hearing students—a place where I'd automatically fit in, instead of standing out in all the wrong ways. What if the financial aid package wasn't enough?

Oh God. I had to concentrate to keep from crying.

Anyway, who's to say what was best for Grace? Mom always called her my baby twin, and if she remained deaf we'd be closer than mere sisters. As she grew up we'd sign nonstop, sharing words that few others could understand. I'd be there for her, help her, allow her to express herself in her own way, not demand that she conform to society's bias toward oral communication. I even came close to saying all this, but then I had an epiphany: My father wasn't indifferent to my deafness; he was mortified by it. For him, Grace's total loss of hearing was an insurmountable disability, something that had needed to be remedied at the earliest opportunity through major surgery. And even though my hearing loss was less severe than hers, the notion that I was also "disabled" struck home. Could it really be that after eighteen years Dad saw me that way—a poor girl struggling to be understood, who achieved self-sufficiency only by virtue of others' help?

Dad interpreted my silence as petulance and shook his head disgustedly as he returned his attention to his *fixed* daughter, leaving me wondering when and how we'd gotten so far off track.

Meanwhile, Mom called Grace's name again and again—from above, from behind, from either side and from the corners of the room. And each time, Grace turned toward her like an obedient puppy, large eyes blinking in wonder, the corners of her mouth turned up, caught between a grin and total bemusement.

"Of course I want the best for Grace," I whispered, hoping that one day my father might understand the million layers separating our ideas of what counts as best.

CHAPTER 4

Finn was late again, and I didn't feel like waiting around while he broke a few more school rules. I figured if he was working on getting expelled, he could at least do it during regular school hours.

It didn't help that I was already in a bad mood. Belson forgot to give us our homework assignment until the bell had already rung, so his announcement was made over the scraping of chairs and the ceaseless chattering of the supermodel wannabes. I couldn't catch what he said, so I had to wait for the room to clear before asking him to repeat everything to me privately. I wish I could say it was an unusual occurrence.

As I trudged back from the parking lot to the school's main entrance I noticed the steps were still blackened, and those stains weren't coming off anytime soon, either. Dumb weren't just the talk of the school, they'd left their mark on the building itself. If Finn needed lessons on how to break school rules with style, he could do worse than learn from the members of Dumb.

As it turned out, that's exactly what he was doing. They'd

just been released from suspension for the day, and a motley assortment of a dozen or so hangers-on had gathered to cheer them. They loitered in the hallway outside the principal's office, presumably to draw attention to themselves, although the principal never emerged. Maybe he was concerned for his safety.

Sensible guy.

At first I kept my distance, so that teachers emerging from their lounge would know that I wasn't connected to the motley crew. But after a few minutes I grew tired of waiting. I signaled to Finn that it was time to leave, but he ignored me. I stepped forward and was about to make a grab for him when Josh Cooke glanced up and waved in my direction. He flashed a smile and I waved back enthusiastically, touched that he must have noticed I was one of the last people to abandon Dumb the day before.

Josh saw me waving and looked confused, then amused as he pointed at something behind me. I spun around and came face-to-face with blazingly gorgeous Kallie Sims, in her trademark miniskirt and knee-high brown leather boots. Designer labels flashed from every item of clothing, like sponsors jostling for space on a winning racecar. Of course Josh wasn't waving at me. Why would any guy notice me when they could be ogling her instead?

Again I signaled to Finn that it was time to go, and again he ignored me. He knew I'd be too self-conscious to call out to him in such a public place, so all I could do was wait while he fawned over the mini-celebs of Dumb. Since he had no more aspirations in life than to get expelled and play guitar in a rock band, they probably seemed like ideal role models.

I think I'd have stayed rooted to the spot forever if Josh hadn't looked over and waved again, and I hadn't accidentally waved back again, at which point he (again) signaled to Kallie just behind me, and she responded with that stupid half smile like she'd just accidentally Botoxed her mouth shut— which seemed completely plausible, by the way.

I guess I must have turned even redder than usual, because Kallie looked almost sympathetic as she glanced my way. Maybe she'd heard the rumor about me never having had a boyfriend. Maybe she knew it was true.

I turned away and tried to focus on a small spot of crumbling wall, but I couldn't stop my eyes from twitching around defensively. Dumb were evidently enjoying their newfound celebrity, and Finn was enjoying their attention. In fact, everybody treated Finn like a long-lost best buddy, like it didn't matter that he was just a freshman. He even gave their amplifiers a thorough checking out, and it took me a moment to realize they must have purchased new amps, like these things were practically disposable; maybe they were, for parents as rich as Josh and Will's. I thought of my own situation—friendless at school, dysfunctional home life, freshly emptied college fund—and something just snapped.

Here's a bizarre fact: When you stride up to a group of people and start signing in exaggerated gestures, conversation stops. It's completely counterintuitive really, since they could keep talking and it wouldn't interfere with my signing at all. But I knew they'd shut up, and I knew Finn would be embarrassed. At that moment, both situations seemed ideal.

Car. Now.

Finn didn't move, wouldn't even make eye contact.

"What did she just say?" asked Josh, clearly unaware that I could understand him without an interpreter. (After sharing the same classes for the past three years, you'd think he'd have noticed.)

"She didn't say anything," said Finn.

That was the final straw. *Tell them they're crap,* I signed.

"What did she say now?" pressed Josh.

Finn looked up at me like he truly hated my guts. "She says you're . . . not living up to your potential."

I raised my eyebrows. Apparently Finn had a gift for improvising. Who knew?

"She seemed to like us when we performed yesterday morning," Josh replied.

All style and no substance, I countered, not waiting for Finn to pass along Josh's words. *Complete amateurs.*

At this point, Finn started relaying my comments verbatim. He probably figured it would increase the odds of Dumb beating the crap out of me right there and then.

But Josh was too smart for that. If he was going down, it was going to be in a war of words.

"Amateurs, huh?" he said, facing me directly now. "And how do you figure that?"

Have you been signed yet?

Finn sighed, passed along the message.

"Course not. We only won the Battle three days ago."

How are you capitalizing on the buzz your win created?

Finn shook his head, mumbled something.

"We did an interview on the University of Washington's unofficial radio station last night."

I wasn't even aware the university had an *official* station. *How much did they pay you?*

Finn's mouth seemed reluctant to open and close. His shoulders slumped even more than usual. I got the feeling he'd never again be late for his ride home.

"Nothing. It's about exposure. You don't make money while you're breaking out."

I laughed in what I hoped was a mocking tone.

Tash shoved in front of Josh, the green spikes in her hair bristling. She flared her nostrils at me in an unflatteringly unfeminine way and turned to Finn, too unobservant to notice I'd been lip-reading all along.

"So, what—she thinks she could get us paid for everything, is that it?"

Yes. If you have any sense, you'll focus on charging for every interview and every appearance, instead of doing free performances on school grounds and getting suspended for it.

Finn swallowed hard. "She says . . . yes."

Tash narrowed her eyes, and I'd swear her daubed-on eyeliner cracked like one of those ancient oil paintings in museums.

"Whatever. There's no way . . ."

She turned away. I couldn't lip-read anymore, and her words became indistinct—a really obnoxious thing to do to someone who's hard of hearing.

I figured she was telling Josh and Will to ignore me, or pummel me, or puncture my tires and set fire to my car or something. But I could also tell from their expressions that what I'd said was NEWS to them, and seriously interesting news at that. As she turned back to face me, even Tash seemed unsure, the metal jewelry peppering her heavily accessorized face twitching like I'd piqued her interest. And flanking them on every side was an ever-growing legion of groupies, all of them staring at me unblinkingly, like they were looking at me for the first time, like I was someone they'd never met before rather than someone they'd simply ignored.

And that was the moment my adrenaline shot of bravado expired. For some reason, they obviously expected me to speak next, only what more could I say? Even if what I'd said was true, I was just venting, and continuing seemed increasingly risky, if not masochistic. Suddenly the eyes trained on me seemed bright with expectation, and I was blinded by the glare.

I turned and strode away, not looking at anyone or anything except the main door. My hand was already shoved deep in my pocket, fingers clasped around the car key that would hasten my escape. I didn't even need to wait for Finn; he was jogging along beside me, as eager to get away as I was.

We tumbled into the car, and I only dropped my keys once before jamming them into the ignition. But somewhere around the twelfth or thirteenth time the engine turned over without starting, I caught a glimpse of Josh, Will, and Tash in my rearview mirror. I exhaled slowly, gave up trying to start the car, and waited.

Josh tapped on the driver's-side window, and there wasn't any point in pretending I didn't know he was there. I gripped the door frame for support as I stepped out of the car, wondering if they'd really dare to beat the crap out of me on school grounds.

Josh glanced at his brother and Tash, then turned his blazing blue eyes directly at me. I couldn't look away.

"Okay," he said. "Here's the deal: You've got one month to get us a paying gig. We'll split the money with you—four ways. Do that and you can be our manager, even when we get big."

I knew I should be laughing. The Piper of five minutes before would have snorted, rolled her eyes, and made grand, sarcastic signs about the unlikelihood of them even making it small, let alone big. But that was five minutes ago. The Piper of the present was suddenly timid and utterly mute. This was a crazy situation in need of immediate resolution, but what was there to say? Josh hadn't even asked me, he'd *told* me this was my job. And even though it would have seemed completely appropriate for the band to break down in bone-rattling laughter right there and then, they didn't. They just stared at me like we'd signed a pact in blood. Suddenly our futures were bound together in a way that was utterly preposterous.

Josh wrote down a series of letters on a scrap of paper and handed it to me.

"Someone downloaded our performance onto YouTube. Check it out. Tell us what we need to do to be more marketable. We're in this for real. We'll listen to what you say . . . or, you know, sign."

I took the paper and studied the website address. I tried to summon the energy for a final refusal, but Josh was smiling his irresistibly large smile, eyes gazing at me and me alone, and I couldn't do it. Without Kallie behind me I had his undivided attention, and I'd be lying if I said it didn't feel very gratifying indeed.

"You're smart, Piper. Everyone knows it. And right now we're too busy to be organizing gigs, whereas you probably have loads of free time, right?"

I sighed, but nodded. What was the point in denying it?

"If anyone can do this, Piper, it's you. Let's get famous . . . make some money."

For someone who'd never spoken to me before, Josh sure had strong opinions on my suitability for the job. What's more, he seemed to have a higher opinion of me than my own father, and was offering to let me make money, rather than siphoning it away from my Gallaudet fund. And while I knew that making money wasn't a sure thing, something told me that if blind self-confidence was an indicator of future success, maybe Dumb was destined for greatness after all.

I looked at the three bandmates again, thought back to the scene outside the principal's office and the crowd of groupies fawning over them like their existence on earth somehow mattered. Sure, I knew I'd never orbit the same social sphere as Josh, Will, and Tash, but knowing they'd begin to acknowledge me around school was another appealing perk. I didn't even pause to consider what that said about me; I simply took Josh's hand and shook it like I was trying to rip his arm off.

Tash immediately turned and sloped away, kicking the ground wildly. And even though I got the feeling Josh's plan had received one dissenting vote, I didn't really care.

Finally, Will looked up for the first time. I'd almost forgotten he was there too. Winding curtains of hair behind each ear, he raised his tired-looking eyes, like he'd just figured out that if I was going to be his manager, he probably ought to be able to recognize me. After much consideration, he offered his hand in painful slow motion, presumably for us to shake on our new agreement. His palm felt cold and clammy.

"Um . . . we're Dumb," he said.

I shook his hand and nodded again and again and again.

Never a truer word had been spoken.

CHAPTER 5

I figured I could do worse than ask Dad for advice. For years he'd compensated for his hideously boring job by immersing himself in rock music. Not that he played it for me anymore, of course—his vinyl LPs were collector's items, and he probably assumed it would be a waste of time for someone in my "condition" anyway—but he owed me after yesterday's remarks, and I was ready to proffer an olive branch.

He was standing before the stove, stirring a large pot of unidentifiable meat. Whatever the animal had once been, parts of it were now spattered across his starched chinos and polo shirt, and I couldn't help wondering when he was finally going to trade them in for sweatpants and T-shirt. I mean, it wasn't like he was fooling anyone—everyone knew his brokerage firm had filed for bankruptcy, offering not a penny in severance pay to its long-suffering employees. Unfortunately, his business experience hadn't exactly prepared him for his new role as Mr. Mom either.

I tried to get a better look at the contents of the pot, then thought better of it. I'd say it smelled like crap, but *that* particular odor was emanating from Grace, who lolled around in her bouncy chair by the kitchen table.

I tapped Dad on the shoulder. *Grace pooped,* I signed, gripping my right thumb with my left hand and then pulling it out—one of my favorite descriptive signs.

Signing was a bad way to start our conversation, as Dad predictably shrugged and looked confused.

"Grace has a poopy diaper," I repeated, this time out loud so he'd understand.

He still looked puzzled. "How do you know?"

"It's my hearing that's impaired, not my sense of smell."

I meant it to come out funny, but Dad must have thought I was being snarky. He sighed dramatically and hustled Grace out of the buckles. A moment later he stuck a finger under her onesie and grimaced.

"Damn. I just changed it."

"Do you want me to do it?"

"No, Piper," he snapped. "I'm perfectly capable of changing a diaper, thank you very much."

I shrunk back as he held her at arm's length and dumped her onto the changing table in the hallway. "I was just offering. That's all," I said quietly.

Dad didn't reply, just huffed and puffed his way through the diaper change like it was a full-contact sport. He didn't even notice Grace kicking her feet into the remnants of her poopy diaper, and when he tried to corral her feet she used her lightning-fast ninja reflexes to smear poop across his shirt, then belly-laughed at his outraged response. It was such an infectious, uninhibited laugh that I almost busted out chuckling too. But then I caught sight of Dad's face. In the end I just watched from the doorway, knowing how much he needed my help, but also how much he needed me not to help. Life in the business world must have seemed so much saner.

Finally he closed his eyes and took a few deep breaths, Grace's smelly feet clamped in his hands. "I'm sorry, Piper. I didn't mean to snap at you. It's just . . . I didn't expect to be in this situation. And I guess I'm really too old to be doing this, you know?"

"Doing what?"

"Raising a child. Being there for her twenty-four/seven, that sort of thing."

I didn't know what he expected me to say, but my silence clearly annoyed him. I guess he thought this kind of honesty and openness would be therapeutic, but all I could think was that Grace wasn't the only child in the house. I was his child too, and I didn't need him to be there for me 24/7—I'd have settled for just a few minutes of undivided attention now and again. There was a time he used to help me with my math homework, and spent long evenings thrashing Finn and me at poker. When was that? It felt like another lifetime.

He shook his head as he realized I wouldn't be bailing him out with some phony line about what a great dad he'd always been.

"I guess I just haven't got the energy for this anymore," he sighed, without a hint of shame or regret.

I looked at him—the thinning salt-and-pepper hair and the poop-stained polo shirt—and thought to myself, *Yeah, but then again, you never did, did you?*

CHAPTER 6

The website Dumb.com had already been taken. Maybe I should have anticipated this, but since registering a domain name was the only part of the plan that I felt comfortable doing, it was a disappointing start. The registration site tried to help me out by advising that related terms such as idiot, moron, dork, and stupid were still available for purchase if I was interested. But although it was tempting, I figured that Josh's ego might have a problem with being the headlining act on Stupid.com. Instead I started a Facebook page for the band, which was free and pretty easy.

I checked out the YouTube video that Josh had mentioned, but the quality was horrendous. The only way I knew for sure that it was Dumb onstage was Tash's green spikes, which glowed like radioactive waste under the freaky stage lights.

I spent a couple minutes tweaking the volume control on the computer, but the quality was awful. At its highest setting, it was plain uncomfortable. I closed my eyes and focused all my attention on the static mess, but the sound was completely distorted. A minute later I turned it off. For all I knew, Dumb may have been the best or the worst band in the history of rock music.

I tried Googling for information about rock bands with three members, but one look at a photo of the Bee Gees assured me this particular line of inquiry wasn't going to be helpful. I searched under "guitar," memorizing words like "headstock" and "fretboard" and "pickups." Then I moved to "singing," wrestling with the possible meanings of "head voice" and "falsetto." By the time I'd blown most of an hour it had become abundantly clear to me that (a) just about the only thing the Web didn't have was a ten-step guide to managing your high school rock band, and (b) the idea of me managing a band was simply . . . well, dumb. Maybe the group knew it too. Maybe this was all a joke—their way of getting back at me for humiliating them—and they were about to have the last laugh.

I closed my eyes and imagined how different things would have been if Marissa had never left. I still recalled every painful moment of that hot August day when she and her parents climbed into the Penske truck and took off for San Francisco: the way she apologized over and over, like she'd had any say in the decision; how she promised that nothing would change, and she'd fly back during winter break; how we'd ooVoo—a video format tailor-made for sign language—every day. And we did, too, until the camera on her laptop stopped working. Then we switched to IM, but it wasn't the same. She couldn't smile on IM, or laugh that ridiculous laugh, or rescue me with a pretend hug before I'd even had a chance to say what was wrong. She felt so much farther away when I couldn't see her anymore.

It was too early in the evening to expect her to be around, so I sent Marissa a text message, asking her to IM as soon as she got in. Then, even though I knew I shouldn't, I waited around in case she replied quickly. I just needed a sign, something to reassure me that she hadn't moved on without me, that she still needed me as much as I needed her. After all, she was the only one who really *got* me, who'd stayed online hour after hour as I complained about Grace's implant, agreeing heart and soul with every word I wrote. Everyone needs a friend who'll sympathize no matter what—for me, that was Marissa.

Ten minutes later, I gave up waiting. Clearly, I'd need to look elsewhere for today's sympathy quota, although something told me I wasn't going to find it at home.

CHAPTER 7

"Piper's the new manager of Dumb," blurted Finn. Apparently the news couldn't wait until dinner had been served.

Dad's eyes narrowed. "What's dumb?" he asked cautiously, like he was afraid of becoming the butt of a philosophical joke.

"You know. They won Seattle Teen Battle of the Bands."

Mom snorted. "Oh, well then, yeah, of course I know exactly what you're talking about."

Finn muttered something, but I couldn't catch a word of it as Grace was babbling and Finn's hands obscured his mouth. *Sheesh.* It was a round table too, so I could follow conversations and read lips more easily. Dad said it was a "concession" they were happy to make.

"You're not serious, are you?" asked Dad.

"Yeah," said Finn, not looking up. "They won it this weekend. I've heard them too. They're really good."

"No. I mean, about Piper being their manager."

"Hello. I'm sitting right here," I groaned. It happened all the time, Dad talking about me as if I weren't sitting next to him.

"Yeah, I'm serious," said Finn. "She told them . . . well, she said she's got some ideas about how to market them more effectively."

Dad nodded, but his fork hung in midair. "No offense, but shouldn't the manager of a rock band have perfect hearing?"

I couldn't believe Dad said that, and neither could Mom.

"Piper can do anything she wants to," snapped Mom, repeating her favorite phrase like a mantra.

"I know that, honey. Piper is as academically capable as any other child, but this is different."

That got me absolutely seething.

"Well, I think it's great, Piper," Mom interjected. "You could do with a non-academic outlet."

I felt my jaw slacken. "Let me get this straight. Dad thinks I'm disabled, and you think I'm a geek?"

They both rushed to defend themselves, so I couldn't decide whose lips to read. "Stop! One at a time." I nodded at Dad first.

"It's not about being disabled. It's about knowing your limitations."

From the corner of my eye, I saw Mom flinch.

"Gee, thanks, Dad. That's especially meaningful coming from someone who can't even change a diaper."

"What's that?" asked Mom, grateful for the change of topic.

"Dad ended up with Grace's poop all over his shirt this afternoon."

"That's enough," he said sternly.

Mom tried to rein it in, but then she let loose an unsavory snort, which got me laughing. A moment later Grace erupted in chortling too, face aglow as she bounced up and down in her high chair. Suddenly I was laughing even harder, and I would have kept laughing if I hadn't realized that in the space of a day Grace had gone from profound deafness to hearing probably more than me. I knew I should have been thrilled for her, but instead I was so overwhelmed with jealousy I wanted to scream. I understood that I was being unreasonable, but if I could I'd have ripped her implant off right there and then.

I looked around the table, wondering how I'd become so frustrated with the rest of my family so quickly. And as I sat there pondering how to escape feeling so wretched, the only thing that offered any relief at all was completely and utterly Dumb.

CHAPTER 8

Wednesday lunch was chess club, an opportunity for me to inflict swift and decisive defeats on anyone who dared to take me on. Which is to say, Ed Chen.

Ed's strengths did not lie in his chess acumen. In fact, it was entirely unclear to me why he continued to subject himself to successive thrashings, but I was grateful for it. Even though I was captain of the school team—a team in name only; we hadn't taken on another school in almost a year—I couldn't get anyone else to play me.

Ed was white again—like having the first move was any kind of advantage—and he commenced with his standard opening, shuffling a pawn forward two spaces. I sometimes wondered if he kept doing it to lure me into complacency, that one day he'd sense my apathy and unleash his full arsenal of devastating moves, his bishops assaulting my defenseless pawns. But after a year of identical openings, I suspected he wasn't holding anything back; there simply wasn't anything there.

Not that Ed wasn't talented. He'd been principal percussionist of the Seattle Youth Orchestra since he was thirteen, and seemed destined to follow in his mom's footsteps by attending one of those prestigious conservatories on the East Coast. He was pretty open about it even, although he never came across as cocky, just confident.

I countered his pawn shuffle by advancing one of my own pawns, blocking his path. It was a throwaway move, but he responded like I'd exhausted his options. He scratched his head, leaving his thick dark hair standing upright, and scrunched his face until I could barely see his deep brown eyes. Even his cheeks had a cute rosy glow. When he speculatively nudged another pawn forward, the move seemed to cause him such grave discomfort I could barely keep a straight face.

"I've agreed to manage that rock band Dumb," I said, breaking the silence.

Oddly, Ed didn't seem surprised. "What do you think of them?" he asked.

I wasn't sure what I thought of them because I couldn't really *hear* them, so I just shrugged. "It's just a joke really, I guess."

Ed's eyes narrowed. "I disagree. I thought their performance on Monday was quite compelling."

I was shocked. "You were there?"

"Sort of. I was watching from the second floor. And for the record," he said, raising an eyebrow, "I noticed that you and Kallie Sims were the only ones who stayed for the whole performance. Odd behavior for someone who thinks Dumb is a joke."

I felt myself blush. Was everyone watching me from behind the safety of a school window?

I stealthily positioned my knight as decoy, while setting up my queen for a devastating attack. Ed responded defensively, throwing a sacrificial pawn in my way. The game could have been over in just two more moves, but talking to Ed about Dumb was helpful.

"Would you look at something for me?" I asked.

"Sure." He seemed relieved to put the game on hold.

As we stood up, I noticed he had finally grown taller than me. Not that he's short—I'm five foot eight—but I'd been taller ever since freshman year. Maybe it's easier to get your ass whipped in chess when your female opponent is shorter than you.

Chess club met in the computer room—presumably geeks who play chess are considered less destructive than other student groups—so I led him to one of the computers and searched for Dumb's YouTube performance. It was no more meaningful for me than it had been the day before, but Ed studied it like it was advanced calculus. When it was over, he nodded several times before turning to face me.

"Okay, well, the good news is that although all three songs are covers, they're imaginative covers, like Dumb's recomposing each song rather than just copying it. That's important—gives them their own identity, which is necessary if they want to stand out."

I had no idea what a *cover* was, but in the context I got the gist of it. So far so good.

"Unfortunately, though, they're very imprecise. They don't listen to one another, and they clearly don't practice enough."

"Really? Because they told me they practice every Friday in Josh and Will's garage."

Ed smiled broadly. "Believe me, there's a big difference between rehearsing and hanging out with each other for a couple hours every Friday evening."

We wandered back to the chessboard, my pieces poised to dethrone his king at a moment's notice. With only two more minutes until the end of lunch, I commenced the endgame.

"Ed, would you do me a favor?"

He perked up. "Sure. Anything."

"Could you come along on Friday and listen to them? You know, give them some pointers."

His eyes shot back down to the chessboard. "I don't think so, Piper. They're not really . . . well, I'm not like them."

"What are you saying—that you think *I'm* like them?"

Ed sighed, passively sending his queen skipping across the board, more fodder for me if I chose to take it. But that seemed unnecessarily cruel. Instead, I moved my rook into position and waited.

"I think you've almost got me here," I said, wiping my forehead for effect.

The corners of his mouth twitched with excitement. "I have?"

"Hmm. . . . Now will you please come on Friday?"

Ed looked closer at his pieces, trying to see the threat that

I saw. He shrugged as he moved his queen all the way back to where it had started the previous move. I sometimes wondered if he thought that the winner was the person whose pieces covered the most real estate.

"If you win, I'll come," he said finally. "But if *I* win"—he smirked—"then it's no deal."

Five seconds later the bell rang. But not before I'd put him in checkmate.

CHAPTER 9

Mom was bouncing Grace on her knee as I entered the living room, and I couldn't help but smile. It used to be a thing we did together—tag-team Grace teasing, we called it—Mom bouncing Grace, me playing peek-a-boo with her. And I'm sorry if it sounds cheesy, but yeah, I liked it. But this time Mom had turned Grace toward her, talking in the rapid-fire patter of a horse race commentator. Visual stimulation was out. Aural stimulation was the order of the day, and I couldn't see how I'd fit into that activity at all.

I was about to leave when Mom stopped, looked past Grace and smiled her honey smile for me and me alone. She tried to sign, but needed both of her hands to hold Grace. It felt symbolic somehow, but I didn't want this conversation to go the way of others, so I stepped forward and took Grace from her, freeing her to communicate.

This must be difficult for you, she signed, not needing to explain what "this" was.

I nodded, rested my chin on Grace's warm, soft head. The delicate scent of baby shampoo was irresistible.

How does Grace's cochlear implant make you feel?

How did it make me feel? Angry and frustrated, yes, but it was more than that. I felt like I'd been judged and found to be inadequate, a problem beyond remedy. But even that wasn't the worst thing. "Alone. It makes me feel alone."

Mom winced, but she didn't look surprised. *You're not alone. You know that, right?*

I buried my face in Grace's soft, wispy hair, felt it tickle my cheeks, nose, lips. I'd forgotten how good it felt to hold her.

Grace isn't you, honey. You had six years before your hearing went, but she hasn't even had a day.

"I know that."

Of course you do. But it changes things. You speak so beautifully, and even now you have some residual hearing—

"Not as much as you think," I protested.

Okay. Maybe not as much as we think, she conceded, her movements fluid and face reassuring. *But some. Grace would have heard nothing. She wouldn't have learned to speak like you. With the cochlear implant she'll have a chance to do those things.*

"You mean she'll hear and speak better than me."

I don't know. Would it bother you?

I shook my head—it was a lie, but I was too ashamed to admit how I really felt. I wondered if Grace would grow up knowing any signs at all, or if that part of our family life would cease the moment I left for college . . . wherever that turned out to be.

"What happens if I can't afford to go to Gallaudet?"

You will. We'll find the money.

"How? You're working so much overtime and it's still not enough."

We'll find it.

"And if you don't?"

Mom sighed heavily and looked at the open door. I almost got the feeling she'd prefer to leave now than continue having this particular conversation. And I suddenly understood why: Because she felt guilty. I'd blamed Dad for raiding my fund because it was more in character for him, but Mom was equally responsible; it had been her call too. They'd had to make a decision about whether it was more important for Grace to get a cochlear implant or for me to fulfill my dream of attending Gallaudet University, and they chose Grace. My grandparents would never have let that happen.

"What do you think Oma and Poppy would have said?" I asked finally. I knew it would make Mom uncomfortable, but I needed her to acknowledge there was another side to all this.

I don't know. Your grandparents were proud of Deaf culture, but it was difficult for me to be an only child in a house of deaf parents. Sometimes they seemed frustrated at me for being able to hear, like it made things easy for me. Other times they needed me to interpret in situations where I didn't feel comfortable.

I knew this, of course. She'd been telling me the same thing for years. But surely I was even more demanding than my grandparents had been. Did she see me as a burden too?

After growing up like that, she continued, *I couldn't allow Grace to be the only profoundly deaf person in a house full of hearing people.* She raised her palm to ward off my objection. *But what would Oma and Poppy have said? I guess they'd have been disappointed by our decision. Let down.*

I knew she was right. After several years I still missed them terribly. They had been the only family members who signed exclusively, which felt comfortable. But Grace's cochlear implant would have been so divisive, and "let down" was an understatement. I think they would have been ashamed of Mom, and I think she knew it too.

"How does that make you feel?" I asked, but then we both cracked up as we realized the conversation had come full circle.

Is there something I can do? Some way I can help? signed Mom, becoming serious again.

"I don't know," I said honestly. At least, I was sure that removing the cochlear implant was a little unrealistic at this stage. But there was one thing. "Is a paralegal qualified to make a contract?"

Mom smiled. *Yes, I am qualified to draw up a contract. What is it for?*

"The band."

The band?

"Yeah. You know . . . Dumb."

Mom looked confused. *Why do you need a contract?*

"Well, the point of me managing them is to get them paid

gigs. And if there's money, we need to have an agreement about how it's divided, and what each person's obligations are, right?"

Mom hesitated, looked everywhere except at me. *Is it really necessary?* Her gestures were typically smooth, but her face betrayed her. I knew she was calculating how long it would take, already mourning the loss of an hour or two with Grace.

Right on cue, Grace eye-locked Mom, fidgeting like she was about to launch herself onto Mom's lap.

"What do you mean—is it necessary?" I asked.

I mean . . . you're making this band sound serious. It's just a little fun, right?

I felt my breath catch. "I thought you supported me doing this."

I do.

"But you don't really believe there'll ever be a paid gig, do you?"

Mom stared at me, tried to gauge my reaction. *I'll draft a contract for you. Okay?* She smiled again, the honey smile. *I'll do it.*

Grace began to writhe in annoyance, and I guessed that screaming wasn't far off, so I kissed her once and handed her back to Mom.

Thank you, I signed. But I already felt guilty for having asked, and deep down I just wanted to scream too.

CHAPTER 10

No doubt about it, Ed was acting weird. As long as we were alone he seemed relaxed and positive, but the moment we arrived at Josh and Will's house, he became tense. And I don't think it had anything to do with the heavy electric gates or the No Trespassing signs.

"I don't think they're going to appreciate this," he said for the hundredth time.

For the hundredth time, I ignored him, concentrating on setting up Josh's video camera on a professional-looking tripod.

"Does this really work?" I asked.

"Hmm?" Ed looked around distractedly, jamming his hands in and out of his jeans pockets. "The video camera? Yeah, it works. There's nothing like visual and aural evidence that you're not playing together."

At the far end of a garage that was almost as large as my house, Will and Tash tuned their guitars. I turned up the amplifier on my hearing aids to hear them better.

"Whatever you do, don't turn up your hearing aids," cautioned Ed. "Something tells me Dumb only has one volume, and it isn't quiet."

Good point. I turned them right back down again.

Josh wandered over. "Ready when you are, geeks." He raised his thumbs and flexed his biceps, stretching his blue cotton T-shirt. His eyes looked even brighter than usual, and he kept smiling at me even when there was nothing left to say.

I didn't look away.

"You should get started," said Ed coolly. "I'm recording."

A minute later the two guitars erupted in an explosion of sound so intense that my whole body recoiled. Josh pulled the microphone stand toward him, wrapped his hands around it caressingly, and opened his mouth—

"STOP!" yelled Ed, flapping his arms desperately.

Dumb fizzled out.

"Start with a song you already know. We'll move on to new material later."

Dumb was uncharacteristically silent.

"That was a new song, right?"

Josh and Will looked offended. Tash looked threatening.

"Okay. Well, never mind. Let's run it again."

Dumb prepared to start again.

"I really don't think they're ready for this," said Ed, and although I ignored him again, I could see that he might have a point after all.

This time, Ed let the band get halfway through the song

before his musical sensibilities drove him to bring things to a premature halt. "That's great. I love the . . . the, um . . . oh, what's the word I'm looking for? . . . I love the . . . enthusiasm."

Dumb were not enthusiastic about Ed's word choice.

"Here's the thing," he added, "you're not playing together. At all. Entire time zones separate you. I feel like I'm listening to three different songs being played simultaneously in an echo chamber."

Josh rolled his eyes. "Okay, we get the picture," he snapped, momentarily letting down that smooth exterior. "What do we do about it?"

Ed unscrewed the video camera from the tripod and carried it over to them. "First, you need to see and hear what I'm seeing and hearing."

He scrolled back until he found the beginning of the song, and pressed Play. Although there wasn't room for me to crowd around the camera's tiny screen as well, I could tell from their expressions that Josh, Will, and Tash were getting the message loud and clear. By the time he stopped the film, I was wondering if I needed to instigate some serious morale-boosting exercises.

"You know, we have Baz Firkin to help us with all this stuff," sneered Tash, "and he's a professional. You might not realize this, but he was lead singer with The Workin' Firkins."

"And he's in prison until next Thursday," I gently reminded her as Ed cowered behind me. "So for now, Ed has kindly agreed to assume Baz's responsibilities. Carry on, Ed."

Ed's Adam's apple wobbled as he swallowed hard. "Yes. Okay.

Well, here's what we're going to do. I'm going to bang out a steady beat and you're going to repeat the opening riff again and again. As soon as you feel comfortable, stop thinking about what you're doing and focus on what the others are doing. Listen to them, not yourself. The emotion is already there, now let's focus on precision."

Ed unearthed a pair of drumsticks from his book bag and looked around for something to bang, eventually settling on a trash can lid. As soon as he established the beat, the others joined in. I couldn't hear a difference, but I could feel the beat as a steady pulse across my hands. And I could *see* the improvement as clear as day.

After three minutes Dumb wasn't just playing in time, they were moving together—not in a choreographed way, just their heads and feet. And they were looking at each other too, escaping from their own personal spheres and becoming a single musical entity.

After five minutes, Tash cut loose, adding something to the standard riff. It still sounded like a fuzzy mess to me, but Ed smiled approvingly. A moment later, Will let go too, slapping his thumb against the strings of his bass guitar, and Ed's smile grew bigger. Then Josh started jumping around like he was adding a trampoline workout to his vocalizations, and Ed erupted in laughter.

They kept going like that for two more minutes, all smiles and pinpoint accuracy. Then Ed cut loose.

He spun the second stick around in his right hand and

brought it down on a metal shelf, incorporating various power tools into his funky performance. While the left stick continued to hammer away on the trash can lid, the right introduced ever more complex rhythms on flowerpots and glass jars, punctuated by occasional stick-twirling displays. I couldn't say if it sounded good, but it looked amazing, and I could feel each object affecting a different part of my body, from my arms to my feet. I was truly experiencing the music, and after a few seconds, so were the others.

Tash was the first to stop playing, her right hand mid-strum when she became too distracted to continue. Will quickly followed, then Josh. But Ed kept going, his arms pumping like pistons, sticks ablaze with motion as he bounced up and down like he was shadowboxing. He bit his lower lip and furrowed his brows in concentration, but instead of looking nervous he appeared transported. I'd never seen him act so confident before. The others seemed awestruck too, although I had to admit that whatever I thought they'd get out of this session, an up-close and personal look at Ed, crazy closet rock star, certainly hadn't been it.

It was obvious: Ed needed to be in the group.

I let him keep going for another minute before I placed a hand gently on his shoulder. He jumped as if I'd woken him from a trance, then turned bright red and burst into nervous laughter. I couldn't help it—I laughed too. Ed's Jekyll and Hyde secret was out, and normal Ed was clearly pretty embarrassed about it.

He peered up and took in the sight of Dumb's slack-jawed members sizing him up. But no one else laughed. To be honest, they seemed more likely to kneel before him than laugh.

"Holy crap," said Tash succinctly. "We need a drummer."

Josh nodded vigorously, but his mouth never closed. "Yeah. And we need one now."

I was still trying not to laugh, so they couldn't have known how relieved I was that we all had the same idea.

Finally all eyes turned to Will, waiting for him to green-light the move, but he seemed overwhelmed by the attention. "I don't know, man," he mumbled, his gaunt face even more troubled than usual. "I mean, think about it. Where the hell are we going to find a drummer?"

I looked at Ed.

Ed looked at me. "Who? You mean . . . no, you must be kidding."

Not the response I was hoping for. This would require another approach. "Does Tash look like she's kidding?"

Ed glanced at Tash and turned pale.

"Good," I said. "Welcome to Dumb, Ed. I think you're the missing piece of the puzzle." I couldn't resist sarcastically adding, *"You complete us."*

Ed scowled, but honestly it felt good to have the last word for a change.

If only I'd actually been right.

CHAPTER 11

Mom shimmied into my bedroom like she was auditioning for the cheerleading squad, waving a piece of paper before me playfully. I squinted at the title and couldn't help smiling. It was the contract, chock-full of phrases like "in accordance with" and "legally binding" and words like "contingent" and "perpetuity." It hadn't occurred to me before, but lawyers really do a first-rate job of making English read like a foreign language.

Is it okay? signed Mom. Her face made it clear that she expected this to be answered in the enthusiastic affirmative.

I nodded, rubbed the edges of the precious document while I wondered how to break the news to her. *It's perfect . . . but I wonder if we could make one small change.*

Mom's eyes narrowed. She was suddenly the anti-cheerleader. *What's wrong with it?*

We have a new member.

Some of the perkiness was back again, so I guess she'd been anticipating something more troublesome. *Who is it?*

I didn't mean to, but for some reason I hesitated. *Ed Chen.*

Chess-playing Ed?

Yes. He plays percussion in the Seattle Youth Orchestra. He'll be our drummer.

Mom grinned like a fool. *So you'll be seeing a lot of each other?*

It's not like that. I rolled my eyes.

She threw up her arms in surrender. *Okay. So what name should appear on the contract?*

I finger-spelled *Ed Chen.*

Which is short for . . . Edward? Edgar? Edmund? This is a legal document. I need his full name.

Edgar.

Certain?

I wasn't certain. *I'll check. I'll get back to you.*

Mom still had a smile on her face, but she didn't seem amused. *Okay, you do that,* she signed, then patted my head like I was the naughty puppy she loved in spite of herself.

The next day, Ed was squinting at the chessboard, as usual. He never really played with any rhythm—which is kind of ironic given that he was a human metronome with a drum set—but this time I really felt he was stalling. And to be honest, I couldn't work out why.

"Did you hear me, Ed?" An unusual question coming from me, but he nodded distractedly. "So what is it?" He shook his head. "I have to know," I said. "It's for the contract."

Ed sighed dramatically. He cast his eyes around like he was

hiding quiz answers from a prying neighbor, then wrote one word on a scrap on paper and nudged it toward me.

I studied the name, and studied Ed. I may have repeated this process several times before I was completely sure he wasn't just screwing with me. "Seriously? Your name is really . . . Edgard?"

"Shhh! Yeah. That's why I go by Ed."

"I get that," I said, not trying to be too personal about it, but—*really*. "And I thought *my* name was weird."

"I love your name," he said simply.

I blushed, and he blushed, and his eyes went all puppy-dog, and then we both pretended to study the board again.

"I've never heard the name Edgard before."

"Yeah, well . . . My mom's favorite composer is this French guy named Edgard Varèse. He wrote these funky, large-scale percussion pieces. And I mean, *only* percussion." Suddenly his lips were moving faster, his face alive with excitement. "No strings, winds, brass . . . just a ton of percussion instruments and sirens and whips and . . . well, almost anything. You name it, he did it."

I didn't know whether to be impressed or amused. "That's weird."

"No, it's great. Seriously. So challenging, but it's like a whole new sound world . . ."

He stopped, took a deep breath like he was afraid he'd just overstepped his mark, but I smiled to let him know it was fine. I could imagine new sound worlds. I was totally okay with that.

"Anyway, Mom started giving me percussion instruments to play when I was still a baby, and Varèse is one of my favorites now as well. It's hard not to like playing the drums after you've immersed yourself in Varèse for a while."

He smiled, emphasizing the dimple on his left cheek. I looked for a matching one on the right and decided I preferred the asymmetry.

"So where are you going to study?" I asked.

Ed's hand hovered over his rook. "I've got an audition at the Peabody Institute in February."

"I've heard of that. Where is it?"

"Baltimore."

"Seriously? That must be pretty close to Gallaudet, then."

"Uh-huh. Thirty-seven miles." He shuffled his rook toward certain death.

"Really?" I was amazed he could put a number on it. Who bothers learning stuff like that? I hadn't even realized he knew that Gallaudet was in DC. "Exactly thirty-seven?"

He looked away, scratched his forehead. "Um, yeah. Something like that, anyway."

"We'll be pretty close then."

Ed nodded, then groaned appropriately as I ignored his rook and put him directly into checkmate. But the faintest hint of a smile made me wonder if it really bothered him at all.

CHAPTER 12

That evening, Marissa finally IM'd me, and I was so excited that I didn't even give her a hard time about taking forever to get back to me.

Once she'd admitted that her new school was everything she'd hoped it might be (and assured me yet again that she wished I were there with her), I told her about Dumb, and how they were really coming together. I was on such a roll that I'd written most of an essay when I suddenly realized I wasn't even sure she was getting any of it.

P1P3R: still there?

MARI55A: yes

P1P3R: what do u think?

MARI55A: you're joking, right?

P1P3R: no. why?

MARI55A: don't u find the name dumb offensive?

P1P3R: they came up with it ages ago

MARI55A: and u think it's a coincidence they
asked u to be manager?

P1P3R: YES

MARI55A: ur sure they're not setting u up?

P1P3R: YES

MARI55A: then why would they want a deaf
manager?

P1P3R: why wouldn't they?

MARI55A: r u serious?

P1P3R: i can do this. i can help

MARI55A: why bother? they always ignored u

P1P3R: they're not so bad

MARI55A: do u actually like them?

P1P3R: they're ok. and ed has joined now, so
that helps. hey, can u guess ed's name?

MARI55A: edgard

P1P3R: wow. how do u know?

A pause. A *long* pause. The kind of pause that's usually followed by a comment like MARI55A HAS LOGGED OFF.

MARI55A: i just do

They were words, nothing more, but somehow I could feel her frustration mounting with each exchange. I needed to bring the conversation to an end, but I wasn't sure how. I began to write a question, then erased the words and typed another, then erased that too. Eventually there was nothing onscreen but the blinking cursor and the aching silence of the distance between us—and it was an entirely different kind of silence to the one that had drawn us together in the first place.

Suddenly another message flashed on the screen:

MARI55A: ttyl. xoxo

She logged off before I could say the same thing.

CHAPTER 13

Arranging our first full rehearsal was like scheduling a UN summit, and the process ended with about the same amount of political goodwill. Monday and Tuesday evenings were out because Ed had piano and marimba lessons (cue eye rolling from Josh). Wednesday was a no-go because Tash's mom's salon had extended opening hours, and she was required to help out. (No one but me seemed surprised that the girl with green hair had a mom who ran a salon.) Thursday had to be ditched when Ed informed us that he worked at a coffee shop (more eye rolling), which left Friday. Even Saturday had to be completely ruled out because Ed had Seattle Youth Orchestra rehearsal and Tash spent all day sweeping up hair at her mom's salon. At that point I put my foot down and said that Sunday may be the day of rest for some people, but it sure as heck wouldn't be for Dumb. Thankfully, faced with the alternative of practicing for only a couple of hours a week, everyone seemed on board with that.

Our first full rehearsal took place back in the luxurious surroundings of the Cooke family garage, with its artfully painted walls, spotlighting, and central heating. There was even an old but fully functioning vending machine I hadn't noticed before, and Josh downed two bottles of energy drink before the others had finished setting up. Thus caffeinated, he generously divulged some of the information he'd inexplicably kept secret until that point, such as:

1. The three songs they played on the school steps were, coincidentally, the same three songs they had played at the Battle of the Bands, which were, "technically," the only three songs they knew.

2. Of those three songs, um, three were covers, which meant that, "in a manner of speaking," Dumb would need to pay the copyright holder before recording them.

At which point I butted in and suggested that maybe it was time to learn some new material, and Josh pointed out that:

3. They'd been rehearsing those three songs pretty much continuously "since the beginning of junior year," and the Battle of the Bands performance was the first time they hadn't screwed up.

And Ed stopped biting his fingernails long enough to ask if it was a coincidence that they'd chosen songs that only used the same three chords, and Josh chuckled and said:

4. No. Not a coincidence at all. In fact, it took a while to find songs that only used C-F-G, although Tash

and Will assured him they were itching for more complex material.

And even though I didn't have a clue what they were talking about, I knew my job was to keep up morale, so I said we'd take our time and make sure we were all comfortable before unleashing ourselves on our adoring general public, and Josh laughed again and said:

5. Yeah, but, you know . . . the first recording session with Baz Firkin is booked for this Sunday.

At which point I stopped biting my fingernails and expressed my incredulity through a choice four-letter word. Then I took a deep, calming breath and suggested that we stick to songs they already knew, at which Josh reiterated:

2. Of those three songs, um, three were covers, which meant that, "in a manner of speaking," Dumb would need to pay the copyright holder before recording them.

At which point I uttered several more four-letter words. And this time, breathing deeply didn't help at all.

Fifteen minutes later, Ed was using an ancient bucket of sidewalk chalk to illustrate how they could insert the chord of A minor between C and F. As far as I was concerned, he may as well have been writing hieroglyphics, but Will seemed to know exactly what it all meant. He leaned back and played a series of rumbling bass notes over and over, while Tash looked on admiringly, although her eyes were locked on Will's face, not his hands. A minute later she joined in with the earth-shattering, paradigm-changing C-A minor-F-G chord sequence, and suddenly I could feel how something indefinable had shifted, like a sentence that had grown by a few words. Finally, Josh got in on the act, composing new lyrics especially for the occasion. By the time everyone was in sync, Dumb had its first original song, and although Josh was bummed when I said he should change the lyrics "Hey ho, make me happy" because they were likely to be misinterpreted, a glare from Tash convinced him I was right.

Meanwhile, I kept busy by e-mailing Baz Firkin, insisting that we put off the recording session for at least a few weeks. Then I pulled out my camera and began taking black-and-white photos of the band at work. I took photos lying on the floor, standing on tables, at forty-five-degree angles, and any other positions I could think of that would make the band look sophisticated and artsy. I loaded them onto my laptop and began altering the contrast, distorting the image, and generally screwing with them until they resembled the grainy, hardcore shots I'd found on other bands' websites.

By the time Dumb took a five-minute break, I was already downloading them onto our Facebook page, so everyone came over to look. Will nodded appreciatively, Ed raised an eyebrow admiringly, and Tash didn't say a word—from her, it was the most approving silence I could imagine. And Josh squeezed my shoulder; just once, but I knew it meant he was impressed, and somehow his opinion mattered most of all.

The second half of the rehearsal was the Ed Chen show. For

the next hour, he was no longer the geek they all ignored at school—he was their muse and cheerleader. With deliberately understated drumming, he kept steady time while Josh serenaded me with ever-evolving lyrics, and Will and Tash experimented with the new chord. Tash even kept her eyes fixed on Will at all times, so that their movements were appropriately synchronized, although I'm not sure Will ever noticed. Truth is, Will was so focused on his guitar that he seemed to occupy his own little bubble. On the rare occasions he glanced up, his cloudy expression suggested he was surprised to discover there were other people playing too. Despite that, I could tell by their relaxed demeanor that the music Dumb was producing wasn't chaotic or mistake-prone at all. It was as if Ed had unleashed them on the previously peaceful kingdom of A minor, and they were laying claim to it for themselves.

As they gave a final rendition of "Let Go, I Feel Crappy," which was loud and pissed enough to sound vaguely impressive from where I stood a safe distance away, it was obvious that Dumb had taken a giant leap forward in only one rehearsal. As long as Ed was around, there was cause for optimism. I even allowed myself to reflect that the positive change was indirectly my doing when a new e-mail arrived in my inbox from Baz Firkin:

> Piper: I'm afraid the date of the recording session
> cannot be changed. I only secured release from
> Washington State's finest boarding facility last
> night, and find myself experiencing pecuniary

difficulties. While this is somewhat ironic considering my charges on tax evasion, I must nonetheless see you Sunday. Baz.

It took me a moment to translate the message into English, but the gist of it was clear enough. Dumb would be spending Sunday afternoon recording a song they'd only just written, and had only rehearsed once.

Okay, so my genius had limits.

CHAPTER 14

I stopped by everyone's houses on the way to the recording session so that we could arrive together. It was a calculated decision to save on gas, make sure we all got there, and to elicit sympathy from Baz Firkin when he realized what a heap of crap I was driving. (USS *Immovable* had always gotten me sympathetic looks from everyone at school.)

The session started at noon on Sunday. Or rather, it *would* have started at noon if we'd realized that the studio was in the basement of a crumbling craftsman cottage. Instead, we drove back and forth through the funky neighborhood of Fremont a dozen times, looking for the snazzy building with tinted windows that turned out to exist only in our imaginations.

There was no doubt whatsoever that the man who emerged from the house a minute later was Baz Firkin. He sported a worn paisley shirt and faded black jeans, a ragged gray-brown ponytail floating down his back like a trail of smoke still lingering from the 1980s. I wondered how he'd made it through prison in one piece.

"Greetings, young ones," he exclaimed as he glided toward us, although he seemed to be addressing only me. (Maybe he was distracted by my hearing aids—I noticed his eyes lingering on my ears as we shook hands.) "And may I say what a beautiful beast of a machine that is," he added, pointing to USS *Immovable.* "I used to have one just like it. That was back when velour seats came standard, of course, not as an extra."

Baz led us to a basement door, unlocking it with a rusty key. As he yanked it toward him, flakes of paint fell off.

"Et voila!" he cried, leaning back to afford us an uninterrupted view of the narrow hallway beyond.

No one spoke.

"Now, don't mind the standing water," said Baz calmly. "I've just laid rat traps."

Ed followed Baz inside, pressing himself against the least mold-ridden wall, as if that might reduce his chances of contracting something contagious.

Baz retrieved another key, this one glinting like solid gold. He slid it into the lock on a second door, pushed the door open, and stood back once more.

I don't know if anyone else spoke, but I'm pretty sure that I gasped.

Behind the door was a studio control room—a real one, with banks of electronic equipment that looked like it had been lifted from NASA headquarters. Behind the controls, separated by at least a couple panes of glass, was the studio. True, it had a peculiar odor, but it was a real studio with microphones on stands, and headphones for the musicians.

I looked at Dumb, and for a split second I could tell we were all thinking the same thing: We'd *arrived.*

Baz ushered the band inside, told them where to sit and how he'd control things like balance and reverb from the control room. To deter him from involving me in decisions about the band's sound, I retreated to the corner of the control room and studied his notice board. One of the notices was for KSFT-FM, a local radio station looking for new bands to promote, so I scribbled down the e-mail address. Then I began snapping more artistic black-and-white photos of Will sweeping his hair back, and Josh manhandling two microphones at once—the kind of pics that would be collector's items once Dumb became a household name (ha!).

It was 12:30 before Dumb was ready to begin recording, by which time Baz's effervescent exterior had cooled somewhat. He signaled that I should stop taking photos, and indicated that my place was on a chair beside him. Then he closed the door and began relaying instructions to the players on the other side of the window. I wondered if their hearts were beating as quickly as mine.

I was delighted to discover that the control room was completely soundproofed, which had the advantage that I could hear Baz surprisingly well as long as he spoke up. I understood his commands, his approach, and what he wanted from the band. I even began to wonder if I was a natural in the recording studio.

Ten minutes later, I was aware of what a *dis*advantage it was to be able to hear Baz. I understood perfectly his confusion, bemusement, and general disgust. I was also able to decode at least one in three of his expletives, which equated to about one every ten seconds.

And it wasn't exactly hard to see why he was so pissed. Tash and Will seemed completely overwhelmed by the experience of being in a real studio, fumbling around like their guitars had grown extra strings. Even Ed looked a little stage-struck. And at the front, the ball of energy known as Josh Cooke squeezed the headphones against his ears as he jumped and jived to a beat that must have been coming from a different song. Baz told him to sit down; Josh said he couldn't. Baz told him that his movements were being picked up by the microphone and would ruin the song; Josh said his movements were an intrinsic part of the song. Baz opened his mouth, but nothing came out.

After two extremely deep, calming breaths, and a few seconds of total silence, Baz turned to me. "Is there another song you'd prefer to work on?" he asked.

I shook my head.

"Okay," he tried again, "let me rephrase that. Which song would you like to work on now?"

"The same one," I said, but timidly.

"It's utter crap. Pick another."

"We don't have another."

Baz's mouth hung open long enough for me to count his

cavities. "Now *that* is the most depressing news I've heard since the judge put me behind bars."

I looked at the clock on the wall. It was 12:50. We had another two hours, but I'd have given anything to leave right then.

"What do you want to do?" he asked.

I peered through the window. I knew Ed was frustrated at himself for letting us down, but Tash and Will still looked freaked out. And Josh was as clueless as before, rehearsing his movements like they had any relevance whatsoever in a recording studio.

When I didn't answer, Baz clapped his hands together. "Okay, here's what's going to happen: Dumb is going to perform the song over and over for the next hour. I'll mark the useable sections of each track, then we'll spend the last hour editing them together into a single track." He smiled, but it was a patronizing smile that made me feel even more useless than before.

I looked at Dumb again, all of them still now, wondering why the instructions had dried up. Which is when I realized that Baz had turned off the connection between the rooms. My conversation with him was for our ears only; no point in battering the band's morale any more. Baz's offer was about as generous as we could hope for, I knew that, but I also knew that a true manager wouldn't settle for it, and I knew I couldn't either.

"Wouldn't it be better for them to do one complete, perfect track?" I asked.

Baz snorted. "You'll be lucky if they can pull off one complete, perfect verse."

I have to say I liked the ebullient Baz much more than the obnoxious one. "Please turn on the speaker in the studio."

"I don't think you want them to hear what I have to say."

"Yes, I do," I said decisively. Baz shrugged as he flicked a switch. "Listen up, guys," I said, staring through the window at the band. "We have two hours left. We're going to run the song over and over, with a one-minute break between each track. If you need a drink, grab a bottle of water from my bag in the corner. Otherwise, sit still, focus, and let's nail this thing."

Baz leaned back and prepared himself, but he wouldn't make eye contact.

After half an hour, Dumb had performed "Let Go, I Feel Crappy" eight times. Seven of those were incomplete versions, aborted mid-song following catastrophic collapses that caused the entire group to surrender en masse. The other one was bad enough that Ed looked deflated and Tash looked psychotic.

Another half hour, another six versions (four of them complete!), but I didn't need to hear Dumb to know they were playing out of time with each other. To make matters worse, they were wearing down now and I knew they didn't have many more renditions in them. Even Josh reluctantly sat down between takes, as dismayed as the Energizer Bunny to discover his batteries were running low.

I told Baz to take five, and I joined the band next door. They all removed their headphones, but only Ed looked up as I walked in.

"So here's the deal. Baz wants to edit useable sections of

each track together to make a single good performance," I explained.

Tash was already nodding vigorously. "Yeah. Let's do that."

I held up my hand. "If that's what you all want, fine. But I think we can get one perfect continuous take."

"Who cares?" Josh shrugged. "No one's going to know either way."

I gave the others a chance to have their say, but no one else seemed to have the energy. "It's true, no one else will know. But *you* will, and I think you can do it. I saw you on the school steps, and you had everyone transfixed. You're too good to cheat your way out of Dumb's first original song."

I don't know what I expected anyone to say, but I certainly didn't imagine that Will would be the one to agree. "Yeah," he said, nodding his head in slow motion. Then: "Yeah."

Suddenly Tash seemed to have a change of heart as well. "I guess it would be more satisfying to nail it."

"Okay, good," I said, breathing a sigh of relief. "So how can we make this work?"

"Well, the problem is, I'm not used to wearing headphones while I play," explained Tash gruffly. "And the clicks are throwing me off. And my guitar sounds weird."

"Anything else?"

"Yeah. I hate not being to hear the others the way I normally do. It's weird."

Everyone else nodded too.

"So leave the headphones off," I said.

"It'll be hard to stay in time without the click track," cautioned Ed. "The acoustics here aren't the same as in the garage."

I couldn't help thinking that these kinds of issues must arise for most bands the first time they record in a studio, and that Baz would know what to do. But having rejected his earlier suggestion, I couldn't bring myself to ask him for advice now. This was my band, and my problem. I needed to fix it myself.

"What about Ed's metronome?" I said finally. "It has a flashing display. You could all watch that."

Ed shook his head. "It's LCD. We'll never see it."

"What if I relayed it to you from the control room?"

"You mean . . . you're going to conduct us?"

It was so completely insane that I expected everyone to laugh. But no one did. Instead, Ed reached behind himself and pulled the little black box from his bag. He moved a dial, set the display flashing, and handed it over. Then he ran out to the hallway and grabbed a broom.

"Take this," he said. "Make sure the handle hits the ground in time with the light. It'll make the beat really clear. But you'll need to go back to the control room, or the microphones will pick up the sound."

A minute later I was standing behind the window once again, smiling anxiously as Baz watched me banging my broomstick up and down. He could have said something sarcastic, but to his credit, he didn't. If anything, I felt like I'd won him over in some small way.

For the next hour I pounded my broom, and Dumb pounded to the steady beat of "Let Go, I Feel Crappy." I felt the broom's beats jarring my body like mini-earthquakes. Blisters formed on my thumb and palm, but I never took my eyes off that stupid flashing display. If Dumb could play through the pain, so could I. When else would I get to feel it too?

At 2:55 Dumb finished the twentieth and final rendition of the song, making it abundantly clear that their favorite version was number 17. At 2:59 Baz burned a CD of it, ejected the disk, and signed off for the afternoon.

"They need to practice harder," he said. "If they're really going to do this, they need to work *much* harder."

"They will," I assured him. "But they got better, right?"

Baz laughed. "Are you going to stand in front of them during their gigs too? If so, make sure you get equal billing. People will pay a lot to see the girl with the broom."

Tash kept up a running commentary for the three miles back to her house, but I didn't make any attempt to listen, or to catch snippets of her monologue by lip-reading in the rearview mirror. I could make a wild, stab-in-the-dark guess about what she was saying, and I wasn't exactly thrilled with how things had gone either.

Eventually it was just Ed and me, but he hesitated when we reached his house. I could see in my peripheral vision that he wanted to say something, so I turned to face him, hoping it wouldn't be too critical.

"I'm sorry, Piper," he said. "I let you down today."

Okay, that was the last thing I expected him to say. "What are you talking about?"

"I made so many mistakes. One of the times the song broke down, it was *my* fault."

I had to keep from laughing. "You feel guilty because you screwed up *once*? Wow, if that's our new standard I should be looking to replace Tash and Will ASAP."

Ed smiled at that. "I don't mean it like that. It's just . . . I don't want to sound cocky, but I've had a little more experience than them, you know? But that session was so new. No audience to distract me. Nothing but one song and a microphone that's waiting for me to screw up."

I held out my hand to stop him. "Look, Ed, if anyone should be feeling dumb right now, it's me. I was the one banging a broom handle on the floor."

"No, you did great! You held us together. Besides, that's how people used to conduct orchestras before batons: They just hammered a staff into the ground." I laughed. "No, I'm serious," he protested.

"But not *real* musicians."

"Absolutely," he gushed, gaining momentum now we were back on his favorite topic. "You're following in the illustrious footsteps of composers like Lully."

I made him spell out the name for me, but it didn't help. "Never heard of him. Was he any good?"

"Sure. Right up to the moment he rammed the staff on his toe, got gangrene, and died."

I snorted. "Now I *know* you're kidding."

Ed bit the inside of his mouth, furrowed his brows. "Actually, I'm not kidding at all. But hey! It looks like your feet are doing just fine. Nice shoes by the way."

He opened the door and climbed out before I could say good-bye. And it wasn't until I started to pull away that I remembered I was wearing a new pair of Chucks.

CHAPTER 15

Determined to prove they were up to snuff, Dumb scheduled an extra rehearsal for Wednesday lunchtime. With Ed on board, we'd even gotten permission to use the large music classroom. Unfortunately, Josh had also scheduled an audience.

I should have realized immediately that Kallie's appearance at the back of the room was no accident. The music block is on the far side of school, and doesn't lead anywhere else. More significantly, Kallie was there to stay—she pulled up a chair and sat down, crossing her freshly waxed legs as though she was discouraging the boys from taking the closer look that her miniskirt seemed to demand.

I stared at her in a way that was meant to say *What are you doing here?* But Kallie just smiled right back, her lips parting by the smallest degree, revealing perfect white teeth.

I'd like to say that Kallie's presence went unnoticed by the band, but nothing could be further from the truth. From the moment she showed up, Josh's performance deteriorated.

Within seconds his focus was on some acrobatic dance moves that seemed more suited to Disney than Dumb. Meanwhile, Tash gripped her guitar like it was an assault rifle. I estimated ten minutes before someone got hurt.

I tried to shut out the madness while I wrote an e-mail to Phil Kirchen c/o WSFT-FM, explaining that Dumb's mentor, Baz Firkin, had made us aware of his call for bands (which was almost true since I'd seen the notice at Baz's studio). A little web-based research revealed that budget cuts and a declining listenership threatened to bankrupt the station, so I added a line saying that if he promoted Dumb I could guarantee at least a thousand new listeners from our high school, where the band had a cult following (again, the sentiment was true even if my numbers were somewhat unscientific). True, the station's tagline—"the softer side of Seattle"—had me a little worried, but I figured minor details like musical style and genre could be negotiated later.

As soon as I'd sent the e-mail, I noticed Josh standing in front of me, stamping the ground as if he were trying to put a hole in it. I peered over the top of the computer and realized all eyes were on me.

"Ed said that stamping my foot is a socially acceptable way of getting a deaf person's attention," explained Josh, confused that it took me so long to notice.

At the back of the room, Ed rolled his eyes. "But not during a band rehearsal, remember? I told you, there are too many other vibrations. Just wave your hand somewhere that Piper can see."

Okay, I admit it—it kind of sucked to have all this explained in front of me, like it was part of a lesson on the care and feeding of the deaf girl. It especially sucked to have it play out in front of Kallie Sims, like we were a study in opposites, textbook definitions of "cool" and "uncool" with real live representations of each (*for illustrative purposes only!*). But at the same time, it was difficult to be too bummed since Ed had obviously told them all this stuff before, when I wasn't around. And although Josh had forgotten, there was something quite comforting about knowing that he'd tried to take note, and that I had some behind-the-scenes help for whenever he (and everyone else) forgot.

Josh accepted Ed's criticism with a curt nod, then looked back at me and grinned like we were sharing a joke that no one else could understand. His eyes twinkled, and I felt myself turn bright red. A moment later he stood beside me, clearing his throat to get everyone's attention.

"Guys," he announced, smiling brilliantly, "I think we can all agree that we're coming together, musically speaking. But there's still something missing. Thankfully Kallie will change that for us."

Tash smacked her right hand against her guitar strings, eliciting an angry response from her amp. "We don't need a stylist."

Josh laughed. "Don't worry, Tash. I wouldn't want to change your style anyway."

Tash narrowed her eyes, but decided to take it as a compliment.

"No," continued Josh, "Kallie's not here as a stylist. She's here as our new member."

I didn't wait for the others to voice their outrage. I just closed my laptop, grabbed Josh's arm, and dragged him into the neighboring practice room. I slammed the door shut and hoped the crumbling soundproofing on the walls still worked.

"What the hell, Josh. You know she can't join."

The smile never left his face. "Why not?"

"For one thing, the contracts have been finalized."

"I don't see any contracts."

"That's 'cause my mom had to redo them to add Ed's name, remember?"

"Oh, yeah, Ed." Josh picked at the wall, flicking a fingernail-sized chunk of white foam across the room. "I'm glad we were able to find a place in the band for your best friend. I really mean that."

"He's not my best friend," I said, wondering why I felt so defensive. "Anyway, we needed a drummer."

"And now we need Kallie."

"Why? What does she play? For all I know she could screw up the band's sound completely."

"The way Geek Boy Ed screwed up our image, you mean? Sure, a dork with bad clothes—that's just what we needed." The words came out faster than usual, and though he tried to salvage the comment by smiling again, it was a smile that didn't extend beyond his mouth. "I don't mean that, of course. It's just that, well . . . *look* at us. My brother looks perpetually stoned even though he's never touched drugs in his life. Tash precisely fits the FBI's profile of a future serial killer. And Ed has all the flair of a bank clerk. See what I'm saying?"

I nodded, half because I was still reeling from his attack on Ed, and half because, though I hated to admit it, I saw his point. Josh was the ideal lead singer—energetic, charismatic, and hopelessly in love with himself. But the band's token feminine influence was Tash, and viewing her in certain types of light was enough to put you off your food. I thought about the photos I'd taken, and how Kallie would change the way people looked at the band. So what if she contributed nothing musically? She'd be a figurehead, a media darling, the paparazzi's dream. But still . . .

"We *need* Kallie," pressed Josh, clearly sensing my waning resistance. "We need someone to make us look good. And believe me, Kallie makes us look *amazing*."

I rolled my eyes. "You just want to hook up with her, don't you?" I asked, hoping he'd seize the opportunity to deny it.

"Don't make this about me, Piper. Dumb needs Kallie. Kallie *is* Dumb."

"Do you mean that literally or figuratively?" I snorted.

He laughed loudly. "Probably both. Does it matter?" He flashed his irresistible smile, confirming that we'd just shared an intimate joke. We were colluding.

OMG! did u hear? piper vaughan and josh cooke were caught colluding in a music practice room!

Josh chivalrously held the door open for me as we left, still chuckling, and it wasn't until we'd entered the classroom that I realized he thought he'd convinced me to accept Kallie. And I guess he had. After all, he knew a whole lot more than me about bands, and his logic seemed flawless. Sure, I still despised Kallie with every fiber of my being, but that didn't seem like an especially persuasive line of defense.

"Okay, guys," he shouted, presumably for my benefit. (He had so much to learn.) "This is a democracy. Let's have a show of hands. All those in favor of Kallie joining Dumb."

As Josh and I raised our hands, Will looked down, and Tash scowled. Only Ed's vote was in doubt. I peered at him expectantly, but he shook his head. If I'd been thinking clearly I'd have realized that Ed's refusal to play along was a last-gasp rescue attempt, a warning sign written large in bright neon lights. Heck, I'm sure I'd have breathed a sigh of relief. But at that moment, all I could see was that Ed was voting against me, and my face must have registered my sense of betrayal. Immediately, as if it had a mind of its own, Ed's hand crept slowly upward, while his eyes studied the floor.

Josh clapped his hands together and attempted to shake my hand like it was all my idea. But I wasn't looking at Josh. I was watching Tash, her nostrils flaring, eyes shooting daggers at Kallie.

Yes, we had our eye candy, but it didn't take a genius to see that she was in danger of being eaten alive.

CHAPTER 16

It was like Groundhog Day: Mom waltzing in with the revised contract as if she were a servant proffering a gift to a monarch. It was supposed to make me laugh, to keep some of the growing tension at bay, but I knew I was about to make things worse.

Before you give that to me, I need to tell you something.

Mom ditched her faithful-servant impersonation. *What is it?*

I need you to add another name.

I already added Ed's name.

Yes. A different name.

Mom's shoulders slumped, but her gestures were surgically efficient, her face suddenly sharper than before. *It's preferable for your band to be able to fit onstage.*

Mom was almost never sarcastic, especially when signing, so I knew she was really exasperated. Or maybe just exhausted, as she was getting back later every day.

It's just one more person—

Today, yes. By the time I redo the contract it might include half the school.

I clammed up because Mom was making fun of me, and she knew it too, because she sighed and changed gear. *So who's new?*

Kallie Sims, I finger-spelled, then added *school goddess* in angry gestures that surprised us both.

And what does the school goddess play?

I was about to answer when it occurred to me that I didn't know, because Josh hadn't told me. I *had* to know, of course. If I didn't, then the band really *was* a joke. How could it not be? And yet . . .

Mom hugged me, saving me from having to incriminate myself. When she stepped back, she tilted her head to the side. *Are you sure you want me to redo this contract?*

I wanted to say that I didn't have a choice, but I didn't want Mom to think even less of Dumb than she already did, so I nodded with manufactured confidence.

Okay. Kallie, right? She finger-spelled the name for confirmation.

I nodded again, but I'm sure a part of me died right there.

Mom was halfway out the door when she stopped. *Would you like me to add a clause about new and departing members? Just something to keep the group fixed at five.*

Yes, I signed with a desperation that must have completely given me away.

An hour later, Mom reappeared with an updated contract. This time she'd printed it on our regular home printer, so it wasn't on the snazzy off-white bonded paper from her office. But I couldn't blame her for that. After all, she probably figured it wouldn't need to last very long.

CHAPTER 17

Apparently, Phil Kirchen at WSFT-FM didn't need long to mull over my request:

Piper: Who's Dumb? Send MP3. Phil.

One line. One freaking line, but the MP3 request sent me into a cold sweat. I figured our chances of getting away with substituting *hard rock* for *soft rock* diminished significantly once he'd actually had a chance to hear the band, and even a DJ who specialized in six-word e-mails was likely to listen to more than the first two seconds of our only track.

I pulled up Google and started reading articles about soft rock, jotting down notes as I went:

- Began as a reaction against hard rock (note to self: bad sign)
- Avoids heavy reliance on electric guitars (note to self: another bad sign)
- Emphasizes inoffensive and inclusive lyrics (note to

self: must try to work out what the hell Josh is actually singing)

- Proponents include: Chicago, Toto, Air Supply (note to self: survivors of these groups all look old and wrinkly now)
- Representative album titles by Air Supply include: *Lost in Love* (note to self: ick); *The One That You Love* (note to self: bleuuugh); *Now and Forever* (note to self: Oh God, I just barfed up my nose)

I took a time-out and thought cleansing thoughts. Then, since it was abundantly clear that Dumb was a million miles from being soft rock, I wrote to Phil and said that we couldn't go any further without assurances that there would be some form of payment.

Ten minutes later I received a new message:

Expenses only. P.

Barf or no barf, that was all I needed. Without wasting another moment I ran out to the car, drove to the local library, and checked out a bunch of CDs. While I was there, I e-mailed Baz to say we were working on a new song we needed to record at the session on Sunday. Then I hopped back in the car and drove to Ed's coffee shop, wondering how I should break the news that he had less than twenty-four hours to compose a soft rock song called "Loving Every Part of You."

Easy.

"You're kidding."

I shook my head. "No, Ed. I'm not."

"You are. You're kidding. Either that or you're completely insane."

"Technically, no. Although there are times I wonder about that," I conceded.

Ed sighed dramatically, but forced himself to perk up as a new customer joined us. I figured our conversation was about to be put on hold, so I took a seat at the back of the shop and studied the ancient black-and-white photos of guys in uncomfortable sporting attire holding gigantic oars.

The photos made sense, I suppose, as the shop was called Coffee Crew, a tiny place sandwiched between a pizza parlor and a dry cleaner's. To be honest, I'm not sure I knew it existed until Ed drew me a map. Half a dozen round oak tables filled the available space, while the warmth of an electric fire lured people to stay a little longer than they might have intended. The seven people who sipped coffee from chunky glasses seemed as much a part of the place as the furniture. I made a mental note to come back again when I wasn't on business.

As soon as another customer had been satisfied, Ed shuffled over and sat down opposite me. "And I repeat: You're crazy."

"It's just one song."

"And you want me to teach it to everyone tomorrow?"

"Yeah."

Ed shook his head like he couldn't believe we were really having this conversation, but he also began to sift through the stack of CDs I was placing on the table, which told me his resistance was waning. I tried to hide my relief.

"So what instruments am I writing for now?" he asked. "What does Kallie play?"

"Uh . . . I don't know."

Ed frowned. "You were the one who wanted her to join. How can you not know what she plays?"

"You voted for her too!"

He sighed and looked toward the door, presumably hoping that a customer would come in and rescue him. "Fine. One song. I'll only use the chords of C, F, and G, and maybe A minor if you can promise me we'll have the whole two hours to work on it tomorrow."

"Deal." I held out my hand.

"Fine." Ed looked at my hand for a couple seconds before he finally shook it, his grip pleasantly firm. Before we let go of each other's hands I noticed dark stains around his fingernails, and looked closer. "Barista's fingers," he explained apologetically, watching me the whole time. "Coffee stains, you know?"

"You have nice hands," I told him, wondering which of us would let go first.

Ed seemed frozen to the spot until reawakened by the sound of the door opening. "I've got to . . . you know," he said, taking his hand away with him. "So get writing that song."

"What!?"

"Get writing. I said I'd compose a song, but I'm not writing the lyrics as well. That's all you."

"What do I write?"

"I don't know. Look at the CD inlays and read the lyrics, then come up with something similar."

I was about to protest again, but Ed clearly valued his job enough to serve customers in a timely manner. Over the next fifteen minutes I scribbled away, penning verse and chorus of the most insipid love song ever composed:

Time has passed since last I saw your face,
The memory of your touch
Your smile, your heart, your grace,
The visions that I once enjoyed have gone without a trace.

I didn't hear Ed rejoin me. I didn't know he was there at all until I saw his reflection in the window from the corner of my eye. I flushed red with embarrassment before he'd said a word.

He sat down opposite me, sipping a large cup of what I hoped was decaf coffee; although, given his usual energy levels, I had a feeling that decaf wasn't part of Ed's vocabulary. He saw me staring at the drink and pushed it toward me, reluctantly taking it back when it became clear I wasn't interested in getting even tenser.

"They're good lyrics," he said finally.

I rolled my eyes. "Whatever."

"I'm serious. I can do something with this."

That perked me up. "Really?"

"Really." Ed smiled. "By tomorrow afternoon Dumb will be performing our first love song."

And then there was silence while we both digested those words.

CHAPTER 18

I'll be home late today, I signed to Mom as she headed off to work the next morning.

Mom shrugged. *Tell Dad. I'll probably be later than you.*

Dad was in the kitchen, banging spatulas against countertops and pans to see how Grace would respond. For her part, Grace was enjoying the entertainment, swinging her head around to follow every sound. Eventually she seemed to get bored, craning her neck toward the front door.

Dad clapped his hands and laid a big fat kiss on her tiny forehead. "Good job, Gracie!" He beamed at me. "Incredible, isn't it?"

"What is?"

"The way she heard Mom closing the front door. I'm not sure she could hear it a few days ago."

I felt my chest tighten. "That's good," I managed, willing myself to believe I'd actually heard it too.

"Correction: It's *amazing.*" Dad bent down until he was at eye level with Grace in her high chair. "Simply amazing."

I wanted to ask him if he'd been as fascinated by the physiology of my hearing loss as Grace's improvement, but I could guess how that conversation would play out.

"I'm going to be home late, Dad." Dad nodded, but he couldn't tear his eyes away from Grace. "I said I'm going to be home late, okay?"

Dad glanced up. "Oh, yeah, fine. Whatever."

Whatever. It was probably one of the top ten words spoken each day at school, but coming from Dad it sounded so very different. I shook my head and was about to leave when he stopped me.

"Hold on. What are you up to?"

"You mean, what am I doing after school?"

"Yeah. That's what I said."

Breathe in, breathe out. Breathe in, breathe out. "Dumb has a rehearsal after school."

"So? You don't play anything."

"I'm the manager."

"Still? I figured you'd be done with that already."

"No."

"Oh. So have you made any money yet?"

And just like that my pent-up anger dissipated, turning me from ferocious tiger to self-pitying kitten. I couldn't even maintain eye contact.

"Oh," he said again. "Well, I guess it's up to you how you spend your free time."

I nodded vigorously, like we could agree on that, but inside

I knew what he was really saying, and I just needed to get away. I yelled to Finn that he had one minute to get in the car, then slammed the front door behind me.

See, Dad, I can hear it too!

Finn used the full sixty seconds, and when he piled into the passenger seat he was out of breath and his shoelaces were untied. *You're angry,* he signed.

I rolled my eyes. "And you're perceptive."

Finn tied his laces while the engine turned over a gazillion times. When I slammed my fist against the dash, he sat bolt upright. "What's wrong? Is it me?"

"No!" I shouted. Finn raised his eyebrows expectantly, waited for me to continue. "It's everything, okay? It's Dad, and Dumb, and the fact that I need them to learn a whole new song today, and I'm still not sure how to get us serious money."

"Forget about the money. Focus on getting them to play better. Add some new songs."

I turned the key again, and this time the engine fired up, blasts of black smoke filling the air behind us. Finn covered his mouth with his scarf, knowing that we'd probably get a lungful as I rolled down the driveway.

I took the car out of first gear—my less-than-ideal solution to a faulty parking brake—and ground the gearstick into reverse. Then I paused. "Sitting in the basement playing guitar with headphones on doesn't make you an expert, you know."

Finn stared straight ahead, blinked twice. "Please don't be mean to me."

I could have responded with something sarcastic, or dismissive, but I didn't. Because for all his faults, Finn looked small in the seat beside me, and I knew he was right. Besides, I was about to say something that would annoy him: "We won't be leaving school until five o'clock tonight."

Finn kept the scarf wrapped over his mouth, but his eyes gleamed as his hands produced an enthusiastic thumbs-up.

I figured he must be kidding, but as I continued to stare at him it was obvious Finn wasn't feigning enthusiasm. For whatever reason, the same kid who seemed hell-bent on expulsion seemed positively thrilled that we'd be staying late at school.

Something was up, and I just hoped I found out what it was before Belson did.

CHAPTER 19

Josh had omitted to mention Kallie's instrument of choice for a good reason: Lo and behold, she was an aspiring guitarist, with the emphasis on "aspiring." Tash saw Kallie removing a guitar from her case and muttered a phrase that seemed to consist entirely of expletives, while Kallie smiled as if it were the most delightful coincidence in the world.

Josh sidled up and grinned at me, presumably to reassure me that this was all for the best. I even believed it until he wrapped an arm around Kallie's shoulders, easing her toward him like he was claiming her. Meanwhile Kallie ran her fingers along a broken guitar string, seemingly unaware of his attention.

"Guess this is a bad time to say I don't have any spare strings, right?" she asked no one in particular.

Josh squeezed Kallie's shoulders playfully and nodded in Tash's direction. "Don't worry, Tash has spares. Can you fix this, Tash?"

Tash glared at Kallie, no doubt thinking of several better uses for a steel string. I contemplated asking Will to bail Kallie out instead, but then I realized that his bass guitar strings wouldn't work.

"I only have one spare set," Tash huffed.

Josh produced a five-dollar bill like so much spare change he'd found in the folds of his pocket. "You can get yourself another, right?"

Tash hesitated, but she took Kallie's battered guitar, wound the string around the nut, and tuned it methodically. Then she tried tuning the neighboring string as well, which instantly snapped. She gazed at her dwindling supply of spare strings and shook her head.

"Have you ever tuned this?"

"Of course," insisted Kallie.

"With what? A tuning fork?"

"No. I only play by myself, so I just tune the upper strings to the lowest."

Tash threw up her hands in surrender. "Okay, I'm done. I'm not going to sit here and replace every single string."

Josh dug into his pocket and retrieved five more five-dollar bills. "Just get on with it, Tash."

He meant it to end the discussion right there, but instead all eyes were drawn to the wad of notes he dangled like a carrot inches from Tash's face. Even Will looked up, his face creased like he'd just detected a nasty odor, or maybe in distaste at his brother's flaunting the family wealth in public.

Tash paused again, but it was just for show. It was clear she'd do it, and was privately hoping that every single one of the strings snapped before she was done.

Which they almost did. Twenty-five minutes later, Kallie had four new guitar strings, Tash had twenty dollars, Josh had his arm surgically attached to Kallie's shoulder, and Dumb had significantly less than two hours to learn a new song and discover they had just been reinvented as a soft rock band.

"*What?*" Tash exploded.

"Soft rock," I repeated. "If we can learn this song today, we'll be heard on KSFT-FM, and interviewed live too." (Okay, so I was getting ahead of myself, but I figured if it all fell through I'd be out of a job anyway, so it hardly mattered. After all, there were only twelve more days until my month was up.) "It'll be serious exposure, the kind we can use to get Dumb's music heard on other stations, maybe even get us paying gigs."

I knew I had Josh at "exposure." At "paying," I had Tash too. I never knew when I had Will, so I just discounted him completely. Then I looked at Kallie—she was technically a member too now, hard as that was to believe—and she smiled back vacantly, which was perfect. Then I signaled to Ed to get started, which he did after an annoyed glance at his watch.

For the next hour and a half I watched with morbid fascination as Kallie tried to coordinate her playing with Tash, Will seemed to slip in and out of consciousness, and Josh sang "I'll stay with you / We'll see this through" like he was dry heaving. By the time it was all over, Ed looked exhausted, Kallie seemed to be having second thoughts about joining us, and I'd discovered that my least favorite song in the whole wide world was the one I wrote myself.

CHAPTER 20

If I'd thought that Dumb's first recording session had taught them a lesson about discipline and studio etiquette, I was sadly mistaken. Tash spent the first five minutes outside with Baz, lecturing him about some aspect of the recording that I probably wouldn't be able to hear anyway. When she finally joined everyone else, she moved her chair as far away from Kallie as possible, even though they were playing roughly the same music.

"You'll be pleased to know I brought an extra broom," said Baz, taking a seat beside me. "You know, just in case you wear out the first one."

He erupted into laughter, which was kind of annoying, so I pretended that my hearing aids had been turned off. By the time I signaled they were on again, he didn't bother to repeat the joke.

Even with several legitimate reasons for the recording to go badly—lack of rehearsal time, ongoing issues with the studio headphones, Kallie's inability to play guitar—Josh decided to spice things up a bit by adding some sound effects (pretend coughing, burping, vomiting) to the first two renditions of "Loving Every Part of You." I couldn't exactly hear what he was doing, of course, but I could see it clearly enough. Meanwhile, the rest of the band plowed on, lost in their own little worlds.

When Josh reprised his hilarious antics for the third run-through, Baz had clearly had enough. He jumped out of his chair, shut down the mixing console, and began pacing around the control room.

"If I spend much more time with your band, I may just check back into prison for a break!" he cried.

"That wouldn't exactly help," I pointed out.

"No, but then, what would? Don't misunderstand me: I need the cash. But I'm still tempted to call the Battle of the Bands organizers and tell them to keep their money."

I couldn't exactly blame him, but flouncing around the room wasn't achieving anything. "Sit down, Baz. Can't you just pretend this isn't about the money? It's your chance to make them sound better."

"And what about you? You're a manager, or at least you claim to be. But you've suddenly got an extra member you don't need, and the group's sound has done a one-eighty. So what are you in this for, if it's not the money?"

I sighed. "Okay, yeah, it's about the money."

He smacked his thigh. "*See?*"

"My parents raided my college fund to pay for my deaf sister to get a cochlear implant, and I thought maybe I could get Dumb some paid work."

Even as I said it I realized how stupid it sounded, but Baz's look of triumph disappeared immediately. He ran his hand along his ponytail, looked through the window into the studio, and rolled his eyes as Josh ogled Kallie from behind. "You seem like a honest person, Piper, and you know these kids better than me. So just tell me they're worth the effort. Convince me this is a band worth fighting for."

I watched Josh strutting, Ed practicing, Kallie hiding, Will spacing, and Tash gazing at Will, and realized that Baz was right. This wasn't a group at all. There was no togetherness, no blending—just five separate flavors of an indigestible dish called Dumb.

Baz opened a magazine and sat down, propping his feet up like he was settling down for a restful afternoon. I didn't even blame him. What else was he supposed to do? Dumb wasn't his group, it was mine. Countless bands had come and gone in the time he'd been running his studio, most of them too insignificant to be mourned by anyone except the members themselves. And yet I already felt nostalgic as I peered through the glass and my eyes glazed over with tears. I wondered what might have been if they could only have put their egos aside and concentrated on the one thing that mattered most: playing music.

And that's when the activity inside the studio stopped, and five pairs of eyes stared right back at me.

I walked through the door and stood before them, sighed deeply as I recalled the opportunity we'd thrown away. It was too wasteful, too frustrating to comprehend. And even though I knew I should apologize for contemplating quitting on them, I couldn't do it. I was too angry. So angry I needed to hit something. Which is how my fist came to make contact with the cinder block wall.

"You idiots!" I screamed. "You've got free use of a studio, a professional mentor, and you still can't even pretend to play together. Well, that's about to change. You're gonna work your butts off for the next hour, or I'm pulling the plug on everything: the Facebook page, the radio shows, *every*thing." Josh raised his hand, but I shut him down. "Whatever the hell it is you think you're about to say, Josh, forget it. Just shut up. Right now, all of you should be ashamed to be heard by anyone. Right now, I'm ashamed to be your manager." No one moved a muscle. "Now, I'm going to beg Baz to give us one more hour. Just one hour. Unless you can make a song work by then, he's done with you. And so am I."

I turned on my heel and strode into the control room, where Baz greeted me with a subtle nod that assured me he approved of the plan. And for the next hour—while my knuckles bled and my hand throbbed—Dumb worked hard. My eyes told me that no single rendition was perfect, but after each one they compared notes, and listened as Baz offered suggestions.

When the session was over they looked exhausted, packing up their instruments in silence. One by one they filed past me without a word of support or dissent, and I realized that in forging a group from Dumb, I might have alienated myself. But then Ed shuffled by, and the grin he wore told me I'd done exactly what I needed to do.

In the far corner of the room, Baz ejected a CD and handed it over. "Here's the best track—not perfect, but useable. If this is who Dumb is going to be, then send it out to radio stations, put it on your webpage. Start generating buzz. Get people listening."

"Okay."

"Look, you've got one recording session left. Do us all a favor and wait a while before booking it, okay? There's a whole world of rock music out there, and you should get acquainted with it. Get everyone up to speed. Learn new material. When you're ready, I'll be here."

He held out his hand and I shook it gratefully, and as our eyes met I had the feeling I'd earned that most elusive prize—his respect.

"One more thing," he said, letting go of my hand. "I know the sacrifices rock bands make for their image, but people are going to notice if one of the members isn't even playing."

I gasped. "What? Who?"

"That new girl. Tash told me you wanted her microphone turned off. . . . Didn't you?"

I didn't answer that question, because I didn't have to. Baz shook his head sympathetically, but as I left the studio I knew that whatever respect I'd just won had already evaporated. Maybe it was deserved too, because instead of thinking about how I should bring Tash back in line, I spent the rest of the day wondering if I could just cover the whole thing up.

But when had things ever been that easy?

CHAPTER 21

The following day I received an e-mail from Phil:

> Got your MP3. Dumb's a go. This Wednesday.
>
> 8PM. Arrive EARLY. Go to 4th floor, suite 416.
>
> Please confirm. P.

Everyone was gratifyingly enthusiastic about the news, even though they still thought soft rock completely sucked. Tash made sure her mom let her off work that Wednesday evening, and after reminding me that school nights are for homework, my mom gave the go-ahead too.

The euphoria even carried over to the extra rehearsal Dumb scheduled for Wednesday lunchtime. I told them Phil would just be playing their MP3 on air, but they didn't seem to care. For thirty minutes I sat back and felt the glimmer of pride that historically precedes the most catastrophic falls.

Rain was misting in from the Puget Sound when we arrived outside the downtown studio of KSFT-FM; or rather, the stained concrete office building within which the studio was buried. Windows reflected amber streetlamps, but there were no signs of life inside. I pressed a buzzer marked KSFT-FM, and waited.

And waited.

When 7:50 came and went, I pressed the buzzer again.

And waited again.

I was practically shaking by the time Ed tapped my arm to let me know the door had clicked unlocked. It was 7:56, so we tumbled inside, partly because we were getting drenched—being true Seattleites, none of us had brought an umbrella—and partly because our interview was due to start in, oh . . . four minutes.

I scanned the not-to-scale map on the wall and hurried everyone toward the only elevator. It was 7:58 when we made it to the fourth floor.

"What kept you?" said the breathtakingly large man who met us as the doors opened. "Never mind that. I'm Phil, and you need to take the second door on the right and get settled in the booth at the far end of the studio. I need to pee."

As we hurried into the studio I realized there was no way we'd all fit into the booth. There was barely room for three people, and Phil seemed to equate to three people all by himself.

"I'll stay out here," I said. "You guys cram in. Just do your best."

Ed placed his hand gently on my arm. "Where's the producer?"

I looked around but there was no one else in the room. I shrugged.

Just then Phil bumbled back in, scanning the room like

he'd lost his keys. "Anyone seen an ugly kid with acne?" he asked.

"No," I said sharply, wondering which of us he meant.

"Damn. He was here a moment ago." He pulled a fistful of gummy bears from his pocket and jammed them into his mouth, and suddenly I had no hope of understanding him. "That's . . . trouble . . . interns," he mumbled. "When . . . no pay . . . disappear." He gawked at me like I was supposed to respond, but at least it gave him time to swallow. "Forget it. So which one of you wrote to me?"

I raised my hand.

"Great."

Phil wrapped an arm around me and led me over to a desk just outside the booth. The pit-stain in his T-shirt was delightfully visible across my shoulder. Through the large window I could see Josh surreptitiously pulling a microphone toward him, ensuring he'd have a starring role in tonight's interview, but everyone else had their back to me.

Suddenly Phil was tapping me on the arm. "You deaf or something?" he chuckled.

I nodded, pulled back my hair so he'd see the hearing aids. Phil didn't seem thrilled by this discovery.

"Jesus," he groaned. "Look, here's what'll happen. You'll hear us through the studio monitors. Whenever I say it's time for a break, you press this." He pointed to a button on which the words "OFF AIR" had been handwritten in thick black ink.

I took a deep breath. "I might not be able to hear you."

"But you can hear me now."

"It's different."

Phil's shoulders slumped. I got the feeling he was a man who was used to receiving bad news.

"Okay, look, when I raise my right hand"—he raised it helpfully to show me which one that was—"you press the ON AIR button. When I raise my left"—the other arm popped up—"press the OFF AIR button. Got it?"

I nodded, resisted the temptation to point out that deafness hadn't yet compromised my ability to tell right from left, but thanks anyway. Besides, Phil was already barreling into the booth, evicting Josh from the office chair and exiling him to one of the off-balance stools on the other side. The office chair dipped about six inches when Phil sat down.

I swung around as I felt the floor vibrate. Ed had stamped his foot to get my attention. "I can do this if you're not comfortable," he said.

"No way." I pointed into the booth. "You need to be in there."

"You sure?" He squeezed my arm, just once, firm and comforting. I could feel the warmth of his hand through my sweater.

I swallowed hard. "Absolutely," I lied.

Ed nodded and turned away while I examined the place where his hand had been. Seconds later, I glanced up to see Phil waving his right arm frantically.

I launched myself at the ON AIR button, and immediately Phil began rambling into his microphone. Then he paused and pressed a button in front of him, and the studio was filled with fuzz and static that resembled Dumb's recording of "Loving Every Part of You."

Behind the glass, Phil glared at me. "Pay attention," he mouthed, all super-slow and super-large and super-duper-patronizing. *Schmuck.*

I took a deep breath and tried to convince myself this interview wasn't just a gargantuan mistake. It would've helped if I could have seen the band, but they all had their backs to me. I tried to read their body language, but they were all sitting bolt upright, which either meant (a) they had good posture, or (b) they were petrified.

One minute down, twenty-nine to go.

When the static fizzled out, Phil leaned forward and resumed his monologue. I could even hear his voice, but the studio monitor inflected everything with a buzzing that obscured the words. It was a full minute before he smiled at Kallie to indicate she could reply, but I couldn't see her lips. She began to hunch her shoulders too, a far cry from her customary breezy movements. I wished I knew what she was saying. I felt so helpless and inadequate, just watching the rise and fall of her shoulders, like that gave me any clue at all. But then I noticed Phil, beaming at her every word. Maybe Kallie had a talent for talking about soft rock after all.

Phil launched into another extended question, then stared at Kallie expectantly. She seemed more relaxed this time. I leaned back and forced myself to breathe normally again.

I was still focused on my breathing when I noticed Phil waving his left hand energetically. I pounced on the OFF AIR button and tried to remain stoic as he rolled his eyes.

Three minutes later I was directed to put them back ON AIR, and this time I never took my eyes off Phil. No matter what, I didn't want to miss another cue.

Phil's questions kept coming, and Kallie's answers seemed to delight him. He laughed with childlike innocence, waggled his finger, clapped appreciatively, then licked his lips and drank from a cracked mug like a man dying of thirst. When he thunked it down on the desk before him, he turned bright red, and it dawned on me that he was acting the way Josh did around Kallie. In fact, he seemed to have regressed about thirty years, practically leering at her.

Oh God. Phil was coming on to Kallie.

Gross.

I checked the other band members and quickly worked out that Phil's crush on Kallie was the least of my worries. Josh had shifted his chair so that it touched Kallie's, and his arm rubbed hers in a proprietary "she's taken, dude" way that made me want to retch. Meanwhile, Tash had fully turned her chair ninety degrees, to get a better view of the girl she evidently planned to dismember later that evening. I glanced at my watch and willed the remaining few minutes to pass without violence.

As soon as Phil signaled for me to take them OFF AIR, I gladly obliged, then pushed open the door to the booth and began ushering Dumb's members away. Phil's eyes remained locked on Kallie's butt as she exited the room, her face caught somewhere between surprise at all the attention she'd received and fear at the vague premonition she was about to suffer a Tash takedown.

"That Kallie is a stunner, huh?" sighed Phil, as soon as we were alone.

I tried not to gag. "She's seventeen."

"That's okay," he laughed, scratching his belly. "I can wait a year."

"You owe us some money," I shot back, trying to redirect the conversation before I called him something offensive.

"Oh yeah, expenses. Ten bucks okay?" he said, reaching into his wallet.

"Thirty."

"What? No way."

"Ten for parking. Five for gas. Five for discretionary refreshments."

"That's only twenty."

"And ten for my producing skills. I normally charge twenty bucks, but I'm giving you the family rate."

Phil snorted. "For thirty, I'll need receipts of course."

"I'll mail them to you . . . of course."

He shook his head as he opened his wallet and took out some bills, and I got the feeling he didn't like me as much as he liked Kallie.

"Five-dollar bills, please," I said, pointing to them helpfully.

He handed them over like he couldn't wait to be rid of me. "You're a pushy one, aren't you?" he said.

I beamed as I pocketed the cash, and I could tell by the disgusted look on his face that pushy wasn't necessarily a bad thing to be.

By the time I got to the elevator, everyone had already gone downstairs. I jabbed the elevator call button, then waited an eternity as it ground its way back toward me. I didn't have a clue what Kallie had said, but whatever it was, she hadn't checked it out with censor Tash beforehand, that was for sure. But it was too late to undo the interview now. I could only hand out the bills as quickly as possible, and hope that Dumb's good graces could be bought for the bargain price of five bucks apiece.

I ran outside as soon as the elevator deposited me on the ground floor, but Tash was already laying into her nemesis.

"Break it up. I've got money," I shouted, stuffing a bill into each of their hands.

"What's this?" asked Josh. He held the bill like it was a piece of used toilet roll.

"It's your share of Dumb's first paid gig."

Josh froze. "Hold on. You don't mean—"

"You told me I had a month to get you a paid gig. I did it."

"By 'paid gig,'" said Josh, curling his fingers into air quotes, "we didn't mean five bucks."

"Fine print's a bitch," I agreed sympathetically.

Our discussion would probably have gone on much longer, except that Tash had pocketed the money and commenced verbally assaulting Kallie again, and I knew I needed to intervene.

"What's going on?"

"Nothing," bristled Tash. "Kallie's just explaining who made her spokesperson for Dumb."

Kallie's eyes brimmed with tears. "I didn't mean for him to ask me all the questions."

Tash rolled her eyes. "Then refuse to answer. Tell him that someone else can speak instead."

"I'm sorry. I really am. I just wasn't thinking."

"Damn right. You didn't even have a single intelligent answer." Tash flicked at the ring in her lip. "We're not just trying to have some fun, as you put it. Maybe that's all this is to you, but it actually *matters* to me."

"I'm sorry. I'm so sorry."

"For Christ's sake, stop saying sorry. I never wanted you in this group anyway."

"But I was voted in."

"Did you see my hand go up?"

Kallie shook her head. Now that her hair was getting wet from the misty rain it seemed to lose some of its life, hanging slick against her head. "I just thought I could probably win you over. I love what we do. And I've been practicing hard. You can tell, right? I really nailed it at the recording session."

Tash laughed. "Are you kidding me? Wake up, Kallie. We told Baz to shut down your channel. . . . You never played a note on that recording."

Kallie looked like she'd just been slapped. "That's not true."

"Of course it is. You didn't really think we'd let you screw it up, did you?"

Kallie turned to me, waited for me to deny it. And although I knew that it was in the group's best interests for Kallie to leave, I still hated not being able to tell her that Tash was lying.

I would have understood if Kallie had said something terrible right then, but she didn't. She simply smiled like she understood, and forgave us all anyway. She studied the five-dollar bill again, proof that she'd lived the life of a rock star for a few precious days, and began walking away.

Josh hurried after her, stopped her and wrapped an arm around her. Kallie buried her face in his shoulder and cried as he ran his hands across her back, up and down, up and down, and down, down, down, until they rested provocatively on her butt. With a shuddering breath, Kallie pulled away and continued her solitary march down the lamp-lit street. I wondered if she knew where she was going. I worried that she was lost.

Everyone shuffled back to the car, until only Josh and I remained on the sidewalk. As he approached me, he waved the five-dollar bill accusingly.

"What did he do, pay our expenses?"

"Does it matter?"

"You think you're clever, huh?" he sneered. "Well, if you're really our manager now, then sort out this mess."

"How, Josh?"

"Kallie is a member of this group, same as everyone else. They don't like it, then too bad."

"She shouldn't have joined in the first place."

"You voted her in."

"It was a mistake."

"Live with it. Just the same as we live with Ed."

I almost laughed. "Not the Ed argument again. We've been through this, remember?"

"Yeah, I remember. And it's the same thing."

"No, it's not. Ed can actually play his instrument. Ed is a musician. Heck, Ed has a functioning brain."

Josh's head whipped up. "Yeah, well, you know what I think? I think that even if Kallie were the best musician in this band, you'd still hate her. So would Tash. And if everyone had treated you the way they just treated Kallie, you wouldn't have lasted a single day as our manager. And you know why we didn't treat you badly?"

I rolled my eyes—I knew what was coming. "Because I'm deaf."

"No. Because I convinced Will and Tash to give you a chance to prove yourself. We gave you a month, but all you needed was three weeks. Don't you think it's hypocritical you couldn't even give Kallie half that long?"

Josh acted like he was waiting for me to respond, but I think he knew there was nothing more to say. For once, he was absolutely right, even if I couldn't bring myself to admit it.

CHAPTER 22

Over breakfast the next morning I stared at Kallie's junior year portrait on my laptop screen. I remembered when I first saw it in the school yearbook, a passport-sized photo with all the mysterious allure of a *Vogue* photo shoot. And now here it was again, blown up to fill the entire screen.

I glanced up from the computer to see if Finn had come downstairs yet, but no. He probably figured there was no need to be on time for school when he was always late leaving at the end of the day. I finished my last piece of waffle and checked out the photo again.

Maybe I should have been thrilled. All press is good press, right? But there was something deeply unsettling about seeing Kallie's likeness gracing a website run by a *concerned parents' support group*. And the photo was just too large, like the authors had decided that their audience would enjoy ogling Kallie even more than reading the text below.

I scanned the article. It was chock-full of phrases like "positive message," "endearingly humble," and "ideal role models." I tried to reconcile these observations with my own experience of Dumb—Josh's overflowing ego, Tash's overflowing temper—but the two just wouldn't mesh, so I kept reading . . . and discovered the article wasn't about Dumb at all, although the band's name appeared often. It was All About Kallie, and whatever she had said on the radio had clearly enchanted concerned parents across Washington State.

And that wasn't the only site dedicated to preaching the gospel of St. Kallie. Even religious bloggers got in on the act, describing Dumb as ideal role models for teens everywhere. Some splashed older photos of Kallie across the screen, ones I hadn't even seen before. Below one of them, a caption read: "Kallie Sims—modest, kind, and beautiful too!" Another described Kallie as "not only stunningly gorgeous, but a supremely talented lead guitarist."

I read that last sentence again, tried to pretend it didn't really use the word "talented" in connection with her playing. Heck, she hadn't played at all on the recording. And while I knew I should be laughing at a situation so completely improbable, I just couldn't. Because as Finn entered the kitchen and stared at me like he was about to administer CPR, it dawned on me that Kallie had just become the face of Dumb—a pretty face that Tash was no doubt eager to rearrange.

CHAPTER 23

It was raining hard by the time school ended, so I stood just inside the main doors and watched a thousand students disgorge like water down a drain. Several of them actually flicked their heads in my direction as they passed, which represented a serious shift from my customary invisible state. True, they didn't actually say anything to me, but as far as I could tell, they didn't often say anything to each other either. In any case, I kind of liked the attention.

Ten minutes passed before I saw Kallie, by which time I'd begun to wonder if she'd taken a mental health day. Turns out she was just avoiding anyone connected to the band—not a positive development, but certainly understandable. She stood with her supermodel posse, all head flicks and lip biting. Every boy who passed by ogled them, including Finn, who almost walked into me.

I sensed that the conversation I was about to have with Kallie might be delicate, and I wanted some moral support, so I told Finn I needed him to interpret for me. It wasn't actually a question, so I was taken aback when he said no.

If you don't help me, you can walk home, I signed, making the stakes perfectly clear.

Finn sighed. "Sometimes I really hate you," he said. But he followed me anyway.

I knew she had seen me—her full lips straightened into a thin line as I approached—but she wasn't about to initiate a conversation with someone as hopelessly uncool as me. She even turned away from me slightly, forcing me to stand right in front of her before signing.

Finn looked crushed, his eyes half closed while he relayed my message: "Piper wants to check that everything's okay."

Kallie curled her lip. "What are you talking about?"

I signed again.

"The band," explained Finn. "She wants to make sure there's no problem."

Kallie stared at Finn, exasperated. "Why are you interpreting for her? I've seen her at band practice. I know she can read my lips."

Finn looked lost, but all eyes were on me, not him. The modelettes shook their heads disapprovingly, like I'd been lying about my deafness all these years. I wanted to scream.

"I'm done, Piper, okay?" said Kallie firmly.

I thrust printouts of the blogs at her—the glowing praise, the Kallie love-fest. She glanced at the text and handed them back. "So what? I'm done. That's my final answer."

I took a deep breath, produced a copy of the contract she'd signed. I pointed to a clause embedded deep on page three, the one that stated no member could leave the band without majority approval, under forfeit of $1,000 fine. Mom said it wouldn't be legally binding for anyone under eighteen, but I was willing to bet Kallie didn't know that.

Sure enough, Kallie's face turned ashen. "No way. You wouldn't."

I signed, *Yes. I would. People want to see you. My mother is a lawyer. If you leave, she will sue you.*

I waited, but Finn didn't pass along the message. I gave him my death-ray stare, but he returned it with interest, then slung his book bag over his shoulder and skulked away with a shake of his head.

I felt myself redden. "If you leave, Kallie, my mother will take you to court for that money."

"That's crazy," she moaned, but she looked worried.

"No one made you sign the contract."

Kallie took a deep breath and readied herself for another assault. But when she couldn't think of anything to say, she began tearing up, right there at the entrance to the school.

I was suddenly acutely aware that our discussion had attracted quite a crowd, most of them gawking at Kallie like she was in the process of spontaneously combusting. Which, in a way, I suppose she was.

"I—I can't believe you're doing this," she cried.

To tell the truth, neither could I, but I didn't have time to say that, as Kallie was already sprinting toward the girls' bathroom.

And however bad I'd felt the night before, I felt a thousand times worse now.

I tried to shut out the incriminating glares as I shuffled after her. My hand was shaking as I pulled open the restroom door. Thankfully we were the only girls in there, which meant there were no other witnesses as she bit her lip to prevent her whole face from creasing up.

"Why do you hate me so much?" she cried.

"What are you talking about?"

She didn't answer. She knew I understood her.

"It's my job to make sure you stay in Dumb," I said.

"And what if Tash wanted to leave? Would you treat her the same way?"

I rolled my eyes. It was a stupid question, but I couldn't exactly deny she had a point.

Kallie leaned against a scraped porcelain sink and ripped a paper towel from the dispenser. She dabbed at her eyes slowly, deliberately, like she needed time to think. "Seriously. Why do you hate me?"

I snorted, considered saying "Why the hell do you think?" Only it occurred to me that Kallie was the one in tears, not me. While I was busily stating my case, she was scrabbling around for a sign that I could tolerate her existence.

"I don't hate you, Kallie. It's just . . . look at you. You're beautiful and popular and . . . you have really nice clothes." (I couldn't believe that with four years to prepare, that's the best I could do, but her crying kind of threw me off my game.)

There were still tears in her eyes, but she looked stronger, more defiant now that she had something to work with. "My mom is a supervisor at Nordstrom Rack," she explained, her voice steady. "All my clothes were bought with her employee discount, and they were imperfect to begin with. Plus, everything is last season."

I tried to think of a suitable rebuttal, but failed.

"I also share a one-bedroom condo with my mom because my dad hasn't paid child support in seven years," she continued.

I should have been sympathetic, but I just felt defensive, like she'd unfairly withheld evidence from the prosecution. "You're still popular though," I said, sounding like an eight-year-old.

"You mean the friends that started walking away when you made me cry? The ones who didn't follow me in here? The ones who like to remind me that my clothes are so last season?"

"Then why do you still hang out with them?"

"Who else should I hang out with? Tash? Will? You and Ed? You've all made it clear how much you want me around."

I felt exhausted, and it wasn't just the strain of lip-reading in a room that echoed like a cathedral. Despising Kallie from afar had always been an unwavering constant in my life, like Finn being late, and USS *Immovable*'s engine turning over twelve times before starting. If I'd been wrong about her, what else had I been wrong about?

"It's only Tash that doesn't like you being in the band," I conceded. "And maybe Will. Why did you even want to join Dumb in the first place?"

"Because I love music. I've wanted to be in that band for ages, and I've been practicing, honestly. I thought there was a chance I could join last year, but then Josh said the others wouldn't agree to it. He said he needed one more member in favor of me joining, so he wouldn't be outvoted. And then you became manager."

As I processed the remark, I tried to convince myself it was all just a coincidence. Surely Josh wouldn't go to the trouble of installing me as manager just to get Kallie on board. But then I pictured him with his hands on Kallie's butt, his come-on as subtle as a sledgehammer. Making me temporary manager had probably seemed like a small price to pay for increasing his chances of hooking up with Kallie. If that had been his plan, he'd have to be disappointed by the early returns on his investment.

"Has Josh asked you out?" I asked finally. I knew it was the million-dollar question, and I didn't have the energy to broach the subject gently.

"No. Well, he did last year, but I wasn't really interested."

"Are you going to date him now?"

Kallie narrowed her eyes. "I like watching him perform. He's funny, and really smart, and he's got so much energy, but . . ."

I didn't need to hear what came next. "But" was the only word that mattered.

Kallie had stopped crying now, but the recent waterworks imbued her with a melancholy beauty that was possibly even more striking than her usual sex appeal. I wondered what she was thinking. Was she contemplating the very real possibility that we were both pawns in a chess game that Josh was controlling like a Grandmaster?

She adjusted her shoulder bag (which may not have been a designer label after all). "I know managing Dumb must be very difficult," she said, "but in the past week I've had my guitar unplugged during a recording session, and been cussed out by Tash. Now you're threatening to sue me if I quit. I don't know what to do."

I swallowed hard. "I'm sorry," I mumbled.

"Me too. But I still want you to know that I think you're a really good manager. And I don't hate you at all. I don't even hate you for having blond hair, and gorgeous blue eyes, and a chest people can actually see. Or for the way people listen when you open your mouth." She began tearing up again. "You're deaf . . . but I may as well be dumb."

She didn't wait for a response before leaving, but that was just as well—nothing I could have said would have made things right.

I leaned over the sink beside me, turned on the faucet, and splashed my face with cold water. Her accusations had been uncomfortably spot-on, yet the line that kept replaying was the one about my appearance. I tried to dismiss her observations, pretend that in the heat of the moment she'd exaggerated for effect, but when I looked in the mirror I saw the same pale blue eyes that she had seen. And while my dirty blond hair wasn't going to turn any heads, it could have been worse. Even my boobs were at least a cup size larger than Kallie's. None of it changed who I was—I was as unspectacular as before—but I couldn't ignore the fact that Kallie had really looked at me, and in doing so had found herself lacking. I grabbed a paper towel and dried my face before I was tempted to undertake any more self-analysis in the mirror.

I waited a couple minutes before leaving the bathroom. I wanted to be sure that Kallie had gone, and I hoped the rest of the foyer had emptied too. But when I pushed open the door I found Finn and Belson engaged in another heated debate.

Finn spun around and pointed at me, like he'd just delivered a decisive blow. For his part, Belson staggered back like a punch-drunk boxer.

"What's going on?" I asked.

"I told Mr. Belson I was waiting for you, but he gave me detention," blurted Finn, signing the entire sentence as well just to be sure I got it.

I couldn't hide my shock. "Mr. Belson?"

Belson furrowed his brow. "He's loitering on school premises again, listening at the girls' bathroom. I just thought . . ." He ran out of steam, clearly unsure exactly what he *had* thought. "I've got my eye on you, Vaughan." He waggled a finger at Finn as he shuffled away.

I waited until we were completely alone. *Were you really lis-tening?* I signed. Finn nodded. *You're a pervert.*

"I'd rather be a pervert than whatever you are," he shot back, no longer even making the pretense of signing.

I'm not discussing this.

I turned away from him, but he grabbed my arm and spun me around. "Some manager you've turned out to be. Kallie gets blistered by the other members of the band, and you go after her instead of them."

You don't know anything about it.

"I know enough."

Don't tell me how to do my job.

Finn closed his eyes, shook his head slowly. "Whatever. Let's just go home."

"Whatever," I droned. "You can walk."

His eyebrows shot up. "You can't do that. It's not your car."

"Then drive yourself." I tossed the keys at his feet.

Finn bent down and picked them up, but his eyes never left me. He wanted to say more, that was obvious, but he had the self-restraint to clamp his jaw shut and stomp away.

I hung around after he left, waiting for him to return and apologize. The lights in the foyer dimmed, and I was aware of how completely the school had emptied, all the pent-up energy of another stressful day sucked out in one efficient maneuver. I felt so tired. I just wanted to go home.

When Finn didn't come back after thirty seconds, I stepped

outside. It occurred to me he'd probably decided to run home, knowing that without the keys I'd have to traipse after him. Quite a smart plan, actually; I should've thought of it.

But I was mistaken. Instead, in the far corner of the parking lot, USS *Immovable* shuddered slightly as the engine misfired. I inhaled sharply, tried to convince myself that Finn wouldn't actually do anything as stupid as I knew he was capable of, but then the car shuddered again. I broke into a sprint, hoping against hope that he'd realize I'd left the car in gear to stop it from rolling backward.

I suspect that of all the sounds in the universe, the dead crunch of metal is the one I hear just as clearly as anyone else. I know I watched in disbelief as the car lurched forward, like it was trying to steal a kiss from the concrete wall.

Finn was climbing out of the car when I reached him, so I shoved him back onto the driver's seat. He looked like he might try to get out again, but then gave up and cowered in the seat, bawling like Grace when you take her pacifier away.

I hadn't seen Finn cry in years, and it made me pause. I didn't feel comfortable shoving him again, even though it seemed like an entirely rational response given the situation, so I inspected the damage: a crumpled front bumper, but thankfully nothing more. I leaned against the car and waited, as the rain drizzled down and the air chilled around us.

A minute later Finn reemerged, clearly distraught. *I'm sorry. I'm really sorry,* he signed with shaking hands.

I just shrugged. *What the hell is going on? Is this about Kallie?*

Finn grimaced, shook his head.

Then what? It can't be about signing for me.

He nodded slowly.

Why? What is it you're so embarrassed about? Me? Or the signing?

He kicked the tire angrily. *Neither. I'm pissed you treat me like your personal slave, even when you don't really need my help.*

I don't treat you like my slave.

You do. You never thank me, and whenever I don't want to sign, you threaten me.

I sensed the blame-balance shifting, and I hated feeling defensive after Finn had just *crashed the car.*

Why is it such a big deal for you? I asked, my face tense, my gestures sharper.

Because when everyone hears your words coming from my mouth, they forget I'm interpreting. They think I agree with you.

No, they don't.

Yes, they do. And you don't even notice. When you and Kallie left, everyone stared at me like I was the one who'd made her cry, even though I'd refused to sign for you by then. It's totally unfair.

What's unfair is how I'm deaf but you're not. Have you thought about that?

But I've done everything I can. Other kids learned Spanish or French, but not me. I'm fluent in American Sign Language, and I did it for you. Not for Oma and Poppy. I did it so that I could talk to you, because you're my sister.

So you want me to thank you more often, is that it?

Finn shook his head. *I don't know. . . . I guess I just want to feel like I have my own identity . . . that when we get home Mom and Dad will stop telling me I'm a shadow of you, that if I had one percent of your work ethic maybe I'd amount to something.*

It was hard to believe this was my brother speaking. Gone was the bravado and the don't-give-a-crap, replaced by a shell in search of reassurance. It occurred to me that a good sister would have known exactly what to say in that moment, to reassure him he was just plain wrong—that he had an identity and that we all loved him for who he was. But something told me that even in his weakened state, Finn's bullshit detector would be functioning perfectly.

"Come on," I said. "Let's see if the car still drives."

CHAPTER 24

Halfway through dinner Finn still hadn't confessed, and I sure as heck wasn't about to put *my* head on the chopping block. Neither Mom nor Dad had noticed the damage, but they would in the morning, and we couldn't drive around forever with a front bumper that was liable to fall off at any moment.

Mom waved at me, stirring me from my reverie. "How is the band these days?" she asked.

I tried to ignore the look Finn gave me. "Good," I said.

"What about the interview last night?"

"It went great. We got some good press."

"That's terrific. What kind of press?"

It was the first time anyone at home had shown genuine interest, and I have to admit, I really liked it. "Well, there are some bloggers saying that—"

Suddenly Mom whipped around and gazed at Grace, then

at Dad. Before I could catch up, Mom had jumped out of her seat and was showering Grace with kisses.

"Did you hear that?" Mom grinned, her hands cradling her face in wonderment. I shook my head. "Grace said 'Mama'!" Mom kissed her again for good measure. "She said her first word. My beautiful, perfect little Gracie said her first word."

Dad was already out of his seat and hugging Mom, while Grace beamed to the delight of her parents.

"Say it again, Gracie," shouted Dad, practically begging her to repeat her death-defying feat of pure awesomeness. "Say it again, you amazing little—"

"I crashed the car today!" The words tumbled out of my mouth so quickly they caught even me by surprise. Mom and Dad turned away from Grace and gave me their full attention. "I left it in gear. I don't know how it happened. I've never done it before."

Dad sat down again, so slow and controlled. "Is it damaged?"

"It still drives."

"That's not what your father asked," snapped Mom, carefully signing every word to be sure I didn't miss anything. "Is it damaged?"

"I think it needs a new front bumper," I said quietly.

Dad slammed his fist on the table. "Well, that's just goddamned wonderful."

Mom touched his arm gently. "Language, Ryan." She feigned a smile, pointed at Grace. "Little ears, you know."

"But I'm insured, right?" I asked hurriedly. "That's what insurance is for."

"You're eighteen, Piper. The best insurance your mom and I could get for you has a five-hundred-dollar deductible. No matter what happens, we come out of this five hundred dollars down."

"I—I'm sorry. It was an accident."

Dad shoved his chair back, threw his napkin on the table.

Mom grabbed his hand before he could leave. "Grace said Mama, honey. She said her first word."

Dad forced a smile and nodded curtly, but when he walked out of the room he didn't look back—not even at Grace.

I stared at my plate, but I couldn't eat. In my peripheral vision I saw Mom glaring at me, like she'd just seen a terrible side of me she hadn't known existed.

Why did you do that? she signed.

I couldn't move, couldn't speak.

We've been waiting for this ever since Grace was born, wondering if it could really happen.

I shook my head, and a moment later Mom clattered her cutlery onto her plate and left the table. When I glanced up again, Grace's lower lip was quivering—she'd obviously sensed the sudden change in mood, and feared she was the cause of it.

When the inevitable flood of baby tears came a few seconds later, Grace wasn't the only one crying. Caught between his inconsolable sisters, Finn reached over and lifted Grace out of her high chair, held her tight against him. I didn't even blame him for choosing her side.

But then he came over and squeezed me too. And I swear, I bawled like a baby.

CHAPTER 25

I had to get out of the house. I didn't care where I went as long as I couldn't be found by anyone with the last name Vaughan, so I just threw myself into USS *Immovable* and started driving. It occurred to me that if Kallie were with me, she'd have been amused to see how quickly my bad karma had come back to haunt me.

I tried to calm myself by remembering that fall semester at Gallaudet began in ten months, but then I remembered The Case of the Amazing Disappearing College Fund. I might not be going to Gallaudet in the next ten years, let alone ten months. And it was looking increasingly unlikely that Dumb was going to be able to change that at all.

I wasn't really conscious of where I was heading, but when I found myself pulling up outside Coffee Crew, I wasn't completely surprised either. Unfortunately, Ed was just turning off the neon OPEN sign as I got out of the car, and he locked the door as I approached. I would have taken it personally, only then he saw me and hurried back to the door, unlocking it and holding it open for me.

"You're closed," I said.

"Clos*ing*," he corrected.

"There's a difference?"

Ed swept his arm across his body in a gesture of welcome. "For my manager, yes." It took me a moment to realize he was talking about me.

In light of recent events the thought of being Dumb's manager was enough to make my stomach churn, but he said it with such exaggerated servitude that I ended up smiling instead. A moment later, I was leaning against a counter and Ed was concocting something inappropriately caffeinated for eight o' clock in the evening.

I couldn't see his face clearly as he worked the espresso machine, so I didn't speak. I just watched him go through the motions, banging out filters and grinding coffee and steaming milk and the other fifty-three steps needed to make a simple cup of coffee. I'd seen gourmet steaks cooked in less time.

While the golden-brown espresso oozed into a glass, Ed steamed a pitcher of milk. It said "whole milk" on the handle, but I had the feeling that objecting to this would be sacrilege to a barista, so I kept my mouth shut and watched him touch the side of the metal pitcher with his fingertips, waiting for it to reach the desired temperature. With the same precise timing that characterized his playing, the espresso stopped flowing at the same moment he shut off the steam, and he placed the glass before me with all the care of someone showing off a delicate antique. I was sure I was about to crack up laughing, but then he began pouring the milk, a steady flow at first, then a gentle shake of the wrist that traced a perfect white flower across the surface of the coffee. Suddenly I didn't feel like laughing anymore.

"It's . . . beautiful," I said, not even bothering to disguise my admiration.

"Try it. It's all about the flavor. The flower is just for show."

I took a sip, the coffee mingling with foam so rich I would have sworn it was whipped cream. I met his eyes. "That's amazing. Seriously. That's the most amazing cup of coffee I've ever tasted. What did you do differently?"

Ed smiled. "Well, first off, I used whole milk. And yes, I saw you twitch when you read the handle of the pitcher. You're not the only one whose peripheral vision works overtime." Okay, now I was *really* impressed. "I also did *not* use any kind of flavoring—it's coffee, not dessert. The other thing I did was to make sure the pour-time was a steady twenty-four seconds—"

"You're losing me."

"Oh. Yeah, maybe that's more information than you need," he said, his mouth crinkling at the corners.

"What's it called, anyway?"

"It's a cappuccino."

"Hmm. Well, aren't *you* a man of many talents, Ed Chen." I

have to admit the words felt deliciously flirty as I said them.

Ed turned slightly red, touched his thick hair nervously. I almost wanted to prolong the silence just to see how flustered I could make him, but that seemed unnecessarily cruel.

"How long have you been working here?"

"Since junior year," he answered, relieved at the change of topic. "I've always been addicted to coffee, and I wanted to learn how to make it properly, so I asked the owner if she'd teach me to use the espresso machine in return for a few hours of dishwashing."

"Seriously? What did she say?"

"She said sure, then paid me for my time and asked if I wanted to come back the next week. Now I close the shop and cash up on Thursdays."

"Except when your boss stops by."

"She never does."

"I mean me," I said with mock seriousness.

"Oh yeah, right." Ed blushed again, a response so endearingly earnest that I wanted to hug him.

"Thanks for this, Ed. I really needed a pick-me-up."

Suddenly he looked concerned. "Why? What's up?"

I took another sip, then another. I wasn't sure I wanted to rehash everything with him, but since he'd asked . . .

"Kallie wasn't very pleased when I told her she had to stay in the band."

Ed waited like there was more to come, then realized there wasn't. "That's not surprising, though, right?"

"I guess not. I just don't know where the band is going right now."

"I can understand that."

I puffed out my cheeks, blew a steady stream of air in an attempt to purge my frustration. It didn't work. "What am I missing, Ed?"

"Honestly?"

I nodded, which was stupid because "honest" is just a code word for "critical," and I should have realized I wasn't ready for that—especially not from Ed.

"Here's the thing," he began, an opening gambit that assured me the list was about to be alarmingly long. "Dumb is a hard rock band. Josh and Tash and Will don't get soft rock *at all*. Meanwhile, we've got an extra guitarist we don't need who can't really play. But because she's hot she's become the face of the band, and now we can't get rid of her, even though she wants to quit. This isn't rocket science, Piper. You need to decide what kind of band Dumb is going to be, and you need to decide quick, because I don't think we'll survive many more occasions like last night."

He'd finished his analysis, but I couldn't speak. I felt the seconds passing and the crushing emptiness of the shop as Ed waited for some kind of acknowledgment that I'd heard a single word. I knew he'd wanted to help, and that under other circumstances I'd have wanted his advice. But at that moment his words stung more deeply than those of Kallie and my mom combined. I didn't think about what that meant—or why it bothered me so much that he'd described Kallie as "hot"—I just nodded like I was strong enough to accept responsibility for everything that was going wrong.

Then I turned away, leaving half a cup of coffee and the remaining shreds of my self-confidence behind.

CHAPTER 26

I needed to distract myself, but none of my homework assignments engaged me at all. And I couldn't shake that look Mom had given me. She hadn't looked angry; she'd looked hurt, like I'd just told her she was fat, or that Grace was an ugly baby. It was the kind of look that left no room for quick retractions. I felt guilty. I hated feeling guilty.

Without thinking it through, I e-mailed Marissa, told her the whole story. I knew it was too late to IM—it was eleven o'clock—but I needed to tell my side of the story to the one person who'd understand. A moment after I'd sent it, Marissa IM'd me:

MARI55A: that sucks

P1P3R: YES. everything sucks at the moment

MARI55A: everything?

I hesitated. Dumb wasn't Marissa's favorite topic—I knew that—but we'd never kept information from each other before. Besides, I needed to vent.

P1P3R: yes. tash and kallie had a blowup after
Dumb's interview last night

MARI55A: kallie sims is in dumb?

P1P3R: didn't i tell u?

MARI55A: no

P1P3R: oh. anyway, i had an argument with her
about staying in the band, and then i went to see
ed and he was kind of mean too

MARI55A: no way

P1P3R: yes. told me i needed to work out what
Dumb was all about

MARI55A: seems fair

P1P3R: i guess so, but i got the feeling he
blamed me somehow

MARI55A: ur the manager. who else should he blame?

She may as well have stabbed me in the heart. I reread the line, tried to inflect it with a positive spin, but it was a million miles from the unconditional support I'd always counted on.

P1P3R: i thought u'd understand

MARI55A: i do. look, i gotta go. hang in there,
okay? xoxo

I would have written back, but she'd already logged off.

I turned off the light and crawled into bed. I wanted to fall asleep, to escape the thoughts clawing at my consciousness, but instead the evening just replayed in my mind, a crappy movie on endless loop. Even Josh made a cameo appearance, smirking as if to confirm that my promotion to manager was no coincidence at all, that he'd planned Kallie's arrival in Dumb as carefully as a military offensive. Unwittingly I'd played my role to perfection. It was enough to make me want to quit, but what if he'd planned for that too? I couldn't bear to give him the satisfaction of being proved right yet again.

Once the clock had yawned all the way to midnight, I resigned myself to not sleeping. I dragged myself out of bed and turned the light back on, then stuffed my pillow at the bottom of the door so Dad wouldn't see the strip of light when he eventually went to bed (even rebels need to pick their battles). Firing up my laptop, I pasted two new reviews of Dumb on our Facebook page, and linked to some bloggers who had discovered the band and thought it was promising. There were also several new messages of the generic "You're an inspiration, Kallie" variety, and even more of the "Oh my! Now I see why Dumb needed Kallie" type from people who had evidently followed the link to Dumb's Battle of the Bands performance on YouTube and suffered emotional trauma as a result. And there was one message from someone called ZARKINFIB that didn't fit any category at all:

get educated u money-grabber. go see kurt at 171 lk wash blvd e

It was like getting a threatening letter—you know you should ignore it, or tell your parents, but instead you read it over and over, like secretly you knew you had it coming all along. And although I was pretty sure ZARKINFIB wasn't likely to bust through the window brandishing a machete anytime soon, I still felt pretty shaken up.

I closed the messages and struggled to focus on the rest of the Facebook page. The main change since Sunday was the number of fans: 6,259. I couldn't actually remember what the number had been before the radio interview, but I knew it was triple digits only, which meant that all those bloggers had directed some serious traffic our way. And even if people were only there to check out extra photos of Kallie, it was still an astounding number. More importantly, it was the ammunition I needed to keep fighting.

I launched the word processor and without pausing to think, I began to type:

> *Piper's Manifesto:*
>
> *Problem: Josh is an asshole. Solution: Suck it up as long as the band makes money.*
>
> *Problem: Tash is bad for morale. Solution: (gulp) Stand up to her.*
>
> *Problem: It's not entirely clear that Will even has a pulse. Solution: That's a problem?*
>
> *Problem: Kallie can't play guitar for crap. Solution: Get Finn to help her—he owes you.*
>
> *Problem: Ed doesn't think I know what I'm doing. Solution: Prove him wrong.*
>
> *Problem: Dumb can't do soft. Solution: Make them hard again.*

Problem: Mom and Dad suck. Solution: Wait until
next summer, then join a commune.

Apart from the last line (which I deleted) the manifesto sort
of made sense. And somewhere in the few minutes it took me to
write it, I'd even begun to formulate a plan.

I Googled "Dumb Kallie Sims" and found links to twenty-
three bloggers who had written about Dumb's resident goddess-
muse. I figured they'd be mostly guy blogs, the kind with
close-ups of Kallie's barely visible boobs and a copy of her
birth certificate proving she'd be fair game once she turned
eighteen the following March. Instead, almost all of the
blogs were written by women, linked to each other like the tenta-
cles of a Kallie Sims fan club that Kallie herself probably didn't
know existed. And there were other common links too, to the
websites of KSFT-FM, the *Christian Family Beacon, Seattle
Today . . .*

I'd heard of *Seattle Today*—one of those breathtakingly dull
talk shows that air in the late morning when the coffee has
worn off and viewers are trapped in a pre-lunch stupor so dis-
abling they can't even summon the energy to switch channels.
The website informed me that the host, Donna Stevens, had
been "guiding" the show with her "effortless blend of gentle
humor and homespun wisdom" for eighteen years, and in all
that time had never once missed a show, even turning up for
work promptly the day after undergoing gallbladder surgery
("!"). (Comparing the almost identical photos of Donna from

her first and most recent shows made me suspect that her gallbladder wasn't the only part of her that had undergone surgery.) The show, it turned out, still aired live, "a decision favored by Donna for the spontaneity of the results and not, as many have suggested, because it puts her in a different category at the annual Seattle TV awards, where *Seattle Today* has won uncontested for the past six years."

It was past one a.m. when I composed my e-mail to Donna Stevens, requesting an invitation for Dumb to appear on her show. I wrote that she was an inspiration to the Vaughan family. I quoted the bloggers who applauded Dumb's "wholesome" values. I provided a link to the podcast of our—okay, Kallie's—interview on KSFT-FM. I even disabled the YouTube link on our Facebook page, just to be sure she didn't accidentally stumble across Dumb's punk alter egos; no need to concern her with details like the band's true musical identity just yet—she'd find out soon enough if they appeared on her *live* show.

I pressed Send.

Over eighteen years, I had done so much to earn the trust and respect of my family and peers—a lifetime of noble works, you might say. And yet it took just eighteen minutes for me to perfect the art of lying, misleading, and perverting truth for personal profit.

Friday October 26, 1:23 a.m.: the moment Piper Vaughan developed a taste for being bad.

CHAPTER 27

Of everything on the Piper Manifesto, I'd thought the easiest part would be getting Finn to help. He knew he'd be stuck at school until Dumb's rehearsal was over, so it seemed like a no-brainer, but he hemmed and hawed like it was actually a tough decision. I figured he was just playing an angle, getting me to beg, so I told him to forget it, which is when he finally said okay. But when he appeared at the rehearsal several hours later, he still looked genuinely conflicted. I wondered what was occupying his time after school ended. Whatever it was, it couldn't be good.

On the bright side, Kallie showed up on time, and took her seat without glaring at me even once. Come to think of it, she didn't look at me at all, but I couldn't really blame her for that. With the cold war between her and Tash still ongoing, I made Finn sit between them—officially, so that he could hear them both; unofficially, so that he could keep them apart. Personally,

I'd have been satisfied if all he did was prevent Tash from assaulting her playing partner, but having sacrificed whatever irresistible plans he'd previously made, Finn seemed eager to make his presence count.

I began by announcing to everyone that Dumb's excursion into the world of soft rock had been a means to an end—and I'd already discovered 6,259 good ends—but that it was time to get back to doing what they did best. (No one begged me to reconsider.) Then I said we needed to concentrate on expanding our repertoire with mostly original songs, and maybe a couple of covers that we could get away with performing as long as we weren't being recorded. (Everyone nodded like this sort of made sense.) Finally, I asked if anyone had written a song that Dumb could work on. Josh said that he and Will had collaborated on nine songs, and that three of them were "amazing."

Josh's definition of *collaboration* was loose, to say the least. Will had clearly composed the songs single-handedly—and even had sheet music to prove it—while Josh contributed angry, stream-of-consciousness lyrics that justified his penchant for screaming into microphones. Once Will had handed out the music, he and Josh performed their favorite "composition" as a duet, including some high-pitched wailing that I think was meant to simulate a guitar solo. When silence prevailed three minutes later, Ed was evidently raring to go, while Tash and Kallie simply looked confused, leaning forward for a better look at the chord symbols decorating the page like hieroglyphics. As for Finn, he seemed to be having trouble coming to terms with the fact that they were leaning across him, Kallie's hair draped over his lap.

"Here," he said, reaching for Kallie's guitar like he didn't trust himself to stay conscious if she remained there any longer. "It's like this."

Finn played the chords perfectly, looking at Tash then Kallie to show them how simple it was. And I didn't know he'd nailed it because I could hear the chords; I knew it because, for a split second, Josh, Will, Tash, and Kallie looked up with expressions of pure awe.

By the time Finn had demonstrated the fingerings three more times, Kallie seemed reluctant to take her instrument back. Even Tash hesitated, afraid of failing Finn's pop quiz. But Finn sat back like a proud grandparent, generous in his praise, gentle in his criticism, always coaxing more from the stage-struck duo. Meanwhile, Ed asked Josh and Will what sort of drumming they'd envisioned. Even though they clearly hadn't thought about it until that moment, Josh naturally had very strong opinions on the matter.

As they all cranked away over the next hour, I didn't spend my time checking Facebook, or trawling Google, or even posting anonymous comments to hard rock fan sites about this incredible new band I'd heard called Dumb. Instead I watched with amazement as Dumb pulled "Kiss Me Like You Mean It" into something resembling a song through Josh's enthusiasm, Ed's discipline, and Finn's ever-patient guidance. My brother Finn, the wayward freshman, had serious skills, and was sharing them with *my* band. I wondered if I'd have done the same for him.

I should have known better than to push my luck, but there were a few minutes left and everyone was pumped up, so I convinced Dumb to attempt a full performance. They seemed so close to getting through it too, but then Kallie stopped playing and the band fizzled out around her.

"Sorry," she said. "I'll get it this time."

Again the band struck up, and again they were in the middle of what I assumed must be the chorus when Kallie dropped out, staring accusingly at her fingers. Finn leaned forward and moved her fingers to the right place, but by then Tash had clearly had enough.

"Just leave that chord out," she snapped.

Kallie peered around Finn. "No. I need to learn it."

"No, Kallie. You need to learn the *guitar*."

I flashed back to the scene outside the radio station and decided I couldn't let things escalate. "Leave her alone, Tash. She's trying, okay?"

Tash pretended to stifle a laugh. "Like that'll help."

I was braced to continue our little spat, but Finn moved the piece of paper with the chord symbols in front of Tash, added a couple of his own, and signaled for her to play. Before she'd even had a chance to sound the first chord, Finn took her left hand and meticulously repositioned her fingers. It was a subtle gesture, but it changed the balance of power in a heartbeat. Suddenly Kallie was beaming at Finn like he was her own personal hero, while Tash stared straight ahead, struggling to work out how she'd been outmaneuvered by a freshman. A day earlier I'd have assumed it was just innocence or cluelessness on Finn's part, but now I knew it was nothing of the sort.

By the time five o'clock rolled around, Tash already seemed to have her guitar halfway into its case. I waved my hands to indicate that I had announcements, but she just ignored me, striding toward the door like I was invisible. I could have let it go, but instead I leaped up and cut her off.

"Guess you and your brother both have a crush on Kallie, huh?" she said, throwing a backward glance at the pair.

"She's getting better," I replied, quietly but firmly.

"Really? And how the hell would you know?"

I felt the flash of anger that always accompanied jabs at my deafness. I wanted to tell her to get over herself, but instead I gripped her arm and pulled her into the practice room around the corner, where even more of the soundproofing seemed to have been sacrificed since my last visit with Josh.

"Why do you always do that?" I asked.

"What?"

"You know . . . those snarky remarks to piss people off. Why do you want everyone to hate you?"

Tash rolled her eyes, snorted, and shifted her weight from one leg to the other, reenacting every well-worn stereotype of the girl who doesn't give a crap. But undermining the whole choreographed routine was her face, flushed red and tense. The girl with rings in her nose, eyebrow, and lip stared at me like she'd never before been pierced so deeply, and I stared right back. I knew that today needed to be the day that everything changed. Today needed to be the day that *she* blinked first, that *she* stormed off in a gesture of defiance that was really just surrender in disguise.

To my utter surprise, she did precisely that.

I felt exhausted as I returned to the classroom, but grateful glances from Kallie and Ed told me they knew how important it had been for me to take a stand. Josh and Will had already taken off, although Josh had apparently thanked Ed for his contribution to the rehearsal. Truly, it was a day of firsts.

As Finn prolonged his private rehearsal with Kallie for one more minute—and indulged his first and last opportunity to brush fingers with the school's resident hottie—Ed traipsed over and sat in front of me, twirling his drumsticks.

"I can't say our rehearsals are completely warm and fuzzy just yet," he announced.

"No," I agreed. "Even our fans are turning on us."

"What? We have fans?"

I laughed. "Well, not the band. Someone wrote *me* a private message on our Facebook page."

Suddenly Kallie and Finn were looking at me too. "What did it say?" she asked.

Against my better judgment I pulled up the message on my laptop and read it to them, omitting the bit about me being a "money-grabber." Everyone was silent. "I don't know what it means," I admitted.

"I do," said Kallie as she put her guitar away. "It's an address. 171 Lake Washington Boulevard East is Kurt Cobain's house."

"I thought he was dead."

"He is. Which begs the question, why does your secret admirer want you to go see him?"

Ed sat down next to me and peered at the screen.

"Actually, the only question it begs is why I read this to you in the first place." I closed the laptop.

Kallie narrowed her eyes. "So that's it? You get a cryptic message from a secret admirer and you just drop it?"

"Yes, obviously. It could be from a serial killer."

Ed tapped his fingers against my laptop. "Whose username is an anagram of Baz Firkin?" he asked dubiously.

ZARKINFIB . . . BAZ FIRKIN. I couldn't believe I hadn't seen it.

"Why would Baz want you to visit Kurt Cobain's house?" asked Kallie.

I thought back to our discussion in the studio. "He said he wanted me to get acquainted with the world of rock music. I guess this is all part of my education."

Kallie sidled up and took my arm. "Well, let's get educated, then." She smiled, like my explanation had been reason enough for her to buy in.

"I'll come too," said Ed.

I shook my head. "No way. I need to get home for dinner. Mom and Dad will be pissed if I'm late."

"I'll tell them you're busy," said Finn.

I was about to protest again. After all, I could think of at least another eighteen reasons why this was a dumb idea. But then I remembered *Piper's Manifesto*, and realized that two of the people who'd spent the previous day chewing me out were being friendly to me again—really friendly, and I couldn't say no. Not even if it meant being late home.

Besides, it beat a Vaughan family dinner hands down.

CHAPTER 28

I dropped Finn at home on our way to 171 Lake Washington Boulevard East. Kallie navigated, taking us on a snaking trail through the autumnal colors of the arboretum and on down toward Lake Washington. Flakes of cloud drifted above us, tinged by the setting sun. On the far side of the lake, the Cascade mountain range jutted through the evening haze.

Lake Washington Boulevard runs parallel to the lake but high above it, a street of large houses and austere fences. Kallie indicated that I should park across the street from a set of especially fortress-like wooden gates. There was no house number, but she seemed sure of the address.

We emptied out of the car and approached the gates cautiously. To the left, an elaborate security system deterred us from getting too close, and all I could see of the house itself were the curved, gabled edges of the rooftop. Ed stepped up to the security system and admired its complexity, while I wondered what on earth we were doing there. I was even more puzzled by Kallie being there with us, but as I glanced over at her, I couldn't help noticing how transfixed she seemed, like she couldn't be anywhere else in the world.

Kallie met my eyes. "There's a park next door," she said, pointing to a hill beside the house. "I think you should see it."

"How do you know about it?"

"My parents. They were big Nirvana fans back in the day. Saw some of their early performances. Mom used to brag about being the first African American to go grunge."

"What about your dad?"

"Well, he's not African American."

"Oh. So what exactly is grunge, anyway?"

Kallie folded her arms, cocked an eyebrow. "You know—the Seattle sound." She gave me a moment to express appropriate recognition, which of course didn't happen. "It was this musical style that started in the mid-eighties. Heavy guitars, angsty lyrics, generally hardcore. You've heard of Nirvana? Pearl Jam? Soundgarden?"

"Nirvana, yes. Not sure about the others."

Kallie's eyes grew super-wide. "Just for the record, I don't think anyone else should ever hear you say that, you being the manager of a rock band and all."

"Point taken," I said, and Kallie smiled.

The park was called Viretta Park, a small, grassy hillside surrounded by woods. We were alone as we traipsed up the hill, the grass lime green from the recent rain. Patches of clover shared the ground with a few stubborn dandelions, leftovers from a summer that was already a distant memory. And in the middle of the park was a Douglas fir, its trunk spray-painted with the letters "RIP."

Beside the tree, two benches had been subjected to the same treatment, every inch of the warm red wood covered in tributes to Kurt Cobain.

"So apart from Cobain, what made Nirvana special?" I asked finally.

Ed turned around. "They took indie rock mainstream."

"Which means?"

"They broke musical boundaries. Their music was only supposed to appeal to a niche audience. They weren't supposed to make it big. But somehow they ended up speaking for their generation in a way that bigger bands just couldn't seem to."

Kallie smiled. "And they had energy. They just . . . rocked."

I looked at Kurt Cobain's house, clearer from the park, and gawked at the size of the place. It was a beautiful house, too, with patterns in the red brick and latticed windows looking out over the lake and mountains. It must have been worth millions of dollars. Suddenly I wanted to get away, leave all that wasted wealth and misdirected adoration behind me.

"I'm sorry, but I just don't get it," I said. "All these people visit this park just because he lived next door?"

Kallie looked puzzled. "No. They come here because that's where he killed himself."

I waited for her to laugh, to cry *gotcha*, but she didn't. "What?" I mumbled. "How?"

"He shot himself," she said. "Didn't you know? He went alone to the greenhouse above the garage and shot himself."

I felt my breath catch, my eyes drawn back to the house magnetically. It looked the same as before, but somehow different too.

I took in the view again, the mountains fast disappearing, the inky black lake stretching into the distance, rimmed by amber streetlights on the other side. "But it's so beautiful here," I said.

Kallie and Ed stood silent, regarding me.

"It's just . . . how could you see such beauty and not find a reason to keep living?"

Kallie stepped forward and took my hand in hers. "He was depressed. He was addicted to heroin. And I think there comes a time when all the beauty in the world just isn't enough."

"But he had so many fans, so much money."

"It's not enough," said Kallie sadly. "I don't think anyone who's motivated by fans or money will ever get it."

"Get what?"

"Music. It's not about those things. It's about a feeling. It's about expressing yourself. It's about letting go."

I couldn't help but stare at Kallie, Dumb's weakest link—the one who couldn't play in time or in tune, whose superficiality had left me speechless for years. Did she really believe a word she'd said?

I sat down on one of the benches, stuffed my hands inside the sleeves of my fleece jacket. On the seat, to my left, someone named Tom D. from Minneapolis wanted Kurt to know that he was gone but not forgotten. Dakota and Phil from Sydney, Australia, told Kurt that he'd live forever. Someone had even left three daisies, wilted and withered now, but a touching gesture all the same.

Ed sat down too, but he didn't speak, just stayed with me as I studied the bench and our breaths condensed in the air. He seemed to know I needed to be quiet, but I was still grateful to feel him there beside me.

In phrases long and short, scrawled and carved, Kurt Cobain's apostles had composed eulogies to their fallen leader. And however much I wanted to dismiss the words as simple graffiti, I couldn't ignore the sentiment or the distances covered on the way to this place, the final destination on the Kurt Cobain pilgrimage. I could have been cynical, of course, but that would have been dishonest. Because the painful truth was that each and every person who had sat on that seat before me had experienced music in a purer, more visceral way than I could even begin to imagine. And I'd be lying if I said that I wasn't profoundly jealous of every single one of them.

CHAPTER 29

Everyone stopped talking as soon as I walked into the dining room.

"Where have you been?" demanded Mom.

I hesitated. "Kurt Cobain's house."

"Yes, Finn told me that. I mean, *what* were you doing at Kurt Cobain's house when you should have been here for dinner?"

I was about to mention the e-mail from ZARKINFIB, but I could tell that Mom wouldn't consider that an acceptable explanation right now. "Kallie said it would be . . . illuminating."

Mom rolled her eyes. "Oh, great. So air-guitarist Kallie is also an air-head."

"I never called her an air-guitarist."

"No, Finn did. The airhead bit I worked out for myself."

"She's not an airhead."

"Oh, right. She just drags you off to the house of a suicidal rock star. Sounds like a shoo-in for Mensa."

Finn looked up suddenly. "Kallie *is* smart, actually. And since you've never even been to Kurt Cobain's house, I don't see how you can call it a waste of time."

Silence. Mom was ready to have an argument with me, but Finn's vehemence surprised all of us. It was like he'd declared war, and she didn't care enough to continue fighting. Or perhaps it had nothing to do with Kallie or Cobain at all. Maybe she was still pissed at me for last night.

"Look, Piper," she said tiredly, "I'm all for you indulging this project, but I'm not going to bend on our rules. You get home in time for dinner or you can forget about the band. Understand?"

I nodded, and Finn returned to studying his plate. He wouldn't meet my eyes until Mom and Dad left the table, and even then I could tell he was still shaken by his outburst.

Do you like Kallie? I signed, trying to keep my facial expressions as neutral as possible, not wanting him to clam up.

She's okay.

She's very popular. You know that, right? I tried, hoping he'd read between the lines and realize she was completely out of his league.

Yes. So what?

Nothing, I lied, then thought better of it. *It was just something Tash said to me tonight, that's all.*

Suddenly Finn was blushing, and I knew I wasn't the only one who'd been lying.

CHAPTER 30

On Saturday morning Dad and I took USS *Immovable* to the shop. He said he'd waited until then so that Finn and I wouldn't be inconvenienced, but the truth is that he just didn't want to give us rides to and from school. It would've meant sticking Grace in her car seat, which, you know, is thirty seconds of extra work.

Also, by waiting until Saturday he made it possible for me to experience every guilt-filled moment, from the ancient mechanic who shook his head incredulously at what I'd done, to the estimate for the work ($400). When Dad found out that the car wouldn't be ready until Monday he almost blew a fuse. Seriously, if Finn hadn't been such a star at the rehearsal the previous afternoon, I might have strangled him when I got home.

It took me thirty minutes to walk to Josh and Will's house on Sunday. Everyone in the band had agreed to an extra rehearsal, even though there wasn't a recording session. Still, that was before I had my blowup with Tash. Just as I'd worried that Kallie might not show after our run-in a few days ago, I now wasted several minutes biting my fingernails and wondering if Tash had made her final appearance. Only I got the feeling that Dumb had an additional attraction for Tash, and that seeing Will was sufficient compensation for having to hang out with Kallie for an afternoon.

Sure enough, Tash showed up just like usual, unpacking her guitar and tuning it methodically. Then she handed her tuning fork to Kallie. It was a simple gesture—essential, really—but it seemed symbolic: Tash grudgingly acknowledging that Dumb needed its two guitarists to be in harmony. What's more, they'd both clearly been practicing—with varying degrees of success— so the band was able to polish up "Kiss Me Like You Mean It" and still have time to learn "Look What the Cat Dragged In," a new number from the Cooke family songbook.

Meanwhile, I sat by the window, engrossed in a biography of Kurt Cobain I'd checked out from the library. It was the story of a life so heartrending that I wanted to hug every member of Dumb just to show I truly cared.

I figured we'd split after the three hours were up, but then a pizza delivery guy arrived and Will said, "Now you all owe me another hour," and no one disagreed. I couldn't decide if I was more amazed that Will had had the forethought to order pizza, or that he had expressed an opinion, but either way, it worked. And when the extra hour was up, nobody mentioned it, and

Dumb pressed on for an hour after that. Maybe it was because they knew that the next full rehearsal wouldn't be until Friday, but even so, it felt momentous, like everyone had finally taken responsibility for making this thing work.

For the first time, Dumb's five flavors were mixing, blending, and forging something altogether greater than the sum of its parts. And I didn't need perfect hearing to know they realized it too.

All of this meant that I was in a pretty good mood on Monday. I even tolerated Dad's eye rolling and steering wheel slapping on the way to school without uttering a single sarcastic remark. There should be medals for that kind of self-control.

At lunchtime I met up with Ed for a game of chess. I was finding it hard to concentrate on anything but the band, so I set goals to help me focus: checkmate in twenty moves or under (not too difficult); execute checkmate through a bishop-queen skewer (significantly harder); mustn't smile—even a small one—when I pulled it off (close to impossible). My assignment worked—for twelve minutes I was focused on nothing but the game, and met every goal except the last one.

Usually Ed was the first to start setting up the pieces again, but for once he just sat back, lost in his thoughts.

"You okay?" I asked.

He nodded. "Just got a lot on my mind."

"I get that. We're still two songs shy of a set, and I want to start selling us as an opening act."

Ed's eyes grew wide. "Why?"

"Well, how else do you think we're going to make any money?"

"But . . ." He broke eye contact.

"But what?"

Ed leaned back and gripped his hair in his hands. "Do you honestly believe that's going to happen anytime soon?"

I wasn't sure I liked where the conversation was going. "It might."

"But it can take years for a band to develop that kind of a following."

"We don't have years."

"I know, but . . . what about Kallie?"

"What about her? I was wrong. She's actually really nice."

"That's not the point. She's not ready to play in public. And unless she and Tash plan to meet with Finn *every* lunchtime, I don't think that's going to change."

I wondered if I'd misheard him. "What did you say about Finn?"

"I said Kallie and Tash are meeting with him, to go over the songs."

"How do you know?"

"Finn told me during morning break. He wanted to check a couple chords out with me."

I was struggling to come to grips with this revelation. "Where are they?"

"In the practice room."

I jumped up and began jogging over there, Ed following close behind. I don't know what I expected to find as I peered through the small window in the practice room door, but the one thing I was certain I wouldn't see was Tash and Kallie hanging on Finn's every word.

Maybe I shouldn't have been so surprised: Finn had been playing guitar since he was eight. He'd even taken lessons for five years, until his teacher brought things to an end over a "philosophical difference" that was never fully explained. I think by then Dad had an inkling he'd soon be out of a job, so I can't exactly say that anyone discouraged Finn from quitting. Except that he never actually quit, of course—he simply changed focus from classical to rock guitar, a shift we interpreted as giving up. And now here he was, a fourteen-year-old leading a guitar master class with two girls on the cusp of eighteen—a freshman boy's fantasy gone wild.

I got the feeling he knew it too. A month earlier he'd seemed awestruck simply by breathing the same air as Dumb, but now he was correcting Kallie's mistakes with a reassuring smile. When she struggled with a chord, he gently moved her fingers to the right place, maintaining the contact for so long I wondered why he didn't just get down on one knee there and then. By contrast, Tash's mistakes were addressed from a safe distance with no physical contact—probably a wise move for a boy who cracked the scales at an even 110 pounds.

I peered over my shoulder at Ed, who nodded somberly.

Whatever his misgivings about Kallie, it was clear he saw the benefits of extra rehearsals with Finn. I wondered if Ed wished he could swap places with him. I hoped not.

The only sign of friction between the girls was when Finn brought things to a close and they both wanted to try out his guitar. At least, that's how it seemed, and Finn was happy to oblige. It was a relatively new-looking guitar too, not like the battered one he'd bought himself at a garage sale when he was eleven. It also faced the opposite direction from the other guitars, presumably designed for left-handed players. I wasn't actually sure I'd seen the new guitar before, which got me thinking about where it had come from. He handed it to Tash first, and she ran her fingers lovingly over the white body, gazed at the neck, and pulled a string with a rapturous expression. Then she gave it to Kallie, who was equally inspired by the moment. It was geek love with a twist.

I stifled a laugh and turned to ask Ed what he made of it, but he'd already gone. And while I certainly didn't expect him to consult with me every time he moved, I realized it was the first time he'd ever taken off without telling me.

With a few minutes of lunch break left, I wandered into the classroom next door and opened up my laptop. Checking e-mail and Dumb's Facebook page was becoming habitual, an itch that never went away no matter how many times I scratched. And it's not like anything ever changed significantly either, although . . .

Dear Piper: Thank you for your kind message. At *Seattle Today* we have always striven to inspire our viewers by highlighting the goodness of the earth, and the warmth of our fellow human beings. After reviewing your materials and reading enthusiastic responses to your recent performance, award-winning host Donna Stevens would like to invite you to participate in next Tuesday's show (November 5), which will focus on the positive contributions of youth in society, featuring no fewer than THREE child psychologists! While this is short notice, you will only be required to perform one song ("Loving Every Part of You" would be perfect) and answer a few informal questions afterward. Please let me know today if this is acceptable, as we have a fourth psychologist on standby.

Sincerely,
Tiffany Myers
(senior producer, *Seattle Today*)
P.S. We will provide an honorarium of $300.

Oh. My. God.

CHAPTER 31

There wasn't time to get Dumb together to approve the show, so I wrote Tiffany back immediately and accepted the invitation, omitting to mention that we'd be using the occasion to return to our hard rock roots. I even threw in some extra fictional-but-complimentary phrases about the show (and other artists that had influenced us) to reassure her we were the kind of band she thought she was getting, rather than the kind of band we actually were. Lying smoothly was an art form that required diligence, but I was getting better every day.

Just before dinner that evening, I found Finn playing his new white guitar in the basement, Dad's enormous old headphones wrapped over his head. I wanted to thank him for working with Tash and Kallie, but he didn't see me, so I just stood in the corner and watched as he ran his right hand up and down the fretboard. He used to practice like that all the time back in middle school, hunched over, eyebrows knitted in concentration.

And whatever the cause of that philosophical difference with his teacher, Finn seemed completely rededicated, like Tash and Kallie had fired his imagination. And even *I* could see how Kallie might have that effect.

I didn't hear Dad coming down the stairs behind me, so I practically screamed when he placed a hand on my shoulder. Finn leaped up and pulled off the headphones like he'd just been caught watching a porno.

"Well," said Dad gruffly, "I'll say again that I'm very disappointed in you for damaging the car. Still, the mechanic managed to find a bumper from scrap that was the right color, so the work was only a hundred and fifty dollars. It's a lot, but I think we can agree we dodged a bullet here. In the future be more careful, okay?"

I nodded, but it didn't make sense. I'd seen the mechanic place the order for a new bumper. I looked at Finn, but he immediately turned his attention to his guitar. And he wasn't alone—Dad seemed transfixed by it, gliding forward like a moth drawn to a flame.

"What's that?" he asked.

Finn cast his eyes around uneasily. "It's a, um . . . *blah* Jimi Hendrix *blah blah*," he mumbled.

"A what?" I asked, slowly and loudly.

Finn glared at me, then finger-spelled *Fender Jimi Hendrix Tribute Stratocaster.*

Dad wasn't paying us any attention at all. He just gazed longingly at the guitar until Finn felt obligated to hand it over.

"Is this the one we bought you?" he asked.

Finn shook his head, kindly omitting to mention that he'd bought the old electric guitar with his own money.

"So whose is this?"

"It, uh . . . belongs to a friend. I've got it on extended loan."

Dad seemed satisfied by that, completely missing the freaked-out expression emblazoned on Finn's face. "How are you handling the switch from right to left hand?"

"Um, okay. Takes some getting used to, but I want to be able to play both."

Dad nodded approvingly. "Man, it's beautiful," he said, running his fingers over the polished surface. "Wasn't it a limited release?"

Finn looked up, narrowed his eyes. "Yeah. How do you know that?"

Dad's head snapped up and the trance was broken. "What? Oh, I must've heard it somewhere. I guess. Probably. I mean, I wouldn't really know, of course." He shuffled his feet as the silence lingered. "Yeah, well, time for dinner. Nice playing, Finn," Dad added, even though he hadn't heard anything. "I'll see you both upstairs."

He took the stairs two at a time.

"How did he know this guitar was a limited release?" said Finn, wide-eyed.

I shrugged. "Who knows? But maybe there's a lot about Dad

we don't know. He can't always have been as hopelessly uncool as he is now."

Finn snorted, and I laughed, and a moment later he started to pull the headphones back on.

"Not so fast, Finn. I don't suppose you know anything about the spare bumper?"

Finn stared at his guitar. "What do you mean?"

"Come on. Don't lie to me."

He rolled his eyes and gently laid the guitar beside his chair. Whatever we were about to discuss was clearly going to take a few minutes.

I paid most of the bill myself, then told the mechanic what to say to Dad, he signed, presumably because he thought it would make me less critical.

I felt my stomach flip. "You did what?"

"What's the big deal?" he moaned, already done with signing now it was clear the magnanimous gesture hadn't worked. "The mechanic didn't care as long as he got all the money."

"How much did you pay?"

Reluctantly, Finn's right hand formed the signs for *278.*

My legs felt unsteady. I was hyperventilating. "Where did you get the money?"

"Shh!" Finn pressed a finger to his lips, stared at the staircase until he was sure no one had heard. "That's my business."

I wanted to throttle him. "What about the guitar? You may be able to fool Dad, but I know it's yours."

"Yeah, but only someone who actually cared about me would realize that."

It was a first-rate self-pitying line, and somewhat true. But he was going to have to do much better than that to throw me off the scent. "How much was it?"

"Not much. It was used."

How much? I repeated, reverting to sharp signs and a fierce face so I could convey my seriousness without having to scream.

Still Finn hesitated, clearly deciding whether or not to lie. *750.*

My mouth hung open in shock. I couldn't make sense of any of it. *Where are you getting all this money?*

None of your business.

It is my business when I have to cover for you after school each day. I closed my eyes, took a deep breath. *Are you selling drugs?*

No! At the mention of drugs, Finn looked like he was about to burst into tears. *It's from the poker games.*

I'd have been less surprised if he'd told me he was growing a bumper crop of marijuana in his bedroom. True, Dad used to play poker with us all the time when we were younger. It was something he could do with me that didn't involve speaking *or* signing, plus he liked winning. But when I switched to chess he bailed, saying a chess game was too great a time commitment. I'd figured that was the end of the Vaughan family's poker playing days.

Or not.

When do you play poker?

Lunchtime, replied Finn, content to sign as long as it kept his secret under wraps. *And we started playing after school too, because you made me wait while you rehearsed. Except Friday, when you made me go to the rehearsal. In a way, the whole thing is your fault.*

I laughed, but inside I was utterly freaked out. *You've really won a thousand dollars playing poker?*

He clearly misread my surprise as admiration. *Almost. I'm a lot better than everyone else.*

And how does everyone else have hundreds of dollars to lose?

I don't know. He laughed suddenly. *Probably selling drugs.*

I didn't laugh. *You've got to stop. You could get expelled.*

"The thought had occurred to me," he said out loud.

I sighed, "And that doesn't bother you?"

"Why would it? All the teachers hate me."

"They wouldn't if you'd try harder."

"Yes, they would. Because no matter how hard I try, I'm not you. But we share a last name, so they're all waiting for me to become class superstar. For as long as I'm there, they'll compare me to you. And I'll always fall short."

"Do you want me to talk to them?"

"God, no! I just want you to admit I don't fit in."

"You were fitting in fine during lunch break today."

Finn looked down, blushed. "What do you mean?"

"You, Kallie, Tash. Quite a cozy threesome."

"We were just going over some stuff. That's all."

I smiled sweetly to irritate him. "But you're still not really interested in Kallie, right?"

Finn's shoulders slumped. "For the last time, no. I'm not interested."

"Isn't she hot enough for you?"

"I'm not talking about it anymore."

Finn leaped up and hurried across the basement. But as he ran up the stairs, I caught him smiling too.

CHAPTER 32

Josh was last to arrive for Friday's after-school rehearsal, sauntering in almost ten minutes late as though prearranged times were optional for Godlike lead singers.

"Glad you decided to join us," I quipped, not bothering to hide my annoyance.

"I'm sure you are. You missed me, I get it," he said, the famous Josh smile intact.

I almost rose to the bait, but managed to keep control. "I have news," I said with forced enthusiasm. "Good news of the paying variety."

Everyone looked up. Apparently, I had uttered the magic word that got their attention.

"The producer of *Seattle Today* wants us to appear on the show next Tuesday," I explained. "We play one song, then do a brief interview."

Will flicked away the curtains of hair obscuring his eyes and leaned forward in his chair. "*Seattle Today* is just a bunch of old women," he droned, seemingly without engaging his face. "They'll want something really boring."

I was taken aback that Will was the one to complain. "Sure, they'd *prefer* a tame song," I admitted. "And yes, it's mostly old women. But right now, that's your main audience."

"That sucks."

"Maybe so. But they're paying . . . three hundred dollars, for one song and an interview."

I let the figure hang in the air, allowed myself to enjoy the stunned silence that signified the band's complete approval.

Will shook his head. "Not worth it."

Tash was up in a second. "Speak for yourself. That's fifty dollars each—sounds like plenty of good reasons to play."

Kallie raised her hand. "I agree with Tash."

"Musically, it makes no sense," moped Will. Then he allowed his curtains of hair to fall back across his face, like a turtle retreating into its shell.

Josh stepped forward, placed an arm on his brother's shoulder while his eyes remained fixed on Kallie. "Kallie's right, Will. It's worth it for an hour."

Kallie nodded appreciatively, and a moment later Josh's arm had been transferred to her shoulder instead. She didn't pull away, but her body tensed, as though his constant physical attention was as welcome as a root canal. Josh noticed it too, and his smile faltered, but he didn't remove his arm, and the awkwardness of the interaction grew steadily for several seconds.

"We need to practice," murmured Kallie, her eyes closed.

Josh finally took the cue and withdrew his arm reluctantly. "Yeah, you do." He ambled to his place at the front of the band. "By the way, Tash, nice costume, but Halloween was yesterday."

"Go screw yourself, Josh."

"Natasha, Natasha," tutted Josh. "Just as rude as ever. After all the time you and Kallie have spent hanging out this week, I figured some of her prim and proper behavior would've rubbed off on you."

"Let it go," she warned.

"Okay, then," I interjected, anxious to get things back on track. "The majority opinion seems to be that we'll accept the gig." (It didn't seem prudent to mention that the majority opinion was irrelevant, since I'd already accepted and mailed back the *Seattle Today* contract; I'd even convinced Mom to glance through it first.) "However, Will has a point. We can't go on selling ourselves as a soft rock band for overprotective parents. It was a means to an end, that's all, but it's not who you are, and it's not who you want to be. I meant what I said last week. You're hard rock, for real. And you're going to stay that way from now on."

Tash shook her head. "They'll never let us play our real stuff on *Seattle Today*."

"Not if we tell them ahead of time, no. But it's a live show, which gives them a choice: Stop the show or let you finish. And from what I've read about the host, there's no way she'll pull the plug." Even Tash seemed satisfied with that argument. "And let's be honest—there's nothing like live TV to send a message. By the time you're done, I'm betting our new target audience will have heard you loud and clear."

I'd never thought of myself as the pep-talk-giving type, although the band seemed to be hanging so intently on my every word that I had to remind them we had gathered for a rehearsal. In particular, Will's mouth had stretched into the uncharacteristic shape of a smile. He was a boy of few words, but I understood that look just fine.

Without another word, Ed and Finn took over, and Dumb did their finest impersonation of a well-oiled machine. From time to time, I even glanced up from my laptop to watch the Boy Wonders at work, marveling at their confidence, the way they isolated mistakes and corrected them without ever making the perpetrator seem nervous. Even Kallie seemed energized by Finn's words of advice, laying into her guitar strings with uncharacteristic vigor before remembering that she was the band's resident wallflower.

By the time Dumb nailed "Look What the Cat Dragged In," I had downloaded more photos and links to our website, taken the bold step of sending MP3s of Dumb's performances to local concert venues, and written to Baz to say we'd like to use the studio again on Sunday. I'd even had time to check our Facebook page, which is how I found a new message from ZARKINFIB:

ur a quick study, but don't forget to enjoy the ride. let hendrix help you at 2010 s jackson

As before, I was shocked to discover the message, but this

time it was balanced by irresistible curiosity. I guessed whom "Hendrix" referred to, and with time to kill I opened YouTube and pulled up some footage of him performing.

Jimi Hendrix was younger-looking and hotter than I'd imagined. When the camera showed a close-up of his hands, his fingers looked slender and strong. The way he closed his eyes and swayed his head made me wonder if he was channeling spirits or had indulged in narcotics, but either way, it was difficult to take my eyes off him.

With the image of Jimi playing on one side of the screen, I pulled up his biography in a new window on the other. As with Kurt Cobain, it made for uncomfortable reading, and I wondered how he'd survived being raised in a home so profoundly broken. By the time I looked up again, six pairs of eyes were locked on me, and Ed was heading toward me, his face tinged with concern.

"Are you okay?" he asked.

"Yeah, I . . . I just got a message from my secret admirer."

Ed nodded. "So where are we off to this time?"

"No, Ed. We'll go some other time. I need to call it a day."

"Uh-uh. I sense the second voyage of the Magical Mystery Tour is about to set sail. Anyone else ready to get educated?"

Kallie nodded enthusiastically, while Tash looked confused.

"What are you talking about?" she asked.

"Nothing," I insisted. "I mean, someone's sending me on a tour of Seattle's dead rock stars, that's all. Apparently, Hendrix is next."

"Then count me in," said Tash. "You coming, Will?" she added, masking her hopefulness with an air of indifference.

Will shook his head, his indifference all too genuine. Josh tried to suppress a smirk as they left the room together. Maybe seeing Tash's advances rebuffed took some of the sting out of his own rejection.

"Come on. Let's go," sighed Ed.

I glanced at my watch. "I really shouldn't. My mom got annoyed last time."

Finn waved my cell phone in the air. "Dad says it's okay. Mom's got some dinner thing at work."

I looked in my bag, wondering when Finn had managed to filch my cell phone. I wanted to ask for more details too, but by then he was heading out the door with the others.

Eventually only Tash remained. She stood by the window, staring into space. I knew what was bothering her, but I wasn't sure what to say, so I figured it was probably best to leave her alone.

Just then, Kallie returned. She padded over to Tash and placed a hand on her arm. I was sure that Tash would pull away, but she didn't. Instead she sighed, just once, then followed as Kallie led her from the room.

CHAPTER 33

USS *Immovable* labored up Capitol Hill. In the rearview mirror, I saw three women in matching Lycra tops powering space-age bicycles, matching us step for step. They were grimacing, and I think it was because we were holding them up, rather than from exertion. I floored the gas and *Immovable* wheezed angrily, but our speed didn't change. I patted the wooden dash encouragingly and prayed that we'd make it all the way to the top.

Finn waved from the backseat, where he'd assumed his now-customary position sandwiched between Tash and Kallie. *Should we get out and push?* he signed.

I stuck my tongue out and he smiled, although it probably had more to do with the aforementioned sandwich than anything I had done.

With a Seattle city map in his hands and a GPS system seemingly hardwired into his brain, Ed directed me straight to the 2000 block of South Jackson Street. It was only a couple miles from Kurt Cobain's house, I realized, but the addresses belonged to different worlds. Instead of mansions designed to maximize views of the lake and mountains, Jackson Street was home to apartment buildings and a mishmash of nondescript warehouses and stores. Instead of the serenity of Cobain's intensely private community, several people loitered on street corners. But the most obvious shift, as subtle as a slap on the face, was that almost everyone was African American. I didn't feel weird about being there, but I had to admit that I couldn't recall having passed through the neighborhood before.

Ed pointed to the side of the road and I pulled over. He prodded the map so sharply I thought his finger might pierce it. "2010 should be here," he groaned.

I looked through his window, but there was only a low wall fronting an overgrown plot of land with a large FOR SALE sign.

"Well, let's find it," I said encouragingly, but everyone took their time getting out of the car.

Tash sloped toward the wall. "Welcome to Jimi Hendrix's invisible house," she deadpanned.

We walked up and down the block, but it was clear that this was where the house misleadingly known as 2010 S Jackson should have been.

Finn waved to get my attention. *I'm going to ask someone what's going on,* he signed.

While I was waiting, I jumped over the wall and onto the

plot, which was engulfed by tall weeds. If a building had ever been there, it had disappeared years ago. I kicked at the ground in frustration, but then something caught my eye.

I knelt beside a bush at the edge of the plot. It looked like someone had dumped trash under the branches, but I knew it wasn't trash. The cardboard boxes had been flattened and covered with moth-eaten blankets, torn wrappers from a Happy Meal licked clean and stashed to one side. Everything was sodden from rain, but someone had lived there for a while, in the cold and wet, on ground that Jimi Hendrix may or may not have ever known.

Ed touched my arm, startling me. "I hope they've found somewhere warmer now," he said.

I nodded as I touched the thin blanket. I couldn't imagine it provided enough warmth to get someone through summer nights, let alone fall.

"Seems symbolic, doesn't it?" I sighed.

Ed crouched down beside me, touched the blanket too. "How so?"

"Jimi Hendrix grew up in poverty," I explained, reciting what I'd learned just an hour earlier. "His mom left when he was young. He often had to scrounge food from his neighbors. I guess it's possible there were days he slept outdoors like this. Same with Kurt Cobain. He got thrown out of so many houses he ended up sleeping in a cardboard box."

Suddenly I could picture them both with painful clarity: two cold, malnourished boys desperately seeking escape from the harsh reality of their lives, whether through music or drugs. Until a month ago I'd never given either of them any thought, and even if I had, I'd have seen only the fame and wealth, never suspecting that fame and wealth were just a veneer—Band-Aids over gaping psychological wounds.

I'd managed to convince myself that Dumb was about a college fund, a simple business decision. But kneeling among those damp weeds, trying to make sense of everything around me, I realized that it had become so much more than that. My college fund was a veneer too, and everything beneath was slowly bubbling to the surface. There was nothing I could do to stop it. And I wasn't even sure I wanted to anymore.

"Come on," said Ed, helping me up. His hand was warmer than mine, and he didn't let go until we got back to the sidewalk, where Finn addressed us with all the enthusiasm of an undertaker:

"It's true. Hendrix's house used to be here, but this isn't where he grew up. In fact, you're not going to believe what I'm about to tell you." That really got everyone's attention. "Jimi Hendrix grew up in a small house a few blocks from here, but that land was sold to a developer to build condominiums. Some fans arranged to save his house, and the city let them move it here. But after a few years, the city wanted to sell this plot, so they told the group to move the house again. Just as the city was about to demolish it, a Hendrix fan picked up the house, stuck it on a truck, and drove it away."

There was stunned silence while we looked at one another,

waiting to see who'd bust out laughing first. It turned out to be Tash.

"You are shitting me," she said with customary eloquence.

"Tash, I am so not shitting you," Finn assured her.

"So where is it now?" I asked.

Finn shook his head. "I don't know exactly, although the guy I spoke to said he thought it was across the road from the Hendrix memorial, which is in Greenwood Memorial Park in Renton."

"Renton? That's way the other side of the lake!"

Tash stepped forward. "Yes, it is. And we're going there now."

Ten minutes later, we joined the rush hour traffic heading east on I-90 across Lake Washington, fighting a stiff breeze that whipped waves against the bridge. I peered in the rearview mirror occasionally, but no one on the backseat was talking. Whatever thoughts we were lost in, we were lost in together.

Ed turned the Seattle map over and examined the streets on the eastern side of the lake, his finger drifting over Bellevue and down to Renton. I could see him tracing our route, but it was several miles before he pointed to an exit sign and I pulled off the highway. As we turned to face another long, grueling incline, I could feel *Immovable* vibrating oddly, and I almost felt sorry for her. Hilly Seattle is a cruel city for a car that should have been retired years ago.

After another mile I saw a cemetery on the right—nothing but headstones and manicured lawns, flanked by evergreens. I signaled to turn, but then Finn jutted between the front seats and pointed to the left instead. I didn't have time to ask why, and as soon as I'd crossed the oncoming traffic and realized he'd directed me into a trailer park, I wanted to curse. But by then he was telling me to stop.

I jammed on the brakes and glared at him, waiting for an explanation. Finn just pointed past me to the shack outside my window: a tiny, dilapidated clapboard house surrounded by a flagging chain-link fence.

"You don't mean . . ." I began, but Finn was nodding.

I dragged myself out of the car and felt my entire body deflate. Tufts of weeds filled holes in the cracked asphalt, and I kicked up stones and dust as I stepped toward the fence. I laced my fingers through the chain-links, icy-cold and battered. The house inside had been painted once, but it was flaking off. In its place, someone had spray-painted graffiti, but that only made the shack appear more neglected.

I was able to walk the entire perimeter of the fence in about twenty seconds. I did another circuit, hoping somehow that I might mysteriously stumble upon the rest of the house— the part where a family could live without being on top of one another the whole time. But there was nothing more to see. The house was tiny, smaller by half than Josh and Will's garage. Whatever the source of Jimi Hendrix's genius, it evolved in a place of poverty.

The rush of cars on the busy road beside us provided a wall of white noise, drowning out the crunch of footsteps and the scratch of voices. Somehow it felt right, so I closed my eyes and savored the peacefulness. When I opened them again, Tash stood beside me, slouching, like the bristling energy that kept her alive had seeped out somewhere between the car and the fence. She wrapped her arm around me and leaned her head on my shoulder.

"He grew up in there," she said, her words distinct so close to my ear.

I nodded.

Tash took a deep breath, exhaled hard. "The greatest rock guitarist in history grew up in this house. Do you understand that?"

I didn't, of course, not really; but at the same time, I did. I got the notion of someone transforming the way an instrument could be played just like I got the way that Andy Warhol and Jackson Pollack could change art, and William Faulkner and Ernest Hemingway could change literature. I told her so.

Tash snorted. "Yeah, well . . . let me know if their houses are falling apart, stuck on the edge of a trailer park, okay?"

"It's not fair," I agreed.

"No, it's not. His home should be a museum. It's a holy relic. It's . . ." She squeezed her left hand through a gap in the fence, willed herself a few inches closer. "Nothing's sacred, you know?"

"I know." I wrapped my arm over her shoulder and pulled her closer. "How did he die?"

Tash cleared her throat. "Drug overdose. He was only twenty-seven, same as Kurt Cobain. Can you believe it? Twenty-seven years old." She bit her lip. "What would you do if you knew you only had nine more years?"

I stared straight ahead, tried not to blink as my eyes dried out in the cold wind and the house became blurry. The sun was setting, casting a warm glow around the place. It reminded me that we'd turn the clocks back the next night, and if we hadn't visited now we'd have missed out on this scene. I didn't want to miss out on moments like this.

"If I only had nine more years," I said, "I'd make the most of every day. Every single one."

Silence again. We kept looking at the house, like we were expecting something to happen—a miracle, perhaps. I thought about all those hours Jimi had spent playing air guitar on a broom. I tried to picture the moment in eighth grade when he received his first guitar, a banged-up instrument with only one string. I imagined him practicing inside those thin walls, in a space so small the only way to be alone, to lose yourself, was through music.

How did he keep playing when money got really tight, and there was no more food in the house? How did he play on when it became clear he was flunking out of school? Was music really enough when the whole world seemed to be collapsing around him? Or was it just the only thing left?

I felt Tash shudder against me, and I knew she was fighting back tears. I would have cried too, but then I pictured Jimi bringing his guitar to life, his whole body transported by the pure power of music. And he didn't look sad or regretful— he brimmed with energy, savoring every stolen moment of untainted joy. *Live in the moment,* he seemed to be saying. And for once, I heard the words perfectly.

Live in the moment. I could do that.

We could all do that.

CHAPTER 34

Tash remained in her silent funk all the way home. Ed had tried to convince her it was a promising sign that fans had bothered to save the house at all, but for once he should have let it go. Tash was beyond seeing the silver lining, and I understood why.

I dropped Ed and Kallie off first. Tash said her mom wouldn't be home until much later, so Finn suggested she head back with us. She even seemed relieved. I guess she didn't want to be left alone with her thoughts.

The house was almost completely dark when we walked in, the only sign of life an overpowering odor of Chinese food. I switched on a light and lifted the lid on each carton, uncovering every variety of meat cooked in every conceivable way. Apart from fried rice (with pork, of course), there wasn't a single grain or vegetable to be found. Dad clearly didn't want the massacre of innocent vegetables on his conscience.

The Vaughan family—reintroducing scurvy, one child at a time!

We ate straight from the containers. After that, we went down to the basement, where Dad was watching the History Channel. The first thing I noticed was his clothes: T-shirt and jeans. True, he'd ironed a sharp crease down the front of the jeans, but it was progress.

He raised his eyebrows as I came into view, which made it difficult for him to express his shock when he caught sight of Tash.

"Dad, this is Tash," I said.

Dad began to extend his hand, then thought better of it, either because he figured she wasn't the hand-shaking type, or because he was afraid she'd rip it off his arm. In the end he settled for a curt nod that looked weirdly self-conscious.

"You're later than I thought you'd be. Just as well your mom is out."

"We wouldn't have been late otherwise," I said.

Dad chuckled, apparently impressed by our cunning. "Where have you been?"

"Jimi Hendrix's house."

That clearly got his attention. "The one in Renton?"

"Uh, yeah. . . . How do you know that?"

Dad waved off my question. "Hendrix was the greatest. The things he could do, the way he transformed rock guitar into something angry and poetic all at once . . . it was miraculous."

I nodded, but I couldn't help wondering if we were getting a glimpse of the *real* Ryan Vaughan at last. It was already the longest conversation we'd had in months.

Tash and Finn sidled up, and together we sat down on the sofa next to Dad's armchair.

"Jimi played at Woodstock in the summer of 1969," continued Dad. "It was a crazy thing—three days of music and drugs and rain. He played near the end, and most of the crowd had given up and gone home, but his set was the most amazing of all." Dad looked up, suddenly remembering that he had an audience. "You've seen it, right?"

Tash and Finn nodded, but I shook my head. Dad frowned, like he couldn't believe he'd been so negligent. He walked over to the far corner of the den and began rifling through a cardboard box. Eventually he pulled out a few LPs, and a DVD.

He handed me the LPs to look at while he put on the DVD. They had cool covers too. The title of one—*Are You Experienced*—was written in a kind of psychedelic bubble lettering, wrapped under a photo of three guys in flamboyant outfits (aka: the Jimi Hendrix Experience). Apart from Tash, I'd never personally known anyone who could get away with wearing such outrageous clothes, and it made me feel kind of envious.

When I'd cycled through the LP covers, I realized that Dad was still kneeling in front of the DVD player, transfixed, unable to contemplate the long journey back to his armchair. So I watched the TV too, where the real Jimi Hendrix had taken center stage, presumably live at Woodstock. He wore bell-bottom jeans and a white jacket with tassels, topped off with a red bandana. He should have looked funny, but instead he just looked incredibly cool.

Dad spun around. "Listen to this," he told me, his hands shaking with excitement.

I could have pointed out that what he was asking was difficult, to say the least, but I just wanted to hang out with this new Ryan Vaughan for a little longer, so I nodded. I wondered if Mom ever saw the version of Dad that emerged during his date nights with Jimi.

Jimi was playing solo now, the crowd cheering wildly. I studied his hands, but the noise coming from the old speakers beside the TV meant nothing to me, gave no hint of the music emerging from his guitar. I'd contented myself with watching Dad instead, when I thought I caught a few notes of "The Star-Spangled Banner." It couldn't have been that, of course, not at Woodstock, but then I recognized a little more of the national anthem. Dad lowered the volume, turned to me and smiled.

"Can you believe it?" he asked, his words clear and slow, like he really needed me to understand. "To do an improvisation on 'The Star-Spangled Banner' at that time, in that place. . . . Hendrix always said he thought it just sounded nice, but it was during the Vietnam War, and his improvisation was so tortured. His guitar spoke for a generation that day."

Finn had stopped looking at the TV now, and his eyes were fixed on Dad instead. Dad was changing before our eyes, and I'm not sure either of us knew what to make of it.

Eventually Dad shrugged, smiled, and turned the volume back up, communing with Jimi once again. The music became denser, fuzzier, but knowing what he was playing helped me. And because it mattered so much to Dad, I concentrated as hard as I could on Jimi and his guitar, as they sang, scratched, and clawed their way through "The Star-Spangled Banner" like it was part patriotic hymn, part heartrending cry. He seemed to sculpt the sound with his bare hands, pulling and shivering a lever, prolonging the agony or ecstasy or whatever was coming out of the instrument at that moment. And although I couldn't make out most of what he did, I could tell by the faces of the crowd, and the faces of Finn, Tash, and Dad, that what he was doing was utterly compelling, and positively transcendent.

As suddenly as it began, the improvisation ended. The whole band rejoined their leader, and the crowd drifted back toward insanity. Immediately Tash unzipped her guitar case and pulled out her guitar, and Finn did the same. Dad grabbed the remote and raised the volume until the speakers rocked on their stands and the walls began to shake. He leaned back and laughed with delight as Tash and Finn jumped up and down on the spot, strumming their unplugged guitars. Then he joined them, and suddenly there was a trio of Hendrix impersonators, egging each other on to ever greater feats of imaginary dexterity. For the first time I saw Tash laughing out loud, basking in her own personal heaven. And Finn was right there with her, matching her step for step, gazing at her like no one else existed.

My breath caught as the scene came into sudden focus. Finn wasn't interested in Kallie—never had been. It was Tash. It was all about Tash. I couldn't believe I hadn't seen it before.

Just then, Mom appeared at the bottom of the stairs, her expression caught between amazement and puzzlement. No one but me even noticed her.

Is your father really doing what I think he's doing? she signed, stifling a laugh.

Absolutely. He's an air guitar genius. Didn't you know?

Mom snorted, but it seemed to require effort. Frankly, she looked exhausted. *What are they listening to?*

I was going to finger-spell *Jimi Hendrix,* but I just lifted the cover to one of Dad's LPs instead.

She nodded, but then her eyebrows shot up, and I knew she'd spotted Tash. She didn't seem as amused anymore.

Is Grace sleeping through this? she signed.

When I didn't respond she stalked up to Dad and waved. "Is Grace sleeping through this?" she shouted. "Where's the baby monitor?"

Dad looked like someone rudely awoken from a very happy dream. He shut off the TV, ran across the room, and turned on the monitor with fumbling hands. Suddenly there was a new sound, as all five lights on the monitor sprang to life.

Dad sprinted across the den toward the staircase, but Mom stopped him with an outstretched arm. "Don't bother," she snapped. "I'll do it myself."

Mom spun around and left the deflated mob in her wake. Dad sighed twice, then shook his head and trailed after her.

Tash knelt down and pushed her guitar back into its case.

"You should stay," said Finn, placing a hand on her shoulder. "I—I'd like my mom to meet you."

Tash peered up scornfully. "Why?"

Finn's eyes darted around the room. "Just 'cause . . ."

She picked up the case and swung it across her back. "This was cool. Thanks."

"You need a ride home," blurted Finn as a last resort.

Tash leaned forward and planted a kiss on Finn's cheek. "I'll be okay, Finn. I've got a bus pass."

Then it was just Finn and me, scurrying around in a last-ditch attempt to clean up the evidence before the interrogation began.

Sure enough, Dad returned a minute later, slumping onto a bar stool and closing his eyes tightly.

A couple minutes after that Mom arrived too, clutching a still hysterical Grace. She popped out a boob and pulled the baby toward it, trying to counteract our neglect through a midnight snack. It seemed to work.

"What on earth were you thinking?" she asked finally.

Dad raised his hand. "I'm sorry. It was my fault."

"No, it's everyone's fault," corrected Mom. "You all know she's up there. Or did you just forget about her somehow?"

"We're sorry, honey. Okay?"

"No, it's not okay. Sorry doesn't make it right. All three of you chose to ignore her because it's easier that way. All so you can prance around the den pretending you're Jimi freaking Hendrix."

Finn shook his head. "We were just having fun, Mom."

"Wonderful. Some new girl comes over and suddenly our family's idea of fun is playing music loud enough to bust the walls, and neglecting the baby."

I could see Finn growing tense, his jaw clamped shut like he didn't quite trust himself to speak.

"You know who she is, Mom," I said calmly. "That's Tash. I told you about her."

"Frankly, I don't care what she's called."

Finn snorted. "I bet you don't. What is it—the green hair or the piercings?"

"Oh, you'd like it to be about that, wouldn't you?"

Dad stepped off his stool, knelt down beside Mom, and squeezed her arm reassuringly. "Hang on, Lynn. Tash was very pleasant. This isn't her fault."

Mom pulled her arm away. "Is that supposed to reassure me? Frankly, I'd prefer to put this down to her influence. It beats the alternative."

"You don't know the first thing about Tash," I groaned.

"And God willing, I'd like to keep it that way. And another thing: This band experiment has gone on long enough. If you're so desperate to go to Gallaudet, then I suggest you get back to studying and focus on applying for scholarships, instead of wasting your time."

I was about to fire back when Grace pulled away from Mom's breast and began wailing again. "I can't even get her to nurse!" cried Mom.

I waited for Grace to settle. "I know you're angry, Mom, and I'm sorry for not paying more attention to Grace, but the band isn't a waste of time. They're getting better every day."

Grace popped off the boob yet again and pawed at Mom's face, leaving an angry scratch across her cheek. Mom flinched as she touched the spot with her fingertips.

"Oh really, honey? And how exactly would you know that, huh?"

I felt my breath catch, her words sharper than a knife. We both knew what those words meant, and so I waited for her to apologize, to point to the bags under her eyes and admit she was too tired to think straight. But when she finally looked up, she just seemed defiant.

"Fuck you." The words came from somewhere deep inside me where the censor had been turned off. I was as surprised as anyone that I'd said it, but I meant it with all my heart.

For a moment no one moved, but then Dad leaped up. "Don't you dare speak to your mother like that."

I needed to back down, I knew I did, but I couldn't. "Oh, that's right. Side with Mom."

"I'm not taking sides. Your mother told the truth, that's all. I'm sorry if that's tough for you to hear."

I could feel the tears coming, but angry laughter slipped out first. "Oh, so I *can* hear now?"

"You know what I mean."

"No, I don't."

"You're deaf, Piper, okay? That may be painful, but it's a fact."

"You're wrong. You're so wrong it's practically a joke. One of these days you're going to work out there's nothing *painful* about being deaf. But I find it pretty significant that you keep using that word. Is that why you spend every waking minute cooing over Grace instead of talking to me? Does it make you feel better to know that at least you were able to cure one of us?"

Dad's hand balled into a fist, and I could feel his anger like a living, breathing presence. In the heat of the moment I willed him to yell at me, to scream obscenities, to declare war once and for all. It would have made it easier for us to admit there was no connection between us—never had been. Suddenly I saw the evening's bonding session for what it had really been: a mirage, brought on by an overdose of Jimi Hendrix, not by me. But then Dad forced himself to relax. "That's not fair, Piper," he said, and I hated him for keeping control, for trying to seem reasonable.

"You're damn right. And it's not fair you never bothered to learn more than fifteen signs, even though you know it's how I prefer to communicate. All these years, and the best you can do is ask how my day went, then pretend to understand my response. You don't know a single sign to express an emotion . . . happiness, sadness . . . *nothing*! Signing with you is like talking to a computer."

I took a deep breath and focused on keeping it together, saying what had always needed to be said, without breaking down. If I broke down, he might feel guilty, and I didn't want him to feel guilty for that moment; I wanted him to see the wrongness of *always*.

"I—I'm sorry, Piper. If I'd known you felt this way I'd have . . ."

"You'd have *what*, Dad? Learned to sign? And you and Mom would've refused to give Grace an implant because you think I'm so perfect you want her to be like me? Don't blame me for this one, Dad. This one's all on you."

I saw the way my words had crushed him, deflated him as surely as a punch to the gut, but I still didn't cry. I didn't even cry when I saw Mom hunched over Grace, a worn-out shadow of a woman with eyes shut tight. It should be them breaking down, not me, I thought.

But then I felt a hand on my arm, warm and comforting. I turned and looked at Finn, his face full of remorse and under-standing, and I began to cry anyway. Through the tears I saw my father help my mother to stand, and together they shuffled out of the den without another word.

I turned back to Finn and buried my face in his shoulder, gave up fighting my battle against tears now that it was blind-ingly obvious I could never hope to win.

CHAPTER 35

"So much for waiting a while longer before using up your final session," said Baz.

"They're ready for this. Trust me."

"Uh-huh. So who are they today? The Beatles? Barney and Friends?"

"No. We're Dumb. And we're going to stay Dumb from now on."

Baz shook his head in disbelief. "Well, you won't get any argument from me. Are we plugging in the eye candy's microphone this time?"

I clenched my fists. "Her name is Kallie."

"Oh, so now she has a name and someone to support her. Where was that last time?"

"I was wrong."

"Sure. Well, let's get on with it. You've got three hours to immortalize Dumb's greatness."

Even though Baz was being sarcastic, I didn't rise to the bait. I knew there was a side of Dumb he hadn't yet witnessed, and I wanted to enjoy his surprised reaction when he found out. But that would have to wait until Josh and Kallie joined the others. Where were they, anyway?

I peered through the window in the control room door and caught sight of Josh's face in a wall-mounted mirror. He looked animated, almost imploring as he dominated a conversation with, I guessed, Kallie. And it wasn't exactly hard to imagine what they were discussing.

He ran a hand through his blond curls, his eyes crying out for a little understanding. Even I'd have hugged him, but when he stepped forward, anticipating Kallie's embrace, it was clear she wasn't playing along. Suddenly he slapped the concrete cinder block with the palm of his hand, and I gripped the door handle in case things were about to turn ugly.

Josh was talking again now, but he was angry, not pleading. I figured his voice must be loud, but Baz was nearby and seemed completely oblivious to what was happening on the other side of the door. I tried to lip-read, but it was hopeless with Josh in profile, so I just watched to make sure Kallie was safe, and let him vent. Sure enough, he slapped the wall again a few seconds later, then waltzed into the control room and on to the studio like nothing had happened.

Kallie didn't immediately follow him, so I opened the door and stood beside her as she fought back tears.

"Are you okay?" I asked.

She nodded. "I guess there was some kind of misunderstanding about me joining the band."

"You mean it came with strings attached?"

"Yeah. I didn't realize, and now . . . now I just wish he'd get it, you know?"

"But he's not getting it. So you need to spell it out for him."

"I can't do that."

"Why not? He's being an asshole."

"No." She bowed her head. "It'll ruin everything."

I was sympathetic, I really was, but her stubbornness was infuriating. "You can't just let him walk all over you, Kallie."

"Yes, I can. Sometimes it's better that way. Anyway, I'll be okay." And with that she took a deep breath and rejoined her bandmates, her insecurity and anguish bottled up inside where no one else would see.

Five minutes later, Ed had Dumb running through the band's original three covers, exactly as I'd instructed him to do. Through my daily dose of web-based research, I'd discovered that while we'd never be able to sell copies of the songs without paying the copyright holders, it was unlikely that anyone would try to sue us for including them in promotional materials. Just as important, it meant that only twenty minutes into the three hours, Baz already had good recordings of all three songs, and Dumb's confidence was high.

The next songs slowed Dumb down, but everyone soldiered on together, and with an hour to go, another three songs had been recorded for posterity. Baz glanced at the clock as if to reassure himself he hadn't lost track of time. I felt vindicated.

I'd only anticipated getting recordings of those six songs, so I was thrilled when Dumb revamped "Loving Every Part of You" as a punk rock anthem. Then they tried a cover version of "Smells Like Teen Spirit" by Nirvana, but Josh was making up new R-rated lyrics as he went along. He was also unusually still, simply blaring into the microphone instead of his usual habit of performing for an imaginary, adoring audience. While Dumb was soaring to new heights as a band, Josh seemed to be in free-fall, rejected by Kallie and probably aware that his dreamed-of greatness might never come to pass after all. So much conniving, yet so few results. I couldn't help smiling.

I spent the session taking photos, posting comments to rock music blogs, and researching *Seattle Today*. But even then I'd run out of projects about half an hour before the session was over. Finally, out of boredom and desperation, I began to draft a letter to the school principal, requesting that Piper Vaughan be granted absence from two periods plus lunch break on Tuesday, November 5 to participate in Dumb's live performance on *Seattle Today*. And since Baz had a printer in the control room, I ran off a copy and forged my father's signature right there and then, before I had time to second-guess myself.

Even so, by the time I folded the letter and sealed it in an envelope, I'd read it at least a dozen times. I wondered if the wording was too formal, or the sentences too long. I imagined that the signature was too legible, the paper too fancy. In my mind I'd been tried and found guilty of impersonating a stay-at-home dad, and the sentence was too appalling to contemplate. I even began to doubt I'd have the courage to hand it in to the school office, but really, what other choice did I have? Ask Mom? Ask Dad? No thanks. Just because Mom knew it was coming up on Tuesday didn't mean she'd let me attend, not after Friday's showdown. Anyway, it was about time I capitalized on my reputation as the school's most upstanding student. The moment had come for Bad Girl Piper to test the theory that it's better to beg forgiveness than ask permission. It usually worked for Finn.

When our three hours were up, Baz ejected another new CD and handed it over. "Tracks one, two, three, five, eight, and ten are good," he said, all business. "And believe me, I don't use that word lightly."

"Thanks."

"I still wish you'd waited longer before coming in. I'm not trying to tell you how to do your job, but Kallie just isn't ready for this yet. When the band got off track, it was almost always because of her."

"She's getting better."

"But how long are the rest of them going to hang around waiting for her to get good enough?" he asked. I shrugged, and Baz seemed to understand that I needed him to let it go. "Seriously, though, they're so much better than the first time they came in here. They just need to attack every song with the same energy and commitment, you know?"

"I know. But we'll be back. And next time I hope we'll be able to pay our own way."

Baz raised his eyebrows like he admired my optimism, and possibly even shared a little of it. "Well, if you do get some paid work and want to book another session, let me know. I really believe we could get some good material—the kind that generates *real* interest."

"Thanks, Baz. Thanks for . . . well, everything."

"You're welcome. You're not exactly in an easy situation here."

I waved off the remark. "Deafness is overrated."

"I'm not talking about your deafness." Baz pointed to a framed poster for The Workin' Firkins—a performance at something called the Showbox back in 1985. "We fired our manager just after this concert. Biggest mistake we ever made."

"Oh."

"Yeah. Thought we'd made it, see? Thought the only way was up, so we figured there'd be a little more cash to go around if we ditched him and arranged things ourselves." He tapped the poster, gazed at it like a long-lost friend. "It worked for a while. We played bigger and bigger venues. Even had one show at Key Arena, back when it was the Coliseum. I'm talking eleven thousand people, you know? It was insane. But by then my brother and I were fighting pretty much all the time."

"Hold on. Your *brother* was in the band?"

"Yeah, lead guitar. And let me tell you, the fights are so much worse when it's family. Just look at Oasis."

"Who?"

Baz frowned. "Never mind. Anyway, it turned out the only

thing that had kept us together was that we all hated our manager. So when he wasn't around anymore, we just went at each other instead. We held it together for one more year, then disbanded."

"I'm sorry." I meant it too, but I wasn't just talking about his band. I felt like I was seeing the real Baz for the first time. The bohemian clothes weren't retro-cool, or even retro, they were relics of 1985, a refusal to accept that the band was over, time had marched on, and he was rapidly becoming an old man. The studio wasn't really about mentoring future bands or making a living, it was his way of reliving the role of pop star vicariously, making all the corrections and improvements he never got the chance to make with The Workin' Firkins. And something told me that Baz was smart enough to know all this too, that in refusing to move on he had come to terms with the desperately held persona, and felt that it was better than any alternative reality.

"Thank you, Baz, for all you do. I'm getting it, I really am."

He nodded. "I know you are." He smiled his crooked smile. "Tell you what, leave me your number. If I hear of any opportunities for an up-and-coming band, I'll contact you."

"Thanks. Although you could just e-mail me through the band's Facebook page," I said nonchalantly, studying him to see how he'd respond.

Baz grimaced. "I don't do Facebook, or any of those other sites. It's all too weird, if you ask me."

It wasn't the response I was expecting. "But you've visited *our* Facebook page, right?"

He rolled his eyes. "No offense, but I've got a million better things to do than trawl through the Internet trying to find your webpage." There was no hesitation, no turning red. Whoever the heck ZARKINFIB was, it definitely wasn't Baz Firkin. "You okay?" he asked as I remained rooted to the spot for several more seconds.

"Yeah. I'm just . . . Yeah. Thanks."

"Okay, that's three times you've thanked me, so we should stop now. I'm not used to it, and it's freaking me out. Besides, I'm supposed to be meeting my parole officer at four o'clock."

It was a good exit line. I just hoped I never had a chance to use it myself.

CHAPTER 36

Tash surveyed the aging audience of *Seattle Today* contemptuously from the edge of the studio. "If one of them drops dead in the middle of our song," she said, scowling, "do we have to stop playing?"

I snorted with laughter before realizing she wasn't completely joking. "That's not nice, Tash."

"Nice, no, but quite likely," she countered, pointing to a couple in the front row who had already fallen asleep.

Selina, the stage manager, glared at us and pursed her lips.

Tash leaned closer. "I don't think that woman likes us."

"And she hasn't even heard you play yet."

Selina hugged a clipboard, her eyes fixed on various people and objects I couldn't begin to identify. A couple seconds later she directed Dumb to take their places on the studio set, exuding all the warmth and charm of an army drill sergeant.

My heart beat wildly as the quintet took their positions and tuned up. I was suddenly glad the audience looked so comatose—watching the old ladies with their knitting had a calming effect I hadn't anticipated when I'd signed the contract. I got the feeling the band was pretty hyper too. All except Will, whose hair may have prevented him from noticing that there was any audience at all.

Selina tapped my arm. "I said, 'They don't look like their pictures on the website. Those black-and-white photos are misleading.'"

I smiled innocently. "Yeah, well, I had to shoot in black and white because Tash's green hair screws with the color contrast."

She rolled her eyes, like my attempt to torment her had actually worked. (Hanging out with Dumb had clearly rubbed off.) Then she left me and walked over to the host, Donna Stevens, who was having her makeup touched up. (She'd only been on air for ten minutes before the first commercial break, and I wondered how on earth she required makeup intervention already.) Donna peered over Selina's shoulder and raised a pencil-thin eyebrow as she beheld Dumb in all their Technicolor glory. I didn't like the look of that, and I liked it even less when Selina paused to talk with someone—the producer or director, I guessed—on her headset, after which she engaged the camera operators in an in-depth discussion. Unfortunately her back was to me, so I couldn't make out what was being said.

As Selina commenced a countdown, I turned my attention to the studio monitors mounted on the wall and waited for the closed captions to begin rolling.

Framed in perfect close-up, Donna was a skeleton-thin fifty-something woman with a sun-bed tan. Despite those extra layers of makeup, she wasn't attractive, although it was hard to say why. Individually her features were perfectly fine, like she'd gone twenty rounds with a plastic surgeon, but the cumulative effect resembled one of those fractured Picasso paintings. She also made smiling seem strenuous. She probably got along really well with Selina.

She returned from the commercial break full of manufactured delight: delight that she had the best audience in the world (cue rapturous applause); delight that she was about to introduce the first live TV performance of a local band called Dumb ("Such beautiful kids," she added, having never met us); delight that it was only a few weeks until Thanksgiving (did she seriously think most of the audience would live that long?). Just watching her made me feel profoundly intellectual.

The camera cut to Dumb, and Ed tapped four strong, steady beats on his sticks. Tash hit her opening riff aggressively, then bared her teeth like she knew the camera would be doing a close-up on her at that moment. Which it did, until she bared her teeth, at which point someone decided to switch to camera two, fixed on Kallie.

Twenty seconds into "Look What the Cat Dragged In" I was pretty sure Josh should've started singing. I even thought I heard him sing-screaming the opening verse, but only Kallie appeared on the monitor screen. She played with grim determination, staring at her fingers to make sure she didn't screw up. I moved away from the monitor and approached the edge of the set.

Sure enough, Josh was in full swing—eyes closed, body rocking, head tilted to one side like he was having a seizure. Everyone except Will exuded raw energy, and the audience looked predictably shocked. I figured it'd be no more than another minute before the security guards started unpacking the defibrillators. In the meantime, the camera was locked on Kallie.

When Josh opened his eyes at the beginning of the chorus, he evidently noticed that neither camera was pointed at him, and his disgust was unmistakable. He began to drive athletically to his right, placing himself between the camera and Kallie, but as soon as he pulled off the complex move, the light above the camera went off. Suddenly the camera on the other side of the stage was fixed on Kallie instead, and Josh had even more ground to cover to get himself in frame. It didn't seem to occur to him to stand in front of her. Or maybe he just wasn't interested in sharing the spotlight. Either way, if his cavorting hadn't been so ridiculously self-absorbed it would have made a fairly compelling spectator sport.

Josh needed only two more tours of the stage before he realized, like me, that Selina had crowned Kallie as the face of the band—that is, the *only* face of the band—and from then on he delivered each line with undiluted venom. I couldn't tell if anyone else in the band had realized what was happening, but in any case, only Josh seemed to care. My sixth sense told me his fuse had been lit, and immediate action was required.

I found Selina in a corridor off the set, barking into her headset. When she saw me coming, she looked away to make it clear she had no intention of talking to me. I had a desperate urge to stride up and whip the stupid headset off her head, but instead settled for scrawling a brief message on a piece of paper and shoving it in front of her face: CHANGE THE CAMERA SHOT.

She spun around sharply. "No way," she spat. "My director says that girl is the only one she wants our audience seeing. The others are punks." I almost laughed at the way she said it, like Dumb had somehow insulted her sensibilities. (I wondered if Ed would be oddly flattered to know he passed as a punk by the standards of *Seattle Today*.) "Anyway," she pressed on, "what was that crap about Dumb being spiritual descendants of the Dixie Chicks?"

"The Dixie Chicks have had a pretty tumultuous past, politically speaking," I hedged.

Selina blinked twice. "And Celine Dion?"

"I was talking about the lyrics," I explained reasonably, pointing to my hearing aids. "I mean, I could hardly be talking about the music, right?"

She huffed in displeasure, then flounced past me to the edge of the set as Dumb ended the song with a screeching blast of pure distortion. It sounded like an airplane landing just above my head.

I turned back to the monitor and saw Josh staring everyone down, especially Kallie. I wanted to call a time-out, sit the band down with a Sharpie and a clipboard and tell them that it was us against *Seattle Today*, and we needed to stick together, present a unified front. Only that was out of the question. They were already piling onto a too-short sofa, and Josh didn't look like he blamed anyone but Kallie.

The camera cut to Donna as she beckoned Kallie over, patting the sofa cushion nearest her. Kallie hesitated, but glided along to her designated spot. With the camera ideally placed to capture the momentous occasion, freaky skeleton lady held out a bony arm and shook Kallie's hand. I was afraid she might never let go, but then Tash plopped down beside Kallie, and Donna pulled away, leaning back in her giant-sized armchair in an attempt to put a safe distance between herself and Dumb.

"Well," began Donna, smiling vacantly, "that was . . . such . . . goodness me . . ."—I wondered if the stenocaptioner was having technical difficulties, but when I looked at Donna's face, it was clear the problem was entirely hers—"such . . . I mean to say . . . tell us how the band formed, Kallie."

Kallie looked like she'd just been asked to explain the theory of relativity. She crossed and uncrossed her boots as her hazel eyes grew large and fearful. Seconds passed like minutes.

"I can answer that, Donna." The words appeared on the screen, but the source wasn't apparent until the camera cut to Josh at the far end of the sofa. (Trust Josh to look up the host's name in advance.) "Dumb was born from the convergence of rock philosophy shared by its original members. Then Ed joined us because we'd cultivated a technique of rhythmic flexibility that some people misinterpreted as, for want of a better phrase, playing out of time. And that leaves Kallie."

"Indeed," replied Donna. "Tell us about Kallie."

"Well, she can't play guitar for *bleep*."

The last word seemed bigger than the others somehow, and I felt my lunch making a bid for freedom. I almost wished the stenocaptioner had just written "shit"—at least I'm used to seeing that word.

"The only reason she's in the band is to expose media bias," continued Josh. "Think about it. We've added a piece of talentless eye candy, and watched everyone fawn over her just because she's hot. It's a *bleep* joke. She's a *bleep* joke."

Selina was beside me in a heartbeat, her breath punching the air in angry whispers. I pretended I didn't know she was there. I didn't even do it to get even with her. I did it because the camera had pulled back to reveal the rest of the band fidgeting on the sofa, and I could tell they weren't exactly thrilled with Josh's word selection either. Actually they looked pretty angry, potentially violent even. It occurred to me that a fight could break out right then and I wouldn't have been surprised. And I don't think I was alone. Donna's face twitched like she was being electrocuted; only her immaculate blond hair remained completely unruffled.

Selina pushed in front of me, waggling her finger and issuing some carefully chosen swear words, which seemed pretty hypocritical, I don't mind saying. Then she pointed to the monitor, where the closed captioning conveyed Josh's latest incriminating sound bite: "Do I have issues with Kallie? No. Why would I have issues with such a superficial, vacant, self-absorbed piece of *bleep*?"

"Let it go, Josh," appeared on the screen, but it wasn't clear who'd said it. It was even less clear whether anyone could slow him down now that he'd opened the floodgates.

I admit it—my mouth felt dry, gummy. Surely the director or producer or *someone* would pull the plug at any moment, but when I looked at the monitor again Josh was still holding court and the camera operator was either too shocked or too traumatized to change the shot. Since no one else seemed able to take charge, I took a deep breath and hurried to the edge of the set, waving my arms frantically. From his place in the middle of the sofa, Ed peered up at me with the widest eyes I've ever seen. He watched carefully as I flattened my hand and placed it against my neck, then moved it sideways like I was slitting my own throat. Would he understand that I wanted—no, *needed*— him to bring the interview to a close?

Ed shook his head mournfully from side to side. Apparently he'd already completed the transition from frightened to petrified. *Great.*

And he wasn't alone either. The oldest members of the studio audience seemed intent on hailing the nearest security guard, like they were seeking protection in case the impending riot somehow extended to them.

I felt Selina's hand clasp my shoulder, but I brushed it away and held her off with my outstretched arm. At that moment I didn't give a damn that her job was on the line too; I just needed to stop the wreckage. My pulse was racing. Sweat trickled down my forehead and back, and I wasn't even the one under the blazing studio lights.

I looked at Josh, studied his lips to confirm that he was still monologuing on his new favorite topic: "The point is, none of us need some stuck-up bitch acting like—"

"Shut up, Josh!" This from Will, not only stirred to action, but shouting loud enough for me to hear clearly. I'd never known him to be so assertive, but it was too little, too late.

I'd seen enough. If the whole crazy ride was ending right there, I was going to have my say. Maybe I was being egotistical, utterly irresponsible, but if the band was about to flame out, it was sure as hell going to be me holding the match.

I took in a final view of them on the sofa—my five flavors of Dumb—and saw the pain and disappointment etched onto the faces of everyone except Josh. Surprising myself, I actually managed a melancholy smile, blew them a kiss, mouthed the word "good-bye."

Then I walked onto the set just in time to see Tash launch herself along the sofa, her hands poised to strangle Josh on live TV. Fists flew. Bodies tumbled to the floor. And at the bottom of the scrum lay poor Ed, our own version of Switzerland. By now Donna was freaking out—she jumped out of her seat and scampered offset, almost knocking me down in her haste.

"They're lunatics!" she screamed. "What the hell are they doing on my show?"

I strode onward. The red lights above the cameras showed

they were still filming, catching the dying embers of the band's impromptu beat down. Frankly, I didn't care. I didn't even hesitate when uniformed security guards joined the fray like they'd waited their entire lives for the chance to throw a few punches in the name of keeping the peace. There just wasn't room in my racing mind to contemplate any of these things.

Ten yards from the melee I narrowed down my choices to breaking up the fight, rescuing Ed, or unleashing a well-aimed shot to Josh's private parts. But then Kallie struggled from the sofa and stumbled toward me. Tash extricated herself too, and grasped Kallie's hand like she'd just appointed herself bodyguard. I looked to see whether Ed was still breathing—he seemed to be—then braced as Tash and Kallie stood before me. I wondered if they'd scream at me, and realized I couldn't blame them if they did. A manager was supposed to prevent situations like this. Instead they moved to either side of me, locking my arms with theirs, and I knew they didn't blame me at all.

Just then, Ed was rescued by one of the older and kindlier-looking security guards, who'd clearly identified him as collateral damage. Ed even locked eyes with me and mouthed the word "go," which reassured me he would survive.

Without a word, Tash and Kallie and I marched off the set, ignoring Donna's wild gestures and threats of retribution. For the first time we were sisters together, and nobody and nothing could stop us. A crowd had clustered in the lobby, eyes glued to the monitors relaying events from the studio, but it parted when we arrived. With looks of surprise, awe, and disgust, they watched us leave the mayhem behind.

As we paraded through the glass doors and embraced the stiff salt breeze, I sensed that all eyes were drawn to Kallie, like always, but she didn't seem to notice. I wondered what she was thinking. Did she need Tash and me to apologize for all the cruel things we'd said? If so, she wasn't letting on.

All the way to Pike Place Market no one said a word, but with every step the past felt more distant. We moved as one body, shared a single mind, and even when the streets grew busier we never unlocked our arms—just forged ahead like we owned the city. And for those few precious minutes, hip to hip like the Three Musketeers, I think that, just maybe, we really did.

CHAPTER 37

When I was little, Mom would take me to Pike Place Market for fresh fruit and vegetables, and sometimes a bouquet of flowers to celebrate the weekend. We used to watch the fishmongers tease tourists with their fish-throwing routine, and breathe in the chaos of thousands of bodies crammed into a space made for hundreds. Pike Place always seemed alive, the beating heart of downtown. I couldn't remember the last time I'd been there.

Tash pulled us into a café, ordered three lattes and paid up-front. There was no use in arguing with her—this was as close as she'd ever come to apologizing for treating Kallie like crap, and we all knew it.

We huddled at a table next to a bay of windows. A month before, Tash and Kallie would have piled onto seats without a thought for me, but now they sat beside each other on one side, with me on the other, so that I could follow the conversation more easily. Such a small gesture, but it meant everything.

I looked out the window, across the dark waters of the Puget

Sound. To the west, the peaks of the Olympics showed off the first snows of winter. I sensed Kallie and Tash gazing out too, immersed in the wondrous scene like they were trying to purge the ugliness of the afternoon. By the time the first hot tears pricked my eyes, I wasn't the only one crying.

"Since Dumb is over now," I said, stating the obvious, "you may as well tell me if you sent the messages from ZARKINFIB."

Kallie frowned. "I thought that was Baz."

"No. I asked him."

"Well, it definitely wasn't me."

"Or me," said Tash. "It sounds like the kind of thing Josh would do."

I'd already considered that, and ruled it out. I'd surmised Josh's motives for being lead singer in his own private rock band, and they were no more laudable than mine had been for managing it. But I couldn't believe he'd waste his time trying to educate me about the deeper significance of rock music when he couldn't even see it for himself.

"I don't think so," I said. "Maybe Will."

Tash snorted. "Not likely. Will doesn't give a crap what you know or do. All he cares about is playing his bass. Right now I hate him just as much as Josh." She gritted her teeth so the muscles in her jawline bulged out. "I've been playing in his stupid band for two years, and he still doesn't notice me."

"Maybe he does notice, but he's afraid to tell you how he feels," I suggested.

Tash brightened a little. "You really think so?"

Actually I didn't, but I liked seeing the effect my words had. "Maybe."

"No," said Kallie, shaking her head. "I don't know why, but he's just not into you."

Tash's face reddened, but Kallie never flinched. And then, as quickly as she'd lost her temper, Tash calmed down.

"I'm sorry. There's a part of me that still hates anyone telling me things I don't want to hear. But it's not your fault."

Kallie took Tash's hands in hers. "Tash, this is no one's fault, certainly not yours. You're strong and devoted and beautiful, but when Will looks at you I think he sees a really good guitarist, a friend, someone he likes being in a band with . . . but that's all."

I didn't know if it was the reality of the situation hitting home, or simply the fact that Kallie was being nice to her, but Tash was struggling to hold it together. She took deep breaths, swallowed hard, and stared out the window like she'd only just noticed the scenery, but Kallie never let go of her hands.

I sipped my coffee, savored the heat from the mug and the warmth of the café. Outside, wind slapped at the windows as gulls fought to hold steady. The fresh smell of salt seemed to seep through pores in the glass. All around us the world kept spinning, but we were caught in a moment of perfect stillness: Tash and Kallie crossing an impossible divide through the simple step of forgiving.

"Thank you for saying that," said Tash finally. "I mean it. If you'd told me you thought there was a chance, I'd have . . ." She stared at her hands, entwined with Kallie's. "I think it's time to move on, you know?"

No one spoke as I added my hands to theirs, but I like to think we all felt the same thing at that moment. Out of the ashes of Dumb, something far stronger and more wonderful had arisen than any of us would have dared to imagine.

I wouldn't have minded if we'd stayed that way, but Tash didn't seem to be in the mood to lose an entire afternoon to silent introspection. She said she needed a pick-me-up, and that we could get free lattes at her mom's salon. And because I was feeling reckless I said count me in, never for a moment considering that coffee was the last thing on Tash's mind.

CHAPTER 38

Tash's mom obviously missed the class where they teach would-be moms about careful language selection and modest clothing. She hadn't gotten the message about blond highlights being a uniform for middle-aged moms either. In fact, she seemed to be competing with her daughter for the most-outrageous-looking award. And make no mistake about it: She was holding her own.

Her name was Cassie, she said, and if we called her Mrs. Hartley or Tash's mom, she'd have to beat the crap out of us. She said it just like that, as if it were perfectly reasonable, while Kallie and I exchanged anxious glances.

Cassie's salon was pristine, with banks of mirrors on every wall, and swirls of burgundy and gold paint embellishing all remaining surfaces. At the cashier's desk, an elderly lady blew kisses to Cassie and her fellow stylist, before exiting with shimmering red hair.

I watched the old lady leave, wondering how on earth she'd

chosen Cassie's salon. But then I noticed Cassie watching me, and I could tell she'd read right through my thoughts, so I smiled and busied myself looking at a book of hair dye swatches on a nearby counter instead.

Once she'd cleaned her station, Cassie wandered over to me and signaled for me to join the others. Tash had obviously told her I was deaf. Equally obviously, she'd been thinking about what she was going to say to us.

"I saw the interview this afternoon, and I'm very disappointed," she began, addressing all of us, not just Tash. "You're all mature enough to know that if a situation makes you uncomfortable, you should just get up and leave. You don't have to stand for anything, and you sure shouldn't attempt to correct things with a few punches."

Tash bristled, but Cassie shut her down with a single cocked eyebrow.

"All the same, I'm pleased you three are still together. Don't let the pricks divide you, you know?"

I wondered if I'd misheard her, or read her lips incorrectly, but no—Cassie was just that forthright.

She clapped her hands. "All right, sermon over. On to business. As Tash has obviously told you, I don't take appointments on Tuesday afternoons because I'm supposed to sort out the accounts. But on a day like this, accounts can wait. Ty needs to be available for walk-ins, though, so it'll just be me. Now which of you two wants to go first?" she asked, waving her finger back and forth between Kallie and me.

I couldn't tell which of us was more confused. "First for what?" I asked quietly.

"A haircut," said Cassie, like it was the most obvious thing in the world. "Surely Tash explained about . . ." She trailed off, her eyes narrowing as Tash tried to keep a straight face.

"Cassie's amazing," said Tash. "And I just thought you both needed a pick-me-up, that's all."

Cassie rolled her eyes, but when she looked back at Kallie and me, I could tell the offer was still on the table.

"Go on," implored Tash. "It's not like the day can get any worse."

Suddenly Kallie seemed to have made up her mind. "Piper will go first," she said.

I didn't even get a chance to decline before Cassie glanced at her watch. "Okay, but I can't promise to get around to you for a couple of hours," she warned Kallie. (*A couple of hours?* I figured I must have misheard her.) "I'll do my best."

"Take your time," said Kallie amiably. "Tash is going to do my hair."

This time I was certain I'd misheard her, but Tash's and Cassie's responses convinced me I'd heard her just fine. Tash was practically shaking—it was the first time I'd ever seen her looking scared. "No way!" she cried. "I'm not qualified."

"I think you'll do great," replied Kallie.

Cassie shook her head. "Absolutely not. I can't have you leaving here with bad hair. It would kill my business."

"Tash won't let that happen," said Kallie calmly.

"No, Kallie," insisted Tash. "Cassie's right. Watching the stylists isn't the same as doing it myself."

"Then I'll just skip the haircut today, thanks."

Tash and Cassie exchanged glances, and Cassie threw her arms up in defeat. "Fine. It's your hair. But don't you *dare* tell anyone it happened in my salon."

I didn't like the way she referred to Kallie's future hairstyle as "it," but I was even more astounded at Kallie herself—calmly offering up her hair as practice fodder to the girl who, just two weeks earlier, would have delighted in dragging her away to a dark corner and shaving it all off.

Cassie caught my eye and beckoned me over to her station, where she pinned a cape around my neck. She ran her fingers through my hair, her eyes betraying her concern. "You need to look after your scalp better," she scolded.

"It's not worth it."

"Yes it is. You have lovely hair."

"It's kind of mousy."

"It's blond."

"Dirty blond."

"Strawberry blond. And I have customers who pay a lot of money for this exact shade."

There wasn't much I could say to that, so I sank into the warm leather seat and wondered if the reason everything felt so good was because it was happening on a school afternoon. Which was also when I realized that I didn't feel guilty at all.

After eighteen years of doing everything right, Bad Girl Piper was embracing the chance to do something really wrong.

In the mirror I saw Cassie waving her comb. "So, what do you have in mind?"

The question shouldn't have caught me off guard, but it did. I studied myself in the mirror and tried to think of an appropriate response. "Maybe, um . . . trim the ends?"

Cassie gawked at me like I'd farted. "Trim the ends?"

"Uh-huh."

Her brows knitted and she continued to stare at me. There was something uncomfortably intense about that look of hers, like she was trying to distill the essence of Piper Vaughan.

"Piper, today I saw a girl stride onto a live TV set to break up a fight, even though she might've gotten hurt. But it turns out that same girl neglects her hair and wears it long enough to hide her face, and her head and neck too. So tell me this: Which one is the real you?"

It seemed like a ridiculous question, but at the same time I knew what she was getting at. "I don't know," I answered honestly. "I think . . . maybe the first one."

Cassie nodded approvingly. "And what should that version of Piper Vaughan look like?"

Her words made it sound like an innocent role-playing game, but my heart was pumping in a way that assured me it was so much more. "She should have . . . shorter hair," I said, staring into the mirror, daring myself to disagree.

"How short?"

I swallowed hard, tried to shut down the frightened part of me. "Above the shoulder. Maybe chin length."

Cassie nodded solemnly, pulled something from the shelf beside her, and handed it to me: the book of color swatches I'd been looking at when I first came in. "What about the color? Dark streaks would go well. Some red would be easy to work in."

I flicked through, let her point out what she meant, but I knew those colors had nothing to do with the Piper Vaughan I was becoming. For good reasons and bad I'd attracted the attention of a whole lot of people recently, and the truth is, it didn't even bother me anymore. I was someone different now, someone new. I was stronger than black, bolder than red. I was . . .

My finger stopped as if it had its own agenda. But when my brain eventually caught up, I knew it spoke for all of me.

Cassie locked eyes with me. "Are you sure?"

I nodded confidently, and the confidence was genuine.

"What are you thinking—stripes? highlights? bangs?"

"Everything."

"Everything?"

"Everything," I repeated, swallowing as I said it.

"Okay," she said slowly. "But first I have to ask: Are your parents going to track me down and kill me for doing this?"

I nodded. "It's entirely likely."

Cassie laughed. "Good. I eat conservative middle-class suburban couples for breakfast. No offense."

"No offense taken. Actually, it sounds like you've already met them."

Cassie laughed again, and so did I, and then I realized that my heart was still beating fast, but in a different way—not apprehensively, but excitedly. I was taking charge, and it felt amazing.

"You're excited, huh?" she asked, watching me.

"Yes. Is that silly?"

"Not at all. It's why people come. They say it's about looking smart, or beautiful, or professional, but it's not. Gray-haired ladies try to recapture their former brunette. Brunettes want to go blond. Other women go for colors that don't arise in nature. Each group thinks it's completely different than the others, but I don't see it that way. I've watched them looking at themselves in the mirror, and they're not interested in conforming or rebelling, they just want to walk out of here feeling like themselves again."

I didn't need to say anything more for Cassie to know she had me pegged; my expression spoke volumes. She patted my shoulder gently and gave me the book of swatches to hold, then turned my chair around so I couldn't see the mirror. While she mixed the dye and began applying it to my hair with a brush, I bade farewell to the old Piper Vaughan, mouthing the words printed on the swatch over and over, like a mantra: *Atomic Pink.*

Twenty minutes later Cassie left me with a head-full of plastic cap, and said she'd be back soon. She didn't exactly give me a ballpark figure for *soon*, but I figured I shouldn't be expecting to make it back to school for last period.

I could have read trashy magazines while I sat there, but I didn't. Instead I turned the chair so I could watch Tash and Kallie. (Cassie had relegated them to the very back of the salon, where they were less likely to unsettle any paying customers.) Tash frowned with concentration as she applied dye in bold streaks to Kallie's auburn hair, but the pair of them kept giggling so hard that Kallie had trouble staying still.

The dye was a brownish color, but the odor drifting along the salon was peroxide, so I knew Kallie was about to be the recipient of blond streaks. I tried to imagine how she'd look—probably like a black animé character. Color-wise, she wasn't being as adventurous as me, but by having Tash do the job, she was taking a leap of faith beyond anything I could imagine. I worried what would happen if her hair turned out terribly. Would everyone at school laugh, or would they simply wonder what had gotten into Kallie Sims?

Or was that precisely the point? Because no matter how it turned out, this was a way for Kallie to turn her back on all that she was perceived to be: an enigmatic beauty—untouchable, beautiful, flawless. Maybe she could untether herself from that world completely. No more rifling through the designer clothes in last season's bargain bucket. No more struggling to concoct a beauty regimen out of the free samples from cosmetic company reps. Kallie could blend. She could disappear. She was ready for ordinary.

It was close to an hour before Cassie returned. I was a little flustered by then, partly because I didn't know if/when she'd be returning, but mostly because I needed to know how I looked. Cassie just smiled and told me to be grateful my hair had started out blond; otherwise she'd have needed to bleach it before applying the pink. And then she tormented me further by turning my chair around again so I couldn't see the mirror as she removed the plastic cap.

"What's the cap for, anyway?" I asked.

Cassie laughed and knelt down so I could see her. "Nothing. It was just to stop you from sneaking a peek."

Before I could pretend to be annoyed, Cassie led me over to a basin, where she placed a soft brown towel on my shoulders. Once I'd removed my hearing aids, I leaned back and closed my eyes. She shampooed the gunk out of my hair and massaged my scalp. The combination of warm water and silence was so blissful that I almost dozed off, but then she turned off the shower and wrapped the towel around my head. She dried my hair and led me back to her station, where she removed the towel like a magician. Which, it turned out, was completely appropriate.

I felt the need to pinch myself. No matter how familiar my face seemed, there was no way on earth that the person before me could be Piper Vaughan. Apart from getting taller and growing boobs, Piper Vaughan had remained unchanged for almost a decade. But the girl in the mirror was holding up her middle finger to that person.

I saw Cassie trying to communicate with me via the mirror, but I couldn't hear a word. I put my hearing aids back in and smiled.

"What do you think?" she asked.

I watched my smile grow into a laugh. "I think it's . . . amazing."

For a moment Cassie's cool exterior cracked and she seemed to exhale. Then she was back to business, picking up her scissors and snipping away entire waves of hair, while I watched her intently. She resembled a grown-up Tash, but without any of the hang-ups. She was, I realized, easier to like than Tash.

Suddenly she was smiling at me. "Thinking deep thoughts?"

"Oh." I blushed. "I was just thinking about Tash."

I regretted saying it immediately. What if she asked me what I was thinking? But Cassie was too kind—or too professional— to do that.

"She's changed since you became manager."

I opened my eyes wide. "Really?"

"Yeah. Really." The scissors paused midair. "For two years she's mooned over Will Cooke like he's the center of the universe, and I've told her over and over she just needs to forget about him, move on. I don't know what his deal is, but I do know that his interest in Tash is definitely limited to her guitar playing."

It's not like what she was saying was a secret, but I was afraid that Tash might hear her.

"Don't worry, they can't hear me," said Cassie, reading my mind again. "Anyway, Tash only joined Dumb to get with Will, but since you took over, she's started talking about the music, and new chords she's learning, and stuff like that. I think she's finally decided the band may be more important than he is."

She resumed snipping from where she'd left off, but her

words stayed with me. She was saying I'd made a difference in Tash's life—a *positive* difference. Basically, she was thanking me. And I was so grateful to her for that.

It took Cassie thirty minutes more to reduce my hair to an artful mess, with dagger-like bangs and a don't-mess-with-me vibe. Then she blow-dried my hair in layers for another twenty minutes. I couldn't believe how meticulous she was. The last time I'd used a hairdryer was for the family's Christmas photo almost a year ago.

The new style showcased my hearing aids in all their glory. Only they were no longer Barbie pink, but rather Atomic Pink— not a relic of my former self, but a statement of my new identity. I didn't even try to cover them up.

When she was done, I glanced at my watch: 2:10 p.m. The last period of the day, Calculus, would be ending soon. Tomorrow I'd go back to school and pick up right where I left off. I'd still be ahead of almost everyone else in the class. The only difference would be my hair, a warning to others never to overlook me again.

I caught Cassie's eye in the mirror. "You look incredible," she said.

"I know," I assured her, and it didn't even feel like bragging. "Be honest, though. Do you think I'm going to like this look a year from now?"

She replaced the hairdryer in its holder with the utmost care. "Does it matter?"

I thought about that for a moment. "Well, I guess I don't want to believe that this is just a stage, you know? That next month I'll wake up and say, 'That's not me at all.'"

Cassie leaned forward like she was about to divulge a secret. "Honestly, one day you *will* wake up and say that. And no matter what godforsaken mess Kallie ends up with today, she will too. And so will Tash, and everyone else who comes in here. But you're worrying about the wrong thing. Don't worry about wanting to change; start worrying when you don't feel like changing anymore. And in the meantime, enjoy every version of yourself you ever meet, because not everybody who discovers their true identity likes what they find."

By the time Cassie removed my cape and brushed away stray hairs, Tash and Kallie had joined us, and Cassie didn't need to say a word for us to know what she thought of Tash's effort. Kallie's hair was shorter by a few inches, the cut unkempt and the blond streaks uneven. Yet through it all she smiled like I'd never seen her smile before. All I wanted to do was capture the moment forever: the image of Tash and Kallie, arm in arm; the discovery that Kallie's beauty radiated from a place that had nothing whatever to do with clothes and makeup.

We hugged then, all four of us, and the tears that followed were the happiest of my life.

CHAPTER 39

I knew the euphoria would end the moment my parents saw me, so I hung out with Tash and Kallie for a couple more hours before driving them home. It was almost dark when I got back, and the front door opened as I pulled up. I honestly believe Mom and Dad would have attacked me as I left the car if it hadn't been so cold outside. I braced myself for their latest offensive.

Instead, entire seconds passed while they stared unblinkingly at my hair. If it was supposed to make me feel uncomfortable, it was working really well.

Eventually Mom shook her head, dragging herself out of the trance. "The school called," she trilled. "I'd ask where you've been, but I think that's obvious."

You like it? I signed, even swallowing my fear long enough to produce a wide smile.

"Don't get smart with me. And don't think we're signing right now. I want your dad to hear every word of this conversation."

I snorted. "Oh, that's right. Let's not make the poor hearing people suffer."

"Don't you—" began Mom, but then she stood up straighter and took a calming breath. "Get over yourself, Piper. You're not the victim today."

"And *you* are?"

"You skipped an entire afternoon of school! I don't even know what to say to you anymore. Ever since you got in with this band, you're behaving like you're on drugs. Are you on drugs?"

"God, no," I groaned, wondering how she could be so off-target, so willfully ignorant of what was really going on.

"Well, what other explanation is there? You fight on live television. You skip school. You're rude and obnoxious. You cut off your hair and dye it pink. I mean, didn't you get the message? It's too late to start rebelling in senior year."

"I'm not rebelling," I said calmly.

Mom bristled. "Of course not. It's perfectly rational to want to look trashy—"

"That's enough, Lynn!"

I'd forgotten Dad was there until he spoke, matching Mom's pent-up anger step-for-step.

"No, Ryan, it's not nearly enough. I want answers. For a start, I want to know who gave Piper permission to leave school in the first place, because it sure wasn't me." She swung around to face me, waiting for the answer she knew would establish my guilt once and for all.

I turned away from her and caught a glimpse of my hair in

the hallway mirror, short and stylish and so very pink—a haircut with attitude. For a while I'd allowed myself to believe that it reflected the new Piper. But the new Piper still had the same old parents. Had I really expected my life to change?

Dad lifted his hand, ran it through what little hair he had left. "I signed the permission form," he said, eyes cast down.

Mom tilted her head to the side. "*You* signed it?"

Dad nodded apologetically, but he still couldn't meet her eyes.

"How could you sign it after everything that has happened recently? How could you do it without telling me?"

Dad looked up slowly, narrowed his eyes. "I don't recall you consulting with me all the times you've signed Piper's forms."

Silence—the kind you feel like a vacuum, sucking everything out of the atmosphere. Mom stepped back like she'd been slapped. She stared at me, then Dad, then me again, her face betraying the realization that we'd somehow joined forces, that from now on she'd be conducting her interrogation alone.

"I see," she said, her hands unusually still. "I . . . I see." She covered her mouth with her hand, then let it fall to her side again. "I'm tired now," she said, her face suddenly implacable, ghostly.

I waited for Dad to say something, but he didn't, or couldn't— I wasn't sure which.

Mom padded away from us and into her bedroom. I expected her to slam the door, practically *willed* her to, so I'd know she was actually pissed as hell, that her worn-out shell act was just that—an act. But instead the door gently swung closed, and suddenly I was the one standing in the hallway with my hands by my sides and my heart in tatters. Amazing how quickly a family can fall apart.

I turned to Dad, knowing that I needed to acknowledge that he'd covered for me, but he'd gone too. At the end of the hallway I saw the telltale strip of light glowing at the bottom of his office door. I walked over, knocked lightly, and let myself in.

Dad was staring intently at a family photo on the wall, the one taken last Christmas, when Grace was still a tiny baby. The photographer took thirty-eight photos that day, and Grace only stopped wailing for one of them. Mom and Dad chose it without hesitation, even though Finn's eyes were closed and I looked like I was having a seizure.

"Where's Grace?" I asked.

"Asleep."

"Finn?"

"In the basement, I think. Practicing his guitar. Or something. I don't know."

Another day, another relaxed, flowing conversation with Dad. I leaned against his desk, took the weight off my unsteady legs. "Thank you for doing that," I said finally. "You didn't have to."

Dad smiled ruefully. "Yes I did. I've gotten used to you and me arguing, but seeing you and your mother going at it just kills me."

I wanted to ask if it hurt him that he and I argued so much, but I couldn't. What if he said no? "I'm sorry things are like this," I said.

"Are you really?"

I didn't know what to say to that, so I looked away, studied the books stacked in piles on his desk—dictionaries, encyclopedias, journals on obscure topics that most sane people haven't even heard about. It was the recurring image of industriousness Dad had portrayed my entire life, but nothing seemed to have moved since the last time I'd been there. Did he actually read any of those books? If not, what did he do during those increasingly drawn-out evenings when he disappeared to the sanctuary of his office?

Only one book was open, its bright white pages out of place amid Dad's predominantly musty, yellowed collection. I leaned over and peered at the photographs of hand and arm gestures. Below each one, a caption translated the sign language into English.

"Whose is that?" I asked, not for a moment considering the most obvious explanation of all.

Dad hurried over and closed the book, and I just had time to catch the title before he placed it under the desk: *The Complete Idiot's Guide to Conversational Sign Language.*

"Good title, huh?" he asked flatly. "A complete idiot . . . that sounds like me."

My heart was doing somersaults, but I didn't know what to say. The book was an olive branch, a chance for us to close the gap, but in all my life Dad had never appeared so vulnerable.

"Are you teaching yourself?" I asked finally, trying to tone down the excitement in my voice.

Dad shook his head. "No. There's a course at the community college. Tuesday evenings." He pulled another book from under the desk, this one called *Master ASL.*

I flicked through it, but I didn't really care about the book's approach, or the quality of the writing. All I cared about were the signs, and the thought that Dad might someday know them. I wanted to drill him with a million questions, but this was my turf, not his, and he still seemed reticent to talk about it.

"How are you finding it?" I asked.

"It's . . . not easy. But I'm getting there." I wondered whether he was talking about our heart-to-heart chat as well as the rigors of learning sign language, but either way, he seemed worn out.

"Thank you for doing this. It means so much."

Dad's head and shoulders slumped. "Don't say that."

"Why not? It's true."

"Because I should've done this years ago, instead of always making excuses. When you started to lose your hearing I tried to learn with Finn, but he picked it up so much quicker than me. And compared to your mom I felt stupid and clumsy. In the end I honestly convinced myself that it would be better for both of us if I didn't even try. But I was missing the point. All that time I think you just wanted me to meet you halfway."

I nodded. "That would've been nice, yeah."

"I feel like I owe you the best part of a decade, and I'm trying to play catch-up. Only I don't know how that's supposed to work."

"You're improvising well."

Dad laughed. "God, Piper, I feel like I'm only just getting to know you now, for the first time."

"You know me."

"No, I don't," he sighed, refusing to play along with the easy lie. "Not really. And it's unforgiveable."

I stepped forward, gave him the briefest of hugs. "Well, I forgive you anyway."

Dad summoned a smile. "Thank you." He turned away and pulled a stack of papers from his bookshelf; the title on the front page read *Financial Aid & Fees*. "It says that more than eighty-five percent of students who apply for financial aid receive assistance. If Gallaudet is what you really want, we'll be able to make it happen."

I flicked through the stack and caught a glimpse of the university's nineteenth-century buildings, familiar from years of browsing the website. It *was* what I wanted, but it still seemed so far off.

"You have to trust us, Piper," said Dad, sensing my concern. "We want what's best for you."

We want what's best for you. Who would have imagined that his idea of best might one day coincide with mine?

"What about Mom? After today she might not be so thrilled about helping with this," I said.

Dad shook his head. "She will. You two are just going through a rough patch, that's all. She feels like you've shut her out."

"No way."

"Hey, I'm not saying she's blameless, but she just can't keep up with everything. She never wanted to work every hour of every day, and I think she'd do anything for things to go back to the way they were." He looked at the family photo again, straightened it carefully.

"But if she'd talk to me, I'd—"

"No." Dad turned to face me, shaking his head decisively. "That's the problem, see? You've moved on without *her*, not the other way around. You need to make the first move here."

"I don't know if I can."

"You can. Just talk to her . . . do that thing you do, okay? You've always been our rock, the one who holds things together—our own Pied Piper. Right now we could really do with some more of that magic."

Even though I was overwhelmed that Dad was learning sign language, I still wanted to say no. I wanted to tell him what a crappy thing it was to put the burden of responsibility on me. But he was gazing at me imploringly. In spite of my pink hair, my anarchic band, and my cutting school, he'd told me *I* was the rock. And in my heart, I knew that he was absolutely right.

I stopped at the doorway. "Thank you for learning to sign," I said.

Dad thought for a moment, then his brows knitted and he opened his right hand, held it palm up and swept it across his body in the sign for *You're welcome*.

And then he smiled at me for the first time in a year.

CHAPTER 40

Mom's room was dark. She lay on her side in bed, hugging the comforter to her chin. Her breathing rose and fell with the perfect consistency of someone who was feigning sleep.

I turned on the light.

Mom fidgeted, but kept her eyes shut tight. After a moment, she produced a sound like a horse. I'm not sure what she thought it would achieve, but I almost laughed out loud.

"Lynn Vaughan," I said solemnly, "future Academy Award winner."

"I was asleep," she protested.

"No, you weren't."

She sat up, propped a pillow behind her. Her face was streaked with tears, mascara bleeding down her cheeks.

"You look awful, Mom."

"Says the girl with pink hair!"

It was such a perfect comeback that I couldn't help smiling, and then laughing. After a few seconds, Mom started chuckling too.

"You look like you swallowed radioactive waste," she said, and laughed louder through her tears.

"It's called Atomic Pink."

"Oh God, so you really *did* swallow radioactive waste!"

We were laughing hysterically as I slid onto the bed beside her and held her hand. It was warm, clammy, like a fever breaking, but she didn't take it away. We twined fingers, and I could feel the barrier between us melting a little.

"I'm sorry, Mom. I think there's a lot going on in your life right now that I don't understand."

She looked at our hands. "Ditto."

"I need you to know that the band was important to me. I don't know if it should've been, but it was. It was exciting. It made me feel . . . alive."

"I know it did, Piper. I wish I'd realized it sooner, that's all. I wish I'd had the energy to keep up with everything."

"Like what?"

Mom lifted our hands and kissed mine, then ran a finger around my nails: the nibbled skin, the split nails, the massacred cuticles. She sighed, and then suddenly she was crying again, and I just didn't understand.

"I'm so behind the times. Months behind . . . probably years. How did I miss it?" As the seconds ticked by in silence, she rubbed my nail beds with her thumb, as if she might undo all those years of self-inflicted damage. "Just today, I

was telling someone at work that things were kind of difficult between us, and she suggested I take you to a fancy
salon this weekend so we could get our hair cut together.
I thought it was such a lovely idea. I even went ahead and
booked appointments for us."

"I'm sorry."

"No, it's fine. Although I must admit that I didn't have Atomic
Pink in mind."

It suddenly dawned on me that she'd been staring at our
hands the whole time. "Look at me, Mom. . . . Please."

Mom looked up, eyes flitting from one part of my head to
another like she was searching desperately for any hair that
might have survived the pink onslaught.

"I like it," I told her quietly, firmly. "I like the color and the
style. And I like knowing that I can't hide anymore."

That really got her attention. "Why would you feel like hiding?"

"Because I don't fit in. I haven't fit in for years. I've been the
nerd at the front of the class, the one without many friends. But
ever since I started with Dumb, people look at me differently."

"You know the teachers will look at you differently too,
right?"

"Yes."

"And you're okay with that?"

"Maybe the teachers don't really know me any better than the
students."

Mom ran her fingers through my hair, tucked it behind my

ears. Half an hour before, I'd have batted her hands away, but I knew she was finally seeing me in the present, not as the girl I used to be, so I let her fingertips continue their gentle sweep.

"It's going to take me some time to get used to everything, you know?" she said finally.

"I know. Me too."

She nodded, continued gazing at me like she wanted to see right into my soul. It wasn't going to be that easy, of course, but at least she was trying.

"What would you say to *Sleepless in Seattle*?" she asked, referring to our favorite romantic comedy, a cheesy '90s chick flick with Tom Hanks and Meg Ryan.

"I've got homework."

She rolled her eyes. "Screw homework. You're already in so much trouble, just for once . . . screw it!"

I stared at her in amazement, then jumped up and slid the DVD into the player. Once I'd got it running, I sat beside her again, and this time crawled under the covers as well.

The movie started and I rested my eyes on the closed captions, but I didn't bother to read them. Somehow I knew that I'd be able to watch the movie a million times in my life, but I might never again nestle into my mother's side, feeling forgiven and so completely and utterly loved.

CHAPTER 41

Dad had a plate of pancakes at the ready when he woke us the next morning, which was almost as surprising as the discovery that I'd spent the night in my parents' bed. He didn't even seem pissed about having spent the night on the sofa, although I felt guilty when I noticed how much trouble he had standing up straight.

I expected him to beat a hasty retreat once he'd delivered breakfast, but instead he shuffled on the spot like a puppy waiting to be taken outside. "Um, I, well . . . Never mind."

"What is it?" I asked.

"I'll tell you in a moment. I don't want to scare you."

"Scare me?"

"Don't worry about it. Just go ahead and enjoy the pancakes. I'll read you the newspaper headlines when you're finished."

The pancake stopped midway to my mouth. "Newspaper headlines?"

He nodded solemnly.

"I need to see them, Dad."

"Believe me, I don't think you want to. For instance, those parent groups that loved you so much . . ."—I nodded encouragingly—"well, let's just say they don't love you anymore. In fact, you've been blacklisted. You've become antiheroes of the indie music scene."

I was about to ask him what he knew about the indie music scene when Finn burst in carrying Grace. "YouTube's gone over a hundred thousand views," he exclaimed. "Can you believe it? A hundred thousand! Holy crap."

Mom coughed. "Language, Finn. Grace is listening."

A moment's hesitation all around, and then . . . nothing. Finn didn't take offense at being called out, and I didn't mind being reminded that Grace could hear now. Something had changed—maybe because there were bigger issues to deal with.

"What are you talking about, Finn?" I asked.

"Your appearance on *Seattle Today*. There's been over a hundred thousand views of it on YouTube."

I had trouble getting my head around that. I had to visualize the number, with all those zeroes, just to reassure myself it was as enormous as it sounded. "How many of those were you?"

Finn looked away. "Seventeen, maybe. Possibly eighteen."

"I watched it too," added Dad. "And I know you're not going to like me saying this, but I thought the behavior was disgraceful."

I rolled my eyes. "No shit, Dad."

Mom pursed her lips. "Language, Piper!" she scolded. "Grace is listening."

"Not so hasty, young lady," added Dad, wagging his finger for emphasis. "What I disliked was the lead singer—what's his name?"

"Josh."

"Yes, Josh. I don't know about his history with Kallie, and frankly, I don't want to know. But no self-respecting person should humiliate another like that. Period."

I was tempted to mention what a coincidence it was that Dad knew Kallie's name but not Josh's, but it probably wouldn't have impressed Mom. Besides, he had a point.

"That's just the way he is," I explained.

"Then you need to do something about it. You're the manager, right?"

"Yeah. . . . I mean, *no!* Dumb is over. Isn't it obvious?"

Dad furrowed his brow like I'd stumped him with the million-dollar question. "Why?" he asked, completely seriously.

"Because they imploded on live TV. They'll probably never talk to each other again."

"You mean . . . that whole thing wasn't *planned*?"

"What are you talking about?"

Mom placed a hand on my arm. "Your father and I just thought . . . well, you know . . . maybe you'd staged it."

"Are you out of your mind?"

"Not at all. Let's face it, you chose a completely inappropriate song for the audience—and don't pretend for a moment that wasn't your idea—so we thought maybe you'd orchestrated a total meltdown as well."

"Why would I want to do that?"

"To generate buzz," exploded Dad. "It's the classic Sex Pistols maneuver."

"The *what?*"

"Sex Pistols," repeated Mom, even finger-spelling the words for me.

"They were a seventies punk band," Dad continued. "Made headlines when they went on a British talk show and used the f-word. And not just once either. It was before tape delays, and no one had the sense to cut away to a commercial break."

I believed Josh was capable of a lot of things, but something like that just didn't ring true. "I don't know, Dad. It didn't exactly feel *planned.*"

Dad almost seemed disappointed. "Well, either way, it had the same effect. Finn's been monitoring your stock value overnight, and right now, Dumb is a definite buy."

"Oh God," I moaned, curling up with a pillow. "So you're saying I might have to keep this thing going?"

Dad shrugged. "That's up to you. But if you do, you're going to have to talk to Josh. His behavior was way out of line."

"But—"

"No buts, Piper. Take charge. It's your job." With the sermon over, Dad's finger relaxed. He reached into his pocket and tossed me my cell phone. "And while you're at it, check your messages. That damn thing's been beeping at me all night."

"For the love of Pete! LANGUAGE! Grace is LISTENING," implored Mom.

I glanced at Finn and we burst out laughing. I couldn't stop myself. Then Dad and Grace joined in, and all I could do was pat Mom's hand reassuringly as she shook her head.

When the laughter died down, I flicked open my cell phone and discovered that I had 143 text messages. I didn't even know 143 people.

"Does that really say one forty-three?" asked Mom, leaning over.

"Yeah."

I looked at the first text message. It was from Tiffany, the producer of *Seattle Today*: SHAMEFUL BEHAVIOR. CONTRACT VOIDED.

I felt my stomach flip, and pushed the plate of pancakes away, much to Dad's chagrin and Finn's delight, as he reached down with his free hand and shared one with Grace.

Mom leaned over and read the message. "Well, I can't disagree with her about the first part, but I've seen that contract, and they're not getting out of paying you."

I leaned back against the pillows and closed my eyes. "Just let it go. It's only three hundred dollars. Anyway, I don't think I can deal with this right now."

Mom cupped my chin, waited for me to open my eyes. "It's your call, Piper, but Dumb has just gone big time. If you want to see this thing through, I can help."

"How?"

"I'll start by asking why no one cut to a commercial break when things started to fall apart. She and the director had so many chances, but they chose to stay with Dumb. And you know what I think? I think they did it because that show has been dying slowly for years, and you guys just gave it an injection of new life. Their viewership is about to take a giant leap, and I'll bet they knew it too. This pathetic attempt to threaten you is just for show, a smokescreen to distract studio chiefs from something they've probably already worked out for themselves."

I looked at the next text, a particularly delightful ditty from someone at school I didn't even know.

"What does it say," asked Dad.

"It says I'm completely screwed."

"Language, Piper! Grace is . . ." Mom rolled her eyes and waved the thought away.

I looked at Mom, her jaw set like she was preparing for battle. By the door, Finn clasped Grace to his hip as he shoveled pancake into her mouth. And loitering beside the bed was Dad, so desperate to make amends, to show that he truly cared. Even though I knew I should be in a state of mourning, or shock, or something appropriately depressed, I couldn't help noticing that for the first time in months my dysfunctional family was together, behaving like a team. All I wanted was to go back to sleep, but I figured that if resuscitating Dumb and taking on *Seattle Today* gave Team Vaughan a mission, then bring it on. What did we have to lose?

"Can we really get paid, Mom?" I asked.

"Yes. If they stall, I'll sue them. And I'll win."

I reached over and hugged her tightly. "Thanks."

Mom hugged me right back. "You're welcome. Although there's one more thing I need to say."

"What?"

"I probably don't need to tell you this, but I love you."

"I love you t—"

"And you're grounded. I mean, totally grounded. Evenings, weekends, everything. I want you home straight after school every day. Understand?"

A part of me wanted to fight her, but what for? She didn't need to tell me I was grounded. I'd have been shocked if I wasn't.

Besides, it was still totally worth it.

CHAPTER 42

I cranked up my laptop before we set off for school, and with Finn riding me like a sadistic personal trainer, I set up a link so that people could download songs from Dumb's Facebook page for a buck apiece. (Even if the band turned out to be history, I figured there was nothing wrong with making a little money on the side while the craziness lasted.) It required hastily establishing a PayPal account and removing all the cover versions we'd done, because I had no intention of wasting weeks haggling with the copyright holders. But as I completed the task, step by excruciatingly painful step, I knew that no one else in the band would have done it. And it made me feel surprisingly . . . well, *managerial*.

I ran into school as bells drilled incessantly through the emptying halls, but I didn't even make it to homeroom before I'd been redirected to the principal's office. As soon as I arrived, a secretary pointed me to one of the hard plastic chairs reserved for the worst offenders, where I awaited sentencing. A minute later, Kallie and Tash sloped in, wearing contrasting looks of trepidation and defiance. I was glad Tash was there—always good to have a veteran when going into battle for the first time.

I think the principal had prepared a speech especially for the occasion—it wasn't every day he got to flex his disciplinary muscle with students like Kallie and me—but he seemed flummoxed by my hair. He clearly hadn't anticipated such a distraction. Every time he tried to hone in on a point, his eyes gravitated toward my head, and he lost track of his thoughts. Eventually he dropped the proselytizing and hurried us on to in-school suspension instead. Josh and Will were sitting outside his office as we left. I gripped Kallie's hand and looked straight ahead.

Being cooped up in a cupboard-sized room with one small window was supposed to have been punishment, but with Tash and Kallie, it was anything but. We spent the whole time corresponding by hand gestures, while avoiding the glares of the secretary sent to keep us from trashing the place. It quickly became clear that Tash and Kallie had picked up some of my signs, and what they didn't know, they made a good attempt to improvise. I wondered if Josh and Will would be joining us, but I guess the principal had envisaged how that might play out, and had decided to put them elsewhere. Thank goodness.

I'd only been in there an hour when one of the secretaries

came in and told me my father needed to see me urgently. My first thought—completely irrational—was that something had happened to Grace, and I left the room in a daze. The secretary led me through to a private office, opened the door slowly, and ushered me in with a wave of her hand. By the window, hands stuffed in the pockets of an ill-fitting tweed jacket was—

"Baz?"

Baz's mouth hung open in shock, his eyes fixed on my hair. It wasn't until I coughed that he seemed to break from the trance. "Oh, right, yes. I'm sorry to disrupt your school day, Piper, but it's your, your . . ." He turned away, took a shuddering breath while he came up with a plausible excuse for showing up unpermitted on school grounds while impersonating my father. "Your grandmother."

The secretary didn't seem terribly interested. Whether or not the news was about to be tragic, I had pink hair, so all I received was a curt nod as she backed out of the door and closed it behind her.

"What the hell?" I barked.

"Don't you ever check your text messages?"

"I had a hundred and forty-three of them. When am I supposed to check a hundred and forty-three messages?"

"Mine was important." He pouted.

I shrugged. "Why didn't you call my parents?"

"After yesterday's shenanigans? You really think they'd talk to *me*?"

Good point. "What's going on, Baz?"

Baz pulled off his jacket, threw it on the back of the nearest chair. "I hate suits," he moaned, tugging at the collar of his pink shirt.

"Then why did you wear one?"

"I was trying to imitate your father, remember? Why else do you think I cut my hair?"

He turned around and sure enough, the ponytail had gone. I almost felt bad for him. "Oh." I had to stifle a laugh. "Dad's into jeans and T-shirt these days."

Baz's jaw dropped. "Seriously?"

"Absolutely. But I must say, you look very sharp. Very corporate."

"Ha-ha." Baz tugged at his collar again. "I'll have you know I had to stop at Goodwill to pick this stuff up. Cost me ten bucks. Don't think I won't be claiming it back from your fee either."

I narrowed my eyes. "What fee?"

"What fee, indeed." Baz sat down, afforded himself a smile now that he'd piqued my interest. "I got a call last night from the manager of ABH, aka Actual Bodily Harm."

He'd lost me already. "What's Actual Bodily Harm?"

"Technically, it's the British legal equivalent of aggravated assault."

"Lovely."

"Yeah, but it's also the name of a Brit indie group, whose American tour has been getting good press." He paused, waiting in vain for me to express admiration. "Anyway, the manager of ABH is considering asking you to open for them at the Showbox on Saturday."

"You're joking, right?"

"No. I know it's short notice, but I think you could do it. The set is forty-five minutes max. You could get away with forty, maybe even thirty-five if you're willing to smash an instrument or two at the end."

I rolled my eyes. "Did you see what happened yesterday?"

"Yeah. Pretty hard core too. I knew you wanted to get away from the soft rock label, but I was impressed by your commitment to faking a meltdown."

"We weren't faking."

"Oh." Baz paused, thought about this. "Look, Piper, bands fall out. But at the end of the day, they're like family. You get back together because you have to, because you're stronger together than you are apart."

"I seriously doubt that."

He nodded solemnly. "Too bad. This would've been a sweet gig for an aspiring band. Great exposure. Good money too."

I finally sat down. "How good?"

"Not so fast. Before he negotiates, the manager needs to know you're still going to be together on Saturday, and that you'll promise to behave."

"Not sure, and not sure."

"If you can make that yes and yes, you might make yourselves two hundred dollars each."

My pulse quickened. "Okay, then. Yes and yes."

Baz threw up his hands in frustration. "Is that a *real* yes, or a *maybe* yes?"

"Baz," I choked, pretending to be offended. "Would I lie to you?"

He leaned forward and massaged his temples in slow circles.

"So what's with the late notice?" I asked.

"They had an opening act lined up, but the band had a, uh . . . falling out. They're not technically together anymore."

"I hear that's happening a lot these days."

"Yes." Baz pursed his lips disapprovingly, but it looked kind of cute on him. "So here's the deal. If Dumb is still together, he wants to meet with you. Five p.m. at my studio."

I shook my head. "No can do. I'm grounded. It'd have to be at school. Say, straight after final bell at two fifteen."

Baz laughed. "You can't really expect me to bring the manager of ABH to a high school for a business meeting."

"Yup. And we'll need to keep it hush-hush. Otherwise I'll probably spend the rest of senior year in suspension."

"Good grief." Baz pulled himself up and grabbed his jacket. "Okay. Two fifteen, by the main doors. But don't be surprised if he's late. He has to come here from Portland."

"If he's late, I'll be gone."

"Oh, for God's sake—"

"I'm not being difficult, Baz! I'm grounded. I couldn't stay late even if I wanted to."

"Okay, I'll make sure he's here at two fifteen," he groaned, like he was guilty of having conceded too much ground. And, truth be told, he absolutely had.

I stole a moment to text Finn, begging him to meet me by the main doors at 2:15. I got the feeling I could benefit from a personal assistant, and Finn was uniquely qualified for the position.

Once we left the room, Baz flounced through the office toward the exit without so much as a good-bye. He was almost gone when the secretary looked up.

"Hello!" she shouted to get my attention. (A gentle wave would have been infinitely preferable.) "Aren't you going to give your father a hug?" she asked indignantly.

Baz stopped and turned around. "Oh, good idea."

My jaw fell open. "No way!"

"What has *happened* to you, Piper?" cried the secretary. "You used to be such a good girl."

"Yeah, Piper," Baz echoed. "What has *happened* to you?" The wicked glimmer in his eye had returned, and suddenly I had to keep from laughing.

I bit my lip. "Come on, then, you dirty old man."

I stepped forward and smacked a kiss on Baz's lips. He looked petrified. The secretary looked horrified. I felt vindicated.

"Run along now, Daddy," I said.

Baz stumbled against a table on his way out, and tried pushing the door marked "pull" several times before correcting himself. He left without looking back.

I turned around in time to catch the secretary shaking her head. I could see her staring at my hair, weighing up my odd behavior, and realizing, at last, that maybe she'd been wrong about me all these years.

You and me both, I thought as I ambled back to suspension.

CHAPTER 43

I didn't get out of suspension until 2:23. The principal wanted to read us the riot act one last time, and slowed down when he noticed how agitated I was. In an attempt to ram his point home with the utmost force, he even started lecturing directly to my hair. I let it go on for almost a minute, then began running my hands through my hair seductively, like an actress in a shampoo commercial. Almost immediately he turned bright red, and seconds later we'd been excused. I sprinted along the corridors and almost knocked Finn over as I turned toward the main entrance.

What's the emergency? he signed.

We have a meeting with the manager of ABH.

Finn's eyes grew wide. *ABH? The band?*

I nodded.

Can I get their autographs?

I'd rather you didn't ask that until the negotiations are finished.

Negotiations?

They want Dumb to open for them on Saturday.

Finn looked as though he might pass out. *So why am I here?*

You're my interpreter.

No! You can do this without me. Finn began to turn away, but I pulled him back around.

I need you, Finn. Not as an interpreter, but to buy me time. Please trust me. You're my trump card.

Finn rolled his eyes, but when I took his hand he didn't pull away. Together we walked outside and greeted Baz, who was loitering on the sidewalk. The manager for ABH stood beside him, shifting his weight from one foot to the other impatiently. He was older than I'd imagined, heavyset and balding, with a Bluetooth earpiece flashing neon and an ugly brown sports jacket with leather patches over the elbows. I couldn't help thinking that as managers went, I looked much cooler than him.

"I'm Mike, and you're late," he barked.

I turned to Finn, who passed along the message in sign language.

"What's this?" Mike asked, with curled upper lip.

"Piper's deaf," explained Baz. "I told you that."

I smiled ambivalently, like I had no idea what was going on.

"Jesus Christ." Mike rolled his eyes. "I thought you were joking."

I already hated Mike, so once I'd pointed in the direction of a nearby picnic table, I walked unnecessarily quickly. I figured I'd at least get him sweating.

I sat down next to Finn and pulled my jacket collar tightly

around my neck. The sky was blanketed in gray, one of those days when it feels like the previous night never completely ended. Mike and Baz sat down across from us and Mike removed his coat, beads of perspiration dotting his forehead.

"So you're her translator?" Mike asked, pointing a stubby finger at Finn.

"Her interpreter."

"Same difference. Well, start by telling her that I need to be sure Dumb is still together. I don't need any more stunts like that crap they pulled yesterday. This is a serious business."

Finn nodded decisively, then turned to me. *Did you get that?*

Yes.

This guy is an utter prick.

Yes.

I want to say something obscene.

Behave!

Finn was in the process of assuring Mike that Dumb was still together when Mike brandished a contract and shoved it toward me. "Tell her to sign here and here."

I glanced at the contract—a single page with details of the location and time of the performance, and a stipulation that all five members of the band attend. The last line had been added by hand, but I couldn't exactly blame him in light of recent events. The contract specified $100 per band member, for a total of $500.

Finn cocked an eyebrow. *Wow. That was easy. I'm good at this.*

I smiled. *Yes, but we're not done yet.*

What do you mean?

Things are about to get interesting. Are you ready to play some poker?

Finn narrowed his eyes, the hint of a smile teasing his mouth. *What do you have in mind?*

I think we have a full house. Three boys, two girls, and I'm playing with house money. I felt my heart racing, the memory of all those poker games I played with my dad suddenly fresh in my mind again. *Take a look at hotshot over there and tell me what he's got.*

In less than a second, Finn glanced across the table and made his decision. I could tell he was looking for more chips. *He's flustered. Could be because he's annoyed about being here, but I think he's actually nervous. He blinks every time you sign, by the way . . . a real giveaway.*

I wanted to hug Finn, but we needed to stay cool. *Good. Now keep signing to me.*

Sign what?

Anything. Doesn't matter. Just keep going until he interrupts.

How can you be sure he's going to—

"What's going on here?" shouted Mike, presumably for my benefit. "Are you going to sign the contract or not?"

Is he angry, anxious, or both? I asked.

Finn rubbed his chin. *Definitely both. He wants you to fold real bad.*

Then he's going to be disappointed.

"Hello!" Mike pawed at my arm—so obnoxious. I just kept ignoring him.

Okay, this is how I see it, I signed. *Rude dude isn't here just to see if we're interested. The gig is three days away, and I think he's desperate. He definitely didn't drive all this way to get turned down.*

Sounds reasonable, agreed Finn.

And that's why you're going to ask for $500 per person, for a total of $3,000.

Finn's jaw slackened. *You've got to be kidding.*

Yes and no. I want you to ask for it, but he's going to refuse. The important thing is what he counters with.

While Finn took a moment to compose himself, I pulled my laptop from my bag and refreshed our YouTube page, which was already onscreen. Thankfully the school's wireless network reached outdoors. I glanced up in time to see Baz choke and Mike turn an inhuman shade of purple. He slammed his fist against the table and stood up.

Before he could leave, I turned the computer screen around and pointed to the view count. It was up to 223,747. I cocked an eyebrow expectantly, and tried to suppress a smile as Mike plopped back down. He turned to Finn.

"Two hundred dollars each. A thousand dollars total."

"What about Piper?" exclaimed Finn, forgetting to pass along the latest bid. "What about her share?"

"She can take it out of the thousand bucks for all I care."

$300 each, $1800 total, I signed.

Finn relayed the latest bid, and I noticed that he didn't seem anxious anymore.

As soon as Mike began to shake his head, I closed the computer and stood up in one swift movement. Sure enough, Mike reached across and grabbed my arm, holding me in place.

"Fine," he said. "Bloody fine."

Mike pulled out another contract and began filling in the revised figures. Two minutes later I signed it.

"Saturday. Get there at four p.m. and you might have half an hour to do a sound check. Then again, maybe not. We'll see," he sneered, desperate to reassert his power.

Baz waited for Mike to leave, then stared me down. "What was all that about?"

"Just doing my job, Baz. I thought you'd approve."

"I did approve of the *original* offer, especially as I was going to get a fixing fee out of it."

Oops. I hadn't considered that Baz's interest in all this might be personal. I patted his hands reassuringly. "Never mind. I won't let you leave empty-handed." Baz perked up. "I'll make sure there's a free ticket waiting for you on Saturday night."

Baz shook off my hands, but as he left I got the feeling he was already laughing about the whole thing.

Finn turned to me then, an awestruck look on his face. *You are tougher than anyone I know. I am so glad you're on my side.*

I grinned like a fool. *I'll always be on your side, Finn. I promise.*

CHAPTER 44

If I'd thought the meltdown on *Seattle Today* would count as the single most uncomfortable experience in Dumb's history, I was wrong. As the band sloped across the student parking lot the next day—we'd been banned from meeting on school grounds, so I chose the most out-of-the-way place I could think of— the tension could have fueled a year's worth of daytime soaps. Anarchic fans trailed every member (except Ed), but the biggest posse was reserved for Josh, whose late arrival was greeted with utter silence and a distinct lack of eye contact from his bandmates.

"I'm speaking first today," I announced, just to be sure everyone knew who was in charge. "It won't be long before a teacher sees us and makes us leave, so listen up. Yesterday I met with the manager of Actual Bodily Harm, and negotiated three hundred dollars apiece for us to open for them this Saturday at the Showbox."

Kallie's eyes flicked up. "You're kidding."

Something told me she wasn't talking about the money. "We can't afford to say no, Kallie," I said, never breaking eye contact. "You know we can't."

"But—" she began, then broke off. She looked like she might cry, but I knew she'd also sign on. I hated that she needed the money so badly.

"Okay, I have to know we're still together," I continued. "It's all or nothing. A show of hands, please."

Eyes stayed fixed to the ground as arms crept slowly upward. Eventually only one person dissented.

"Ed?" My voice caught in my throat, but Ed shook his head. "You have to," I insisted, refusing to take my eyes off him.

Ed looked around at the other band members, then at the crowds of students staring at him unblinkingly as the future of Dumb rested in his hands. He continued to shake his head, but it was more an act of surrender than a refusal, and we both knew it. A moment later, he raised his hand.

"Okay, then," I said, relieved. "Here's the plan: Our set is still a ways from being ready, so practice by yourselves tonight and be ready to play tomorrow lunchtime. We'll meet here in the parking lot."

Tash stuffed her hands in her pockets. "Why bother? The teachers will never let us play here."

"Yes, they will. Trust me."

Tash raised an eyebrow, but I could tell it was out of respect, not suspicion. And then I recognized the same look on the faces of the forty or so kids who were watching the meeting.

"We need all of you here too," I told them. "Nothing like a live audience to make us focus." An apologetic cheer went up in response, but I knew I had their attention now, which was the main thing. "And finally, before we go, I think we all need to hear what Josh has to say to Kallie."

Josh's look of surprise was the most honest response I'd ever seen from him. "What are you talking about?"

I shrugged. "Oh, I don't know. How about an apology? How about a promise to stop stalking her?"

Tash snorted with laughter. Josh turned red. The portion of the crowd clearly marked as his entourage took a step back.

"Fine. I'm sorry I was rude to you, Kallie. And I'm sorry I sabotaged our performance."

I'd been so certain Josh wouldn't apologize that I wasn't sure where to look when he'd finished. Neither was Kallie, although she nodded in grudging acceptance.

"And while I'm at it," continued Josh, "I'm sorry that our performance has been viewed a quarter of a million times on YouTube." He looked at me, steely-eyed. "And I'm sorry this notoriety has allowed Piper to start selling our songs for a buck apiece over the band's Facebook page."

Suddenly all eyes were on me. "Oh, yes. I was going to mention that," I said.

"I'm sure you were. So how much have we raised so far?"

"I—I don't know. I forgot to check."

"You forgot?"

I nodded mutely.

"Well, you be sure to tell us as soon as you know. We don't want anyone thinking you're hiding something from us, and I'm certain Tash and Kallie will want to hear the good news."

Will began to wander off before Josh had finished, and everyone else followed straight afterward. And even though I hadn't done anything wrong, I felt like I'd just been found guilty of embezzlement. How did he do it?

Eventually it was just Josh and Ed and me. Ed signaled that he'd meet me at chess club, then ran off before he risked getting into any trouble. As the only member of Dumb to escape Tuesday's misadventures without getting suspended, he was clearly eager to maintain his clean slate.

"You, Tash, and Kallie—quite the cozy threesome," said Josh finally.

I ground my teeth. "Ever thought of putting your evil powers to good use?"

Josh shook his head. "No. Have you?" He laughed at my angry expression. "Look, we need to call a truce. Trying to humiliate me like that isn't going to help Dumb move forward."

"An honorable sentiment given that you tried to destroy the band two days ago."

"Ooh, great comeback! Shame there's no one around to hear it. But then, that's the story of your life, isn't it? So assured as long as things are going by the script, but you can't improvise to save your life."

"What are you talking about?"

"*Seattle Today.* I saw you hovering at the edge of the studio.

You could have stopped things by telling the stage manager to cut the feed. You could have walked onstage and ended it yourself, but you didn't. When things turned ugly, you froze—not a way to win anyone's trust. And now everyone's concerned about where the money from the song sales is going."

"That's bull. Everyone knows I'll share it evenly."

"Is that what you think their looks meant? Interesting."

I wanted to hit him so badly. I could probably have gotten in a good right hook before he was able to defend himself. "What is it you really want, Josh?"

"I want to undo my worst mistake. I want us to let Kallie go."

"I think the whole world got that message on Tuesday."

"I know, and I really am sorry I did those things. I just got so mad about the way Kallie contributes nothing musically but gets all the attention. I was even willing to break up the band if that's what it took to get rid of her, but I'm grateful to you for keeping us together."

I wanted to roll my eyes, but the line sounded so genuine. *Josh Cooke: snake oil salesman.*

"You know I'm not going to get rid of Kallie," I said.

"And you know that Dumb is on life support if you don't. We can only go so far with a guitarist who can't play guitar. Record label executives can spot that kind of thing from a mile off."

"Forget it, Josh. I've already had to threaten her to keep her in the band, and the only reason she's agreed to keep going now is because she doesn't want to let me down."

"If she's so ambivalent, she won't be too disappointed when you tell her she's out."

"No. Dumb stays as it is. If you've gotten sick of one of the flavors, that's your problem."

"And if you don't make it clear to Kallie that Saturday is her final show, I'll be *your* problem too."

I hesitated just a moment. "Oh, really? What are you going to do this time—set fire to the Showbox?"

Josh laughed. "You're funny, but unimaginative. I can do so much better than that."

CHAPTER 45

Our first chess game only lasted seven minutes. I was furious at Josh, and channeled my anger into bludgeoning Ed in just fourteen moves. For his part, Ed seemed to be concentrating even more poorly than usual. He was constantly glancing at my hair, but looked away whenever I made eye contact. It was making me feel really self-conscious.

"Are you ZARKINFIB?" I asked.

Ed narrowed his eyes. "I thought that was Baz."

"No."

"Oh. But you can't possibly . . . I mean, why would I do it?"

I shook my head because I was certain Ed was innocent, and besides, he wasn't responsible for my foul mood. "So how long are you grounded?" I asked as we set up the board for another game.

"I'm not grounded," said Ed, his eyes flicking from the chess pieces to my hair.

"How come?"

"I wasn't the one fighting, remember? I was the one on the

bottom of the pile. I think even on our low-def eighteen-inch TV my parents could work that out."

That was enough to make me break a smile. "You have enlightened parents."

"I do," he agreed. "Plus, I didn't exactly play hooky and get my hair dyed pink."

"Oh, that," I said, like I'd already forgotten about it, instead of spending every other second checking myself out in reflective surfaces. "I take it you don't approve."

"No, no. I like it."

"Really?"

"Yeah." Ed paused, furrowed his brow. *That's good,* he signed jerkily.

I was impressed he'd learned any signs at all, and immediately returned *Thank you.*

You're welcome.

I laughed, mostly because I was so touched, but I got the feeling Ed thought I was laughing at his attempts to sign. "You sign well," I assured him. "And I'm glad you like my hair."

"It's good to see you emerge from your shell. You've been hiding too long."

I felt myself blush, and I wasn't sure how to reply, so I stared at the board and concentrated on that. Over the next minute— two moves each—I put Ed in checkmate. Fool's mate, it's called, because only a fool wouldn't see it coming.

As I watched Ed struggling to come to terms with what I'd done, I couldn't help laughing. I expected him to laugh too, but he just stared at the board like he suspected I'd cheated.

"How did you do that?" he asked.

"It's just fool's mate."

"What's fool's mate?"

I narrowed my eyes, waited for him to say he was kidding. "It's just, well . . . you know . . . fool's mate. You know what that is, right?"

He looked hurt. "No, Piper. I don't."

"How can you play chess this long and not know that?"

"I guess I'm slow."

"I didn't mean it like that," I added quickly. "It's just . . . you spend so long playing, aren't you interested in knowing about classic maneuvers, and defensive plays?"

Ed stared at his pieces for a moment and then toppled his king roughly.

"I'm sorry, Ed. I figured you weren't paying attention."

He stood up and grabbed his bag. "Yeah, well, at least I'm not alone, then."

"What's that supposed to mean?"

"God, Piper. Dumb died on *Seattle Today*. Anyone could see that. And the only reason my parents didn't ground me is because I promised them the band was over."

"Why do they care?"

"Are you serious? They care because my grades are falling, and they never see me anymore. I have an audition at Peabody in the middle of February, but I don't even have time to practice. I haven't had a marimba lesson in a month."

"So why did you say you want to keep the band going?" I shot back defensively.

"I didn't, at first. But then you made me, and I didn't want to let you down."

"So everything is *my* fault?"

Ed shook his head. "Look, Piper, however bad the past two days have been for you, they've been a whole lot worse for me. A quarter of a million people have watched me getting my ass whipped on YouTube. And if that wasn't bad enough, I waited by your car for an hour after the security guards threw me out of the studio. You were supposed to give me a ride back to school, but you never showed up. I caught a bus, but school was almost over, so they gave me my first ever detention."

I swallowed hard. "I'm sorry. I didn't know that."

"And until now you hadn't thought about it either."

He was right, of course, and I felt terrible. "I really am sorry."

"It's okay," he said, too decent to remain angry even when it was called for. He looked at the chessboard. "Look, I didn't ask for any of this. All I wanted was . . ."

"What?"

His mouth was open, but the words just weren't there. "Nothing." He didn't look back on his way out the door.

It was the first time we'd argued. And something told me it had nothing to do with my hair.

CHAPTER 46

There was only one message in my in-box that afternoon when I got home, but it was from Marissa, so I opened it right away. I figured that I might as well deal with all fractured friendships on the same day.

Surprisingly the e-mail was an apology—for not being in touch, for not listening better, for not realizing how much the band mattered to me. Most of all, it was to check that I was okay. I sent a reply asking her to IM me as soon as she got home, and half an hour later a message appeared on the screen.

Marissa asked me about the *Seattle Today* incident. Her questions were really detailed too, like she'd watched the YouTube footage at least a dozen times. When I said the band was still together, she seemed pleased rather than shocked. Then she said that Ed looked cooler now that his braces had been removed.

P1P3R: i'd forgotten about his braces. how did u
remember that?

MARI55A: r u kidding? ed = cute. i had major crush

P1P3R: u never told me

MARI55A: cuz he liked u, not me

P1P3R: no way

MARI55A: yes way. why do u think he joined chess club?

I sat bolt upright, feeling like a coach doused in Gatorade when the game has been won.

MARI55A: ok, don't answer that. what about rest of dumb? u like?

I tried to stop my hands from shaking.

P1P3R: yes. tash and kallie hang out with me

MARI55A: they ignored us for years

P1P3R: they're different now. u'd like them

MARI55A: if u say so. just promise me u won't get green hair

P1P3R: lol. no way. got pink instead

MARI55A: ha!

P1P3R: srsly!

MARI55A: omg. ooVoo me

P1P3R: can u ooVoo again?

MARI55A: yes

I shifted to the browser, loaded ooVoo, and made the connection with Marissa. A few seconds later she appeared on my screen, and then there was nothing but stillness and silence.

It was Marissa, but not the Marissa I remembered. Gone was the mousy brown hair, replaced by cascading blond curls. She wore dangly earrings and a chunky necklace color-coordinated with her form-fitting flower-print T-shirt. Unless the color was way off on my laptop screen, she wore half a cosmetics store on her face. She looked like she'd undergone a complete makeover with one of Kallie's supermodel wannabes, or more likely, Donna Stevens's stylist.

You look different, we signed simultaneously, then laughed nervously.

You look great, I signed, realizing that my face had probably already betrayed my surprise, and, also, my disappointment that she'd changed so much without me.

You too.

Silence. I could feel her slipping away from me with every second that passed, but I didn't know what to say. I didn't even know who she was anymore. And I knew Marissa was thinking the same thing, right up to the moment that she raised a hand to her face and brushed away a tear.

I'm so sorry. I've ruined everything, she signed.

What are you talking about?

Marissa disappeared for a moment and returned with a tissue. She dabbed her eyes gently, careful not to disturb the artfully applied mascara and eyeliner. *My computer was never broken. I just didn't want you to see me.*

Why not?

Because I look like one of Kallie's friends. Admit it, it's true.

I nodded. There didn't seem to be any point in lying.

It was so hard for me when I moved out here. You weren't around, but then I started to make some new friends, and I just wanted to be different than I was in Seattle, you know? I just got tired of blending in.

A part of me wondered if she might not blend in even more now than before. But I couldn't blame her for wanting to change. Anonymity hadn't been a problem as long as we'd had each other—hiding out together had barely felt like hiding at all—but apart, it became unbearable. I understood that completely. I really did.

You're beautiful, I said.

As Marissa peered at me through her tears, I got the feeling she was looking at my hair.

Not like you. You were always prettier than me. And so much stronger. I wouldn't be brave enough to get pink hair if my life depended on it, but it looks amazing on you. You're amazing.

So are you.

Thanks. Marissa smiled bravely. *So have you and Ed hooked up yet?*

No. I didn't know he was interested in me until just now.

Marissa rolled her eyes and cocked an eyebrow at the same time—a new gesture in her repertoire. *How could you not know?*

I just didn't. I shrugged. *I wish you'd told me.*

I'm sorry. I was jealous, remember? I used to watch Ed in the cafeteria, and for a while I thought he was staring at me every time he looked over at us. But then he joined the chess club, and I knew it was you he liked.

That must have been tough.

Marissa smiled ruefully. *Torture. I'm not sure how he could have been any more obvious. You're deaf, but there's no excuse for being blind as well.*

I nodded, accepting the criticism. But inside I felt shaken up. The old Marissa was kinder, gentler than that. Maybe her make-over wasn't limited to the outside.

I miss you, she signed, summoning one last bittersweet smile.

I miss you too, I signed back. But I worried that what we really missed were versions of each other that might no longer exist. And as I closed the computer, I wondered what it meant that my thoughts had already turned to making up with Ed, not Marissa.

CHAPTER 47

"Anyone want a latte?" I asked as I left the dinner table. I needed to see Ed, and right away.

Mom looked at me like I'd grown an extra head. "Where are you going to get a latte?"

"Coffee Crew."

"You're grounded."

"It's just a cup of coffee."

Dad stood up. "Actually, I'd like one too. But Mom's right, you're grounded. So I come as well, and I drive."

Mom's eyebrows lifted to her hairline. "Hold on a minute, I . . . Oh, heck, just bring me one too."

Before she could change her mind, I dashed outside and waited for Dad to join me.

Five minutes later, we pulled up in front of Coffee Crew. "That looks like Ed Chen," Dad said, looking through the shop windows.

I was about to feign ignorance when something dawned on me. "How do you know Ed?"

"He's taking the same signing course as me." Dad narrowed his eyes, deep in thought. "He's the drummer in your band, right?"

I tried to answer, but I couldn't get past the fact that Ed was learning to sign . . . for *me.*

Dad leaned back in his seat, smiling like the pieces of the puzzle had just fallen into place. "All right. I want a double tall two-percent. Same for Mom. I've got to pick up some milk from the grocery store. I'll be back in half an hour, okay?"

I swallowed hard. "Okay. Thanks, Dad."

He smiled. "You're welcome. . . . Oh, and Piper," he added, "don't forget the coffees. Crucial for our alibi."

I snorted and jumped out of the car, then waited a couple seconds while he drove away.

Ed was brushing coffee grounds off the counter when I walked in, and hesitated when he saw me. When he resumed, he seemed to be moving slower than before.

"Can we talk, Ed?"

He dropped the grounds into the trash and turned to face me. "What about?"

I picked up a green Magic 8-Ball on the counter and read my fortune: *Buy pork bellies.* Not likely.

Ed handed me a yellow 8-Ball with a smiley face instead. "Try this one."

I turned it over and read the message: *You're fantastic.* I felt my face redden, like I'd always dreamed of being admired by a Magic 8-Ball.

"What does it say?" he asked.

I swallowed. "It says I've been incredibly dumb."

Ed bit his lip. "Seems a bit harsh to me."

I looked up, fixed his eyes. "Not really."

He rested his hands on the counter. They were only inches from mine. I wanted to touch them.

"You were wrong about the distance from Peabody to Gallaudet," I told him. "I looked it up. It's actually 36.98 miles."

"I was rounding up."

"The gas will be expensive."

"Worth every penny."

"Why didn't you ever tell me how you felt?"

Ed turned away, breaking the connection. After a glance at his watch he switched off the OPEN sign. Then he lingered beside the espresso machine. "What can I get you?" he asked.

I reached across the counter and placed my hand on his arm, made him face me again. "Don't do that, Ed. I may be deaf, but I'll listen to everything you have to say."

He removed a filter from the machine, pounded it against a container to knock the coffee grounds out.

"Okay," I tried again. "Let's do it this way. I'll be Ed, and I'll tell you how things really are. Just stop me when I get something wrong." Ed shrugged in tacit agreement. "So, first off, I don't actually like chess. In fact, I hate it. And in spite of an IQ that would place me in Mensa, I completely suck at it." Ed stifled a laugh. "Good. Piper's getting warmer. . . . So anyway, the reason I started playing is because it was the only way I could get Piper away from her clique. Except she didn't know that, because she thinks the only cliques are ones everyone else wants to join." Ed's head bobbed up and down like it was agreeing with me without his consent. "And I even joined her freaky rock band, and saved it on several occasions, without so much as a word of thanks from that skanky ho manager."

Ed spun around, palm raised. "Now you're putting words in my mouth."

"More or less, yeah," I agreed. "Why? Did I get something wrong?"

He smiled, cleaned the filter with a cloth, and placed it back in the machine. Then he turned to face me again, to make it easier to read his lips, even though he wasn't ready for eye contact just yet. "I really like you, Piper. I've liked you for a long time. . . . I like being near you."

"Then why didn't you say so?"

"Because I was nervous, I guess. About what you'd say if . . . if I asked you out."

I was rocked by the urge to kiss him and punch him for wasting so much time. "I'd say yes, Ed. Definitely yes."

He started tapping the counter, his nerves palpable in the cozy surroundings of the coffee shop. "Look, if you're going to be hanging around here when I'm trying to close up, you need to learn to make your own coffee," he said, pretending to be stern. "Come around the counter and I'll show you how."

I sighed, realizing yet again that neither of us had said what needed to be said. I wondered if we ever would.

Ed positioned me in front of the espresso machine and stood behind me. I turned my head, tried to begin the only conversation I cared about, but he brought a finger to his lips, silencing me. As he reached around me, I felt his breath across my ear and his chest pressing against my back. I held my breath as his hands rested over mine.

Like a gentle puppeteer he guided me to the grinder. Our left hands placed the filter underneath, while our right hands switched the grinder on and pulled a lever, releasing fresh, powdery coffee in cascading heaps. Then we lifted a metal object that looked like a paperweight and pressed the coffee into the filter. Our fingertips brushed with each movement, and although my hands felt weak and useless, he guided me with strength and patience. It was a wholly new and bewildering situation, yet I wanted there to be at least another fifty steps before the coffee was ready.

As we put the filter into the espresso machine, his face brushed my hair and I felt my heartbeat quicken. We placed a glass under the filter, and with the press of a single button, golden-brown liquid poured in like syrup. I let him lead me as we first steamed the milk, then mixed it with the coffee. But this time there was no flower gracing the surface of our drink—just a plain, simple heart.

I tilted my head back against his shoulder and cheek as I lifted the glass. I took a sip because it was *our* drink, and I even smiled approvingly too, but I had no idea how that coffee tasted. Every part of me was focused on Ed, daring him to pull away, but hoping he wouldn't. Hoping, even, that he'd push things further.

I placed the cup on the counter and felt his cheek press against me, his hand pulling me around so I could see him. He cupped my face between his hands, and when our lips touched, his skin felt soft and warm. It was the smallest, gentlest, most earth-shattering kiss in the long and glorious history of kisses, and it took my breath away.

"What would your boss say if she walked in right now?" I asked, just needing a moment to stop hyperventilating.

Ed continued to gaze at me like the rest of the world had ceased to exist. "I think she'd say I've got good taste."

I leaned forward and kissed him again, our mouths gently pressed together, fingers running through hair, over skin irresistibly electric.

Ed looked positively serene. "You have no idea how long I've waited for this to happen."

"I'm sorry," I said, feeling anything but sorrow at that moment.

"Don't be. Apart from this afternoon, I've never regretted a second I've spent with you. You inspire me."

I felt the impact of his words, the forgiveness and longing and, incredibly, the love.

"It's going to feel like a long thirty-seven miles," I whispered.

Ed shook his head. "Shortest thirty-seven miles in the world."

He leaned into me and we kissed with mouths open. Ed Chen—virtuoso, genius, hero—became my universe for a few precious seconds until the door opened and cold air rushed in.

I spun around and saw Dad in the doorway. He was bright red, and I was pretty sure it had nothing to do with the chill breeze.

He looked everywhere except at us, then reached for the glass on the counter and drained it in one big gulp.

"Where's Mom's?" he asked.

My turn to blush.

"Yes, well, never mind," he continued. "Just be sure to make it before I get back."

"Where are you going?"

"Oh, another errand," he said, waving off the question with a flap of his hand. "I just called your mother, said you'd been delayed. She told me to give you another ten minutes. . . . I'm not sure either of us is terribly good at the whole grounding routine. You've never given us much practice."

Dad shuffled away without another word, and I turned to face Ed, his features glowing with delight.

"I *love* your dad," he gushed.

"Yeah, me too," I said, realizing that in spite of our difficult history, it was true. "How could I not love someone who learns to sign, just so they can talk to me?"

Ed reddened. "He told you, huh?"

"Hmm. Is that why you've been missing marimba lessons?"

Ed shrugged in that maddeningly boyish way that simultaneously made me want to chew him out for jeopardizing his future and to kiss him harder than ever for putting me above everything.

"I guess he told you who's top of the class," said Ed, breaking the silence.

"You, I suppose."

"Ha! Not even close." And then he smiled again, his eyes teasing me mercilessly. "Now where were we?"

It didn't take us long to remember.

CHAPTER 48

The clouds threatened rain, and our breaths condensed in the air. Tash pulled on a pair of fingerless gloves and smiled like it wasn't the most ridiculous situation imaginable. Ed twirled his drumsticks and pretended to tune the sheet metal beneath him. Everyone was acting dumb, but what else could they do?

"So before you begin," I announced, "you'll probably want to know that our songs have been downloaded over nine hundred times, which means a hundred and fifty dollars each. Unless anyone has a problem with it, I'll add it to the three hundred you're each getting for opening at the Showbox tomorrow."

No one had a problem with that, of course, but the present situation wasn't so straightforward.

"There's no room for my guitar," said Tash.

"Yes there is," I said. "Just swing your legs over the side. You too, Kallie. Will, hang your legs over the windshield. Josh, just stand on the hood."

"What about me?" complained Ed. "You can't seriously

expect me to drum against the roof of your car. It'll ruin the paintwork."

"Then you can come over this weekend and we'll wax it together," I said, which shut him up spectacularly well.

No one seemed especially thrilled about the idea of rehearsing on top of my car, but in my opinion it was the finest use of a Chevy Caprice Classic in the history of oversized planet-destroying automobiles. Sure, they'd be uncomfortable if it rained, but until then Dumb would keep warm by thrashing through Saturday's set. Which they did, flying through the first four songs like they just wanted to go back inside ASAP.

I knew we wouldn't get away with such a blatant assault on school rules for long, but of all the teachers who should stagger out to arrest us on that delightfully gray afternoon, it seemed appropriate that it would be Boy Scout Belson. As soon as he emerged from the school he removed a white napkin from his breast pocket and began waving it above his head. I couldn't tell if he was trying to get my attention or surrendering, so I pretended not to notice. The way I saw it, forcing him to walk fifty yards across the parking lot bought Dumb at least an extra minute of rehearsal time; two, if he needed to stop for a breather.

When Belson got within ten yards, I pretended to see him at last, rushing forward with the same carefree smile he claimed to enjoy seeing each time I destroyed an opponent at chess. I even held out my hand in greeting, but he was in no mood to shake it.

"What's going on here, Piper?"

I signaled that I couldn't hear—which was completely true, as it happens—and led him a few steps back toward the school buildings. In the background, I heard the blurry mess that was Dumb's fifth song end with a chaotic flourish.

"Your band has been banned from performing on school grounds," said Belson sternly, clearly tired of walking.

"My band has been what?" I shouted.

"Banned."

"Yes, the band. What about it?"

"It was banned," repeated Belson, matching my shouts.

"It's still a band," I explained, waving my hand at Dumb as though he was being dense.

I expected Belson to call me out for willfully misunderstanding him, but he didn't. "They're not allowed to play on school grounds," he sighed.

"They're not on school grounds."

"What? What are you talking about?"

"They're on my car. All five of them. I'd never let them break a school rule, Mr. Belson, you know that."

Belson stared at me, but he didn't seem angry, just resigned. "I'm going to look for the principal now, Piper. He's almost certainly too busy to deal with this, but if he gets around to it, I think he'll be furious." He nodded to himself a few times, then adjusted his tie and began walking back toward the school.

If the principal was busy, then so much the better. I was prepared to debate the legal definition of "school grounds" with the highest authority in the land if necessary, but there were only ten minutes until the end of lunch break, and I preferred not to risk further suspension if it was avoidable.

With half an eye on the school doors, I returned my attention to Dumb. I figured they must have been doing okay, as they'd been moving swiftly through their set, but suddenly they seemed to be in shambles. Still, I couldn't be certain that things sounded as bad as they looked, so I scanned the faces of the audience for confirmation . . . and got exactly that. Ed's car-top drumming had been reduced to a single pounding beat as he struggled to keep everyone in time. Josh was moaning as if lyrics were an optional extra. And Kallie was staring at her fingers imploringly, willing them to find the right notes. She barely seemed to notice that she was so out of time the right notes wouldn't help one bit. And it wasn't for lack of practicing—she mouthed the lyrics like she'd been playing along with the song for hours—it was just lack of skill. At the end of the day, Kallie just wasn't up to the level of the others, and I hated knowing how unavoidable that truth had become.

When the song fizzled to an apologetic close, Josh hopped off the car's hood and bowed deeply (and, I hope, ironically). He faced me and shrugged like the whole freaking mess had nothing to do with him. But then Tash leaped off the roof and pounded toward us. Instinctively I threw myself between them. The last thing we needed was another suspension for fighting.

"What's going on?" I shouted.

"Josh wants to cut 'Smells Like Teen Spirit,'" spat Tash. "I've been practicing it for hours."

I whipped around to face Josh. "You're kidding."

Josh shook his head nonchalantly.

"You were pretty close to nailing it last Sunday. What's wrong with it now?"

"Too many new lyrics. It's not as easy to learn the music *and* lyrics as it is to master a little guitar solo, you know."

"But we agreed on the set—"

"And you can play everything for all I care. It's just that I'll have already left the stage."

I couldn't believe it was happening again. And yet, I could believe it too. Josh's schizoid act had become so common I was already trying to formulate alternative plans, knowing he'd never budge.

"Look, Josh, we're contracted to play—"

"For forty-five minutes. I know. But that's a time *limit*. No one's going to complain if we get offstage early and let the real band on."

Tash had clearly had enough of my brand of diplomacy. She placed a hand on my shoulder and eased me aside. "I don't want to fight over this, Josh," she said with uncharacteristic calm, "but I've practiced that opening riff a thousand times. I've nailed it. I won't let you take that song out."

Josh shrugged. "Then go ahead and play it as an instrumental. You can even—" He broke off and peered over my shoulder, then started laughing.

I looked around. Kallie was still sitting cross-legged on my car, her guitar in one hand and the other raised high above her head like a shy kindergartner just itching to be called on in class.

"I, uh, don't think we should drop it," she said. "It's a Nirvana song. It just feels wrong to cut a Nirvana song."

Suddenly Josh was laughing, utterly unself-conscious as the ever-growing crowd stared on with morbid fascination. "And why the hell would you care, Kallie?" he fired back. "It's not like you're actually contributing anything."

Kallie's head drooped. She stared at her guitar intently. "You're such an asshole, Josh."

"And you're so superfluous. Which is why I'd still rather be me."

And with that, Josh began to walk away. Just like normal, he'd fractured the band and was executing his exit strategy before anyone else could have the last word. And that's when I knew I'd had enough.

I shouted for him to stop, but he didn't even pause, just kept striding toward the school door. I began to follow him, walking faster and faster until I caught up with him just inside the building. Students poured out of the cafeteria beside us, a mass of bodies streaming around us like we were rocks in a river. Within seconds the spectators from outside hurried to join us, either because they wanted to get warm or because they didn't want to miss Dumb's latest train wreck.

"I won't let you do this, Josh."

Josh rolled his eyes and turned away, but I grabbed his arm and pulled him around to face me again. "Did you hear what I said?"

"Yes, Piper. I'm not deaf."

I brushed off the remark, refused to play the role of easy victim, but inside, my heart was pounding. The crowd was getting larger, their persistent hum obscuring Josh's words. I focused all my energy on watching his lips, knowing this was a fight I couldn't afford to lose. "We're sticking to the set we agreed on, Josh."

"Or what?"

Or what? It was a good question actually. For a few seconds I didn't know what to say. "Or I'll cancel the gig on Saturday."

Josh smiled, cold and calculating. "No, you won't. You need the money. You and Tash and Kallie—you all need the money."

His words dripped with scorn, like our lack of wealth was a personal failing. I despised him for thinking that, and for outing us in front of so many people.

"Whether or not I need the money, I'll cancel. Only I have the power to say whether or not this goes ahead. *Me.* Do you understand?"

"Oh, sure. You're so important that—" He turned around as he continued speaking, like something had grabbed his attention. My heart sank, but I knew exactly what he was doing.

"You'll have to repeat that, Josh," I said calmly as soon as he turned to face me again.

"I said that—" Again he looked over his shoulder and I couldn't read his lips.

By now there must have been a hundred people grouped around us. I'd never felt so public in my life. And then Belson strutted up, ready to hand out detentions like so much confetti if the occasion called for it. Which, to be honest, I suspected it was about to.

I fingered the ends of my hair nervously, reminding myself of the pink strands that represented the new Piper—the *real* Piper. The Piper who wouldn't hide or back down. What would *that* Piper do?

Suddenly I felt calmer, more in control. I put Belson out of my mind—if he wanted to break up the fight, so be it, but until then, I needed to focus.

"Oh, Josh Josh Josh," I said sweetly. "You think that nobody here knows what you're doing. But you're wrong."

For the first time, the sheen wore off Josh's performance. He shifted his weight from one foot to the other.

"Everyone knows I'm deaf, Josh. They know I'm reading your lips," I continued, even though I realized this was probably news to at least half the people there. "So stop trying to humiliate me. I'm not disabled, Josh, and trying to make out that I am just makes you look like an even bigger jerk than usual."

I waited for the witty comeback, the one-liner that ended the faceoff in Josh's favor. I knew it was coming, but as Josh looked around, I think he saw in everyone's faces the same look I saw: a mixture of sadness and disgust. All of them were muttering, and even though I couldn't hear a word, I knew that every one of them was ripping Josh, not me.

Josh turned on his heel and stormed off, and for a moment I wondered if he'd just quit the band. But then I felt Belson's hand on my shoulder, and he was pointing in the direction of his office. Amazing—after Finn's tireless efforts to break every rule in the book, I'd still be the first Vaughan ever hauled into Belson's office. It took me twenty-eight steps to get there, plenty of time to wonder how my parents would respond to yet another disciplining.

Once we were inside and the door was shut, Belson lowered himself gingerly onto his ratty black chair. "Your hair is pink," he said, like he'd only just put his finger on what was different about me.

I nodded.

"Ed told me he's leaving the chess club."

I nodded again. "I told him he should."

Belson heaved a sigh. "May I ask why? It's not as if we're inundated with members."

"He was only in it because he had a crush on me. He's actually a terrible player. So I figured we should just date, and then he could stop pretending he had any interest in chess."

Belson's eyebrows seemed to have taken up permanent residence along his hairline. "I see." And then he smiled, and laughed, and I was utterly confused. "You know, Piper, I've always thought of chess as a form of civilized combat. It allows even the most peaceful folk to unleash their inner dictator. It's a game that rewards the more aggressive player, the one who outwits the other. And then, when the game is over, we can go back to being polite, and meek, and shy." He paused, tapping his finger against his cheek. "But I've also wondered if it wouldn't just be better for us to unleash those inner demons for real, you know?"

I shook my head.

"Oh, I think you do. Ever since you arrived at this school you've been the most calculating, conniving, and generally vicious chess player I've ever met. But away from the chessboard, everyone has walked all over you. Now something's changed."

I looked down at my hands. I had a feeling I wasn't going to like what he said next.

Belson waited for me to look up again. "I appreciate good students, Piper. I like it when they're polite, and prompt, and attentive. But I also like it when the best students finally catch on to the fact that they really are *better* than the poor students . . . when they realize they need to stop hiding out, hoping no one notices them. What I'm saying is: What took you so long?"

Suddenly he was smirking, and it dawned on me there would be no detentions given out today. And because he couldn't seem to stop smirking, I had time to work something else out too.

"You didn't tell the principal we were playing in the parking lot, did you."

The smirking stopped, but the eyes kept twinkling. "He's a hard man to find at the best of times."

I nodded appreciatively. "Thank you. And thank you for finding us before any of the other teachers did."

Belson rubbed his chin. "Well, as long as I was there, it saved anyone else from having to discipline you. Believe me, no teacher wants to give up their lunch break arguing with the second coming of Kurt Cobain."

I felt like he'd paid me the ultimate compliment, but I kept that to myself. Belson had me pegged as the next chess Grandmaster, and it was clearly working in my favor.

CHAPTER 49

Finn was hiding out in the basement, eyes closed, headphones practically swallowing his head while he strummed his guitar. When I touched his arm he leaped up, and the headphones clattered to the floor.

What's going on? he signed.

Will you go to the Showbox for me tomorrow? I'm grounded, but I want someone there to make sure it goes okay.

Finn shook his head, which surprised me.

Please? Tash will be there, I reminded him.

No, I can't. I'll be watching Grace.

What? You're babysitting?

Yes. Mom and Dad don't think a rock concert is a good place for a baby.

I couldn't believe it. *My concert?*

Finn was trying hard not to grin. *They want to go. And they only trust me to look after Grace.* He paused, thought about that. *That's what they said, anyway.*

What about me? I asked, hurt by the implication.

You're busy.

Why?

You'll be at the concert too. He pretended to study his guitar, which made it clear he'd had a hand in this development.

What have you been up to?

Finn picked out a few chords that I couldn't hear, then gave up. *I told Dad about the contract you negotiated. You know he loves anything that makes money.*

I wanted to be mad at him, but actually I should've thought of it myself. *And now he's going to let me go to the concert? Just like that?*

I said you'd have to cancel if you couldn't be there.

Damn. Finn was really good. *And he believed you?*

Finn snorted. *He was seeing dollar signs. He didn't question anything.*

I couldn't believe my parents were going to see Dumb. I began to panic, wondering what they'd think of the band.

Right on cue, Dad appeared on the stairs, Grace pinned to his hip.

Are you sure you'll be okay with her? I signed hurriedly.

As Dad approached, Finn put his guitar on the floor and held out his arms to take Grace. She seemed to enjoy it too. "Yes, Piper, I'll be okay," he said.

I stared into Grace's bright blue eyes and ran my fingers over her dimpled cheeks. "What'll you do with her?" I asked Finn.

"I'll just stick her in the baby carrier, wander around downtown. Maybe meet you all afterwards. I'm sort of hoping people will assume it's my kid and give me dirty looks."

Dad cocked an eyebrow but didn't say a word. I think that privately he was relishing the thought of an evening without diaper changes. When he headed back upstairs, I decided to stick around. Finn's company was comfortable, calming. I even began to wish I were a little more like him.

"Did you ever find out why Baz was sending you all over Seattle to check out dead rock stars?" he asked, conducting Peek-a-boo 101 with Grace.

"It wasn't Baz."

Finn looked up suddenly, and Grace arched her back in disgust. "So . . . that whole ZARKINFIB thing was, what—just a diversion?"

"Yeah. A good one too. I wouldn't have gone if I'd known the messages weren't from . . ." A thought crossed my mind—a single, momentous thought. I was sure I must be mistaken, but even more certain that I wasn't. "How did you know the username, Finn?"

He only hesitated a second, but it may as well have been an hour. "You told us."

"No. Ed told you the username was an anagram of Baz Firkin, but he was the only one who saw it on my computer."

Finn's poker face was eluding him when he needed it most. "I don't know how I know."

I suddenly remembered how it had been Finn who "discovered" the details about Hendrix's house being moved. But even though I'd solved the mystery, it still didn't make any sense.

"Why did you do it?" I asked.

Finn resumed peek-a-boo with Grace, but his mind was clearly elsewhere. "I saw you the day Dumb played on the school steps . . . the way you watched them, and screamed at the end. Everyone there knew how ballsy it was for Dumb to do that, but when you saw them later on, you totally dissed them."

I raised my hand to interrupt, but Finn shook his head. This was his confession, and he needed me to hear him out.

"They totally should've called you on it, but instead they made you manager. And the next thing I know, you've got them playing soft rock on some pathetic station no one listens to anymore, and when that backfires, you threaten Kallie. It was a freaking disaster and it was all your fault. And it really pissed me off that you had this chance to do something amazing, but you didn't care about anything but the money. I just wanted you to see there was more to it than that, so I sent the message. I never thought you'd tell anyone, and I definitely didn't think you'd go . . . but you did." Now that he was done, he seemed surprised to find he was still playing peek-a-boo.

"I get it now," I said quietly. "I really do."

He nodded, but he wouldn't make eye contact. "You must hate me, huh?"

I leaned forward, caught a glimpse of my reflection in a mirror on the wall. "No, Finn, I don't hate you at all. How could I hate you for being right?"

A smile crept across his face. "You have to admit, that trip to Hendrix's house—"

"Was kind of surreal, yeah."

We both laughed then. And when we stopped and there was nothing but silence, we laughed again. After so much chaos, so much noise, it was sublime.

CHAPTER 50

We never got around to discussing dress codes for the Showbox performance—not that we'd have agreed on one anyway—and as they took the stage, Dumb certainly presented an eclectic mix. Ed looked casual-cool in a tight yellow T-shirt that read "Roll over Beethoven." Josh had the preppy J. Crew thing down cold. Even Will looked okay in that black-jeans-plus-black-shirt, undertaker-in-training kind of way. Tash had dyed her spikes a freaky purple for the occasion (in honor of Jimi Hendrix's "Purple Haze," she said). And Kallie wore an unflattering gray cardigan that looked like it belonged to a man twice her size. She wasn't even wearing makeup, and her lank hair seemed to be crying out for whatever nourishing product it was used to receiving on a daily basis.

Although they were nothing to write home about individually, together they looked like the real deal. And it had less to do with their clothes than the venue, an art-deco palace with deep red walls and an immense ceiling supported by fluted golden pillars. The decor seemed to inspire Dumb too, and as soon as ABH allowed them onstage, Ed took control and had them up and running without so much as a word of discussion. Instead of being intimidated by their surroundings, they behaved like they'd been waiting for this opportunity to show exactly what they could do. After countless hours of rehearsing, and (most likely) a sleepless night, Dumb's five flavors were ready to rock.

Or rather, four of them were.

It almost made me cry: Kallie Sims, twenty-first-century grunge girl, hiding at the back of the stage in self-imposed exile, shrinking into the folds of her cardigan like she was hoping no one would notice she was even there. Only, the Showbox stage hadn't been designed as a place to hide. Instead it showcased her rhythmic deficiencies in all their spotlighted glory. This time no one needed to take the initiative and turn down her amp—she did it herself as soon as the first song was over.

To their credit, ABH had given Dumb more than an hour to run a sound check and rehearse their set. I wanted to celebrate every minute of it too—the seamless transitions, the subtle-but-constant eye contact, the way they seemed to be having fun for the first time in a long time—but Kallie bowed her head throughout. And when it was all over, I noticed someone was waving at me from a seat across the bar table where I was sitting.

In the low light it took me a moment to recognize the lead singer of ABH. He was scary thin, with thick bags under his eyes. He smiled without opening his mouth, but spoke with his whole face when he introduced himself as Joby Barrett. We shook hands, and then there was an awkward but meaningful silence.

"Our manager says you're deaf," he said speculatively. He waited for me to show signs of recognition. "Severely deaf, or profoundly deaf?"

I was surprised he knew the difference. "Moderately severe."

"So you heard some of what was going on up there?"

"Some, but it's kind of a mess."

"I won't tell them you said that," he laughed. "But seriously, I'll tell you what I heard, just in case you're interested, okay?"

"Okay," I said, although I knew I wasn't going to enjoy any conversation that began with a disclaimer.

"Look, Dumb is a really promising band. You can't fake that kind of energy. But—and I'm just being honest here—it took me a while to realize that girl in the cardigan was actually part of it."

There didn't seem to be any point in pretending I didn't understand, so I just nodded.

"Like I say, this is just my opinion, but you can't be carrying around dead weight. Audiences aren't dumb, if you'll excuse the pun. It'll kill the band eventually. So if you really have high hopes for them, you're going to have to cut her loose. Not today, obviously, but sometime."

I couldn't hate him for speaking his mind, but a part of me wished he'd never stopped by. Especially not when he looked up and nodded at someone behind me.

I looked over my shoulder and saw Josh, seated alone a couple of tables down. He took the opportunity to come over and introduce himself to Joby, then pulled up a chair and joined us. Before Josh had even begun to speak, Joby excused himself, and suddenly we were alone.

"I heard what he said," Josh announced.

"Of course you did."

"So what are you going to do?"

I rolled my eyes. "Right now . . . nothing."

Josh leaned back, conjured that infamous smile I'd once mistaken for attractive and misread as genuine. "Tonight is her last show, do you understand?"

"Or what?"

"Or Dumb is history. And that's not me being melodramatic. It's just the truth. You know what that guy said."

"Yeah, Josh, I do. And you know what? Kallie may still be the weak link, but I don't think that's what bothers you at all. You just want her out because it's clear she's not into you."

His smile only grew. "So you admit she's the weak link?"

I didn't say anything. Really, what could I say?

"Go be a manager, Piper. You know what needs to be done, so try earning your money for a change."

CHAPTER 51

It was after seven p.m. and the first ABH groupies were already starting to filter in. One middle-aged trio pointed to the other seats at my table. I realized I was taking up prized real estate, so I excused myself. I took my belongings to the "other" greenroom—ABH had claimed the one with windows and a coffeemaker—and tried to feel at home amid the dark carpet and dark walls and dark vinyl sofa. There was a round table in the far corner, and since no one else was around—they'd all gone in search of food—I sat down and opened up my laptop.

The Showbox had Wi-Fi, so I checked my e-mail. There were good luck messages from Finn, and Mom and Dad, and Baz, and Marissa, and I knew that every one of them genuinely wanted to see things go well. The clock said 7:14 p.m.

I was feeling light-headed, so I decided to get a bite to eat as well. But I'd barely stepped outside the building when I turned around and walked right back in. Who was I kidding? There was no way I'd be able to stomach eating anything.

Just inside the main doors of the Showbox was an enormous plate glass window, engraved with the names of all the bands that had preceded us. It was a list that made me want to crawl away and hide: Duke Ellington, Dizzy Gillespie, the Ramones, The Police, Blondie, Iggy Pop, Pearl Jam, Dave Matthews, and hundreds more. Seriously, when even I recognized several of the names, we were clearly out of our league.

Audience members were turning up in droves now, the crowd evenly split between casually dressed adults and over-caffeinated kids. It wasn't hard to guess which band each group was there to hear. Some of them even stared at me like there was something familiar about my face, but the pink hair was enough of a disguise that I was able to make a clean escape.

The Showbox staff were frantically busy. Unlike me, they had jobs to do—they could *control* things—and I suddenly felt completely useless, just counting down the minutes until I fired Kallie, or Dumb screwed up one last time. When the meltdown came, would Mom rush to my aid and take on ABH too?

I paced back to our greenroom, just for a little peace and quiet, but Kallie was already there, perched on a stool in the corner. (I guess I wasn't the only one who couldn't stomach the thought of eating.) She had her back to me, and was clearly engrossed by something on my laptop. Every few seconds she paused to scribble on a scrap of paper, then wiped her nose on the sleeve of her cardigan. I couldn't be certain, but I was pretty sure she'd been crying.

She didn't hear me padding through the room, and it wasn't until I sat down beside her that she noticed me. Even then she didn't say a word, just smiled bravely and returned her attention to the laptop.

It looked like she was watching an old home movie on YouTube—a kid about our age in front of a graffitied wall, then another kid waving a kite from a roof, the footage suddenly in black and white. It was all very strange. Then there was another image: two older guys playing guitar in a room that resembled Baz's studio, although they seemed oblivious to the camera, like this was a performance for themselves, not for anyone else. Eventually a third guy came into view, a drummer I was sure I recognized. Above the movie the title read: "Nirvana—Seasons in the Sun." And that's when I realized that the drummer was Kurt Cobain, only I was sure he'd been the band's lead guitarist. The other two guys had swapped instruments too.

"1993," said Kallie, turning to face me. "The year before he died." She ran the sleeve across her nose again. "Look at them. They weren't so different from us—just screwing around on each other's instruments, feeling like there was a place they actually belonged." All the while her head nodded slightly, propelled by a beat I couldn't really hear. "There was pain in his voice even then. Just . . . anguish, you know?"

I didn't really know, but I nodded all the same.

She restarted the song from the top, a black-and-white title screen followed by footage of the men when they were boys, as earnest as Kallie, as gawky as Ed. Even the film of them playing in the studio in 1993 had a similar quality, their movements ever so slightly awkward, like they were surprised to find the wrong instruments in their hands.

Still gazing at the screen, Kallie reached out and took my hand and squeezed it. With her free hand, she picked up the scrap of paper and handed it to me. It was worn, creased, like it had been folded and unfolded a hundred thousand times. Some of the ink had bled in the perfect circle of a teardrop. I took a deep breath and read the words at the top: "Seasons in the Sun." Slowly, painstakingly, she'd written down every lyric to the song:

Good-bye my friend, it's hard to die
when all the birds are singing in the sky
and all the flowers are everywhere.

I stopped reading and looked at the screen again, and the three guys fooling around with each other's instruments like they knew this whole crazy trip was nothing but a magic carpet ride, something they needed to cherish now because all dreams die eventually.

Kallie took the volume down and turned to me. Even with tears running down her face, she was still beautiful.

"My parents used to fight," she said finally. "A lot. I heard it in my bedroom, even when I closed the door, even when I played music on my stereo. Nirvana was the soundtrack of my parents falling apart." She blinked and fresh tears tumbled down her cheeks. "One day he . . . he threatened her. And I said he was wrong, and I meant that he was wrong to threaten her, but maybe he thought I meant he was wrong about everything. And, I don't know, maybe I did mean that. And I'll never forget the look he gave me, like that was the final straw. He could take it from Mom, but not me. So he left. He left, and we never heard from him again. Not once. Not ever."

I didn't know what to say. I'd figured Kallie had a story to tell, just like the rest of us, but certainly not that kind of story. "I'm sorry, Kallie. I'm so sorry."

"If I'd just kept my mouth shut, maybe he'd have stayed," she said, like she was replaying the scene for the millionth time, tweaking and refining it until it had a happy ending. "Maybe everything would be okay. Maybe I'd actually be the girl everyone thinks I am."

I thought of the way she'd been so honest with Tash in the café. But who can view their own life with that kind of clarity?

I swallowed hard. "That's not true, Kallie. If you'd kept your mouth shut, he'd have hurt your mom and left anyway, and you'd be telling me that you had the chance to do something, and you let her down. You'd have spent the past six years regretting your silence."

Kallie managed the slightest nod as she turned back to the screen. "I just . . . I just want to go back and make everything right," she said, and I couldn't tell whether she was talking about her family or the guys onscreen.

"You have to live in the present, Kallie. Make now the best it can be," I said, meaning every word, but hating how prophetic it felt.

Kallie didn't speak after that, just watched me. She even summoned the infamous Kallie half smile, and it suddenly struck me that it didn't make her look sexy, or teasing, or any of the other things I'd always thought. It made her seem uncertain, even vulnerable. In the end, the half smile was her instinctive reaction to uncomfortable situations—nothing more.

I took a deep breath and realized I didn't feel anxious anymore, just tired. The movie had ended again, but Kallie immediately replayed it, and I could only guess at how many times she'd watched it over and over, memorizing details, struggling to make sense of it. She even pointed to the handwritten lyrics, her finger guiding me through each line so I could keep up with the song I couldn't properly hear:

We had joy, we had fun, we had seasons in the sun
but the hills that we climbed
were just seasons out of time.

I looked back at the screen and watched the home movie of Nirvana, all off-balanced colors and amateur camerawork. There was an honesty about it, an unscripted innocence that was heartbreaking. Then the movie cut to one of Kurt's bandmates, at the very moment his face crumpled and he sobbed, just once, as if he knew so much more than he could ever really know. I felt Kallie's shoulders shaking gently against me, her hand gripping mine so very tightly, like she was afraid of losing me as well. And as I pulled her toward me and hugged her tightly, let her cry warm tears against me, I wondered how I'd never seen it before—how horribly broken Kallie was.

Meanwhile, the others had begun drifting back into the room, implacable exteriors intact, just business as usual. That's when I realized with a degree of shame that of all of us, Kallie was the one who felt it the most—the raw emotion, the power of a single song to change her world. She'd never come close to Ed's calm professionalism. She couldn't walk the walk like Will and Tash, or talk the talk like Josh. She simply felt every lyric as if it was a message composed especially for her. Improbably Kallie needed Dumb more than anyone. So much more. And I knew that if Dumb was to have any soul, any meaning at all, it needed her too.

Just then I felt Kallie's body stiffen, and I looked up to see Josh standing beside her. He even looked genuinely distressed to see her crying, placing a hand on her shoulder as she tried to pull away.

"I guess Piper told you you're out, then, huh?"

CHAPTER 52

For a moment Kallie didn't react. It was like all her energy had been focused on getting away from Josh, and luckily for me there simply wasn't room for her to digest a bombshell like the one he'd just dropped.

I jumped up and pulled her away before Josh could say anything more, but I knew that she needed an explanation, and fast.

"Ignore him, Kallie. He's full of crap."

Kallie shook her head. "It's okay, Piper. Seriously, it's okay."

"No, it's not okay. You're staying."

Josh was beside us in a heartbeat. "What about our deal?"

"There was no deal, Josh."

"Bullshit. Kallie's the weak link. You said so yourself."

I never took my eyes off Josh, but from the corner of my eye I saw Kallie's face fall. I wanted to get out of that room so badly. Earlier it had just felt small, but now it felt as claustrophobic as a phone booth. I needed space to breathe.

Kallie reached out and touched my arm. "It's okay if you want me to leave," she said, and I swear she didn't even look angry, just resigned.

"No, Kallie. I absolutely do not want you to leave."

Josh spun around and punched the wall, releasing a tiny fountain of plaster dust. Then he smiled in that demonic Mr. Hyde way that made me want to employ a bodyguard. "You know what, Kallie, you're out. *I'm* telling you because our manager is too much of a flake to do it herself, okay?"

Then Ed joined the fray, putting himself in my line of vision to make sure I could follow everything he said. "No, it's not okay. Kallie stays."

"Then I go!" Josh shouted.

The room was only still for a moment before Ed made it clear that was fine with him, and then Tash did too. Even Will didn't seem bothered, just stayed out of the way, cleaning his bass strings.

"Let's not be hasty, guys," I interjected, aware that things were spiraling out of control. "We need Josh, remember?"

But Josh was clearly unnerved by the extent of Dumb's mutiny. "No way. You guys want Kallie more than me, well . . . fine! I'm gone."

"You can't leave," I reminded him. "You leave and I'll sue you for a thousand bucks, and you know I'll do it."

"Okay. Let's put it to a vote. Hands up who's willing to let me go."

Suddenly Ed, Tash, and Kallie had their hands high in the air, and Josh was smirking like he'd won the lottery.

"Good. Then the thousand bucks are off the table. But you'll want to think about tonight's contract," he added, pulling a copy from his pocket. "It stipulates that all five members must be present onstage."

Tash simply laughed. "You're so full of it, Josh. If you wanted to leave, you'd have gone already. But then who'd give a crap about you?"

"Are you testing me?" He waved the contract for emphasis.

Will stopped cleaning his strings, blew hair out of his eyes. "Come on, Josh, cut the drama."

"No, Will. I'm leaving for real. Dumb's history, and Piper's about to be sued for breach of contract unless we make a new deal right now. And the deal is that after tonight, Kallie's gone."

Suddenly no one was laughing anymore. We'd called Josh's bluff, believing he'd never actually follow through on his threat, but here was an ultimatum. (Where was poker master Finn when I needed him?) Never mind the extraordinary and devious lengths to which Josh had gone to get Kallie in the band in the first place—he was tired of her now, so it was time to move on.

With the stakes so high, it was a no-brainer: Contractually, we'd get sued without him; musically, we'd be retaining one scene-stealing lead singer instead of an air-guitarist with limited acting skills. It was such an easy call that I waited to see which of us would fold first, swallow our pride and accept Josh's terms for the greater good of the band. I just couldn't bring myself to be that person.

The problem was, neither could Ed, or Kallie, or Tash, or even Will. And Josh didn't wait for us to reconsider.

The second he walked out the door, I expected someone to run after him and drag him back, kicking and screaming if necessary. I even had half a mind to do it myself, only the other half was stronger. So instead of tracking down our dysfunctional lead singer, we looked at each other like developing Plan B was top priority.

For once, I knew exactly what it should be.

I pulled out my cell phone and speed-dialed Mom, then thrust the phone at Ed. "Who's answering?" I asked.

Ed raised an eyebrow. "How the heck would— Oh, hi there, Mrs. Vaughan!" He turned an adorable shade of scarlet as he realized he'd just sort of sworn at my mother. "Actually, I'm not sure what I want," he said, visibly deflating.

"Ask her if Finn has Dad's cell."

Ed relayed the question, then nodded vigorously. "Oh, good. In that case—"

I snatched the phone from him and hung up. There wasn't time for polite good-byes, although I made a mental note to tell Mom it wasn't Ed's fault he'd hung up on her. I dialed Dad's number and shoved it back at Ed. "Tell Finn we need him here right now."

Ed was still bright red, and had begun pacing around the

room in tiny circles. I got the feeling I was killing him softly, but it was already 7:55, and although I knew all rock shows started late, I figured that wasn't really our call to make.

"Finn? Finn?" cried Ed. "Hi. It's Ed."

Ed grimaced as he tried to make out Finn's reply. Eventually he gave up and held the phone away from his ear. "It's really hard to hear him," he complained.

I rolled my eyes. "Welcome to my world."

"Oh, right. I see what you mean." Ed brought the phone back to his ear. "Look Finn, we need you here right now. Josh has bailed and we need a fifth member. . . . Oh, I see. Well, never mind."

"What?" I exploded. "What's going on?"

"Finn's hanging out with Grace in Pacific Place Mall. He says it'd take at least ten minutes to get here."

"Then tell him to leave now!"

"She says you need to leave now. . . . What's that? A poop. Right now? Oh." Ed frowned. "Finn says make that fifteen minutes."

"Tell him forget the poop. Mom and Dad can deal with it when he gets here."

Finn obviously heard me well enough, because Ed immediately shook his head. "He says no go. This is his chance to show that he's a responsible babysitter."

I ripped the phone away from Ed and gave it to Tash, who took over seamlessly: "Hi Finn, it's . . . You are? . . . Great!" She hung up. "He's on his way," she said triumphantly.

While Ed struggled to work out what had happened, Kallie appeared before me, tugging her sleeves anxiously. "What's Finn going to play?" she asked.

I sighed, but there was no use in lying at this stage. "He's going to play guitar."

"So who'll be singing?"

"You know who'll be singing, Kallie."

Her eyes grew wide and she shook her head. "I can't. I couldn't. I'm just . . . not like Josh."

"Which is exactly why you're still here and he's not." I could feel her pulling away, taking refuge in her pessimism. "You can do this, Kallie, I know you can. I've seen you mouthing the words to the songs. Josh has pushed you around for too long. It's time to push back."

Before Kallie could respond, Mike poked his head through the door. "You're on in three," he shouted. When I pretended not to understand, he held up three fingers helpfully.

Then the games really began.

"Okay, Ed," I said. "Mike doesn't know I can understand him, so from now on I need you to act like you're interpreting for me. I'll watch his lips carefully, so don't worry about signing correctly, just drag it out as long as you can."

Ed twirled his drumsticks and raised his thumbs in agreement.

Next I sent Kallie to the ladies' room so she wouldn't be around when Mike came to find out why we hadn't gone onstage. After Ed and I had spent thirty seconds going back and forth with meaningless signs, Ed informed Mike that Kallie had stage fright and was barfing in the bathroom. (Coincidentally, this turned out to be true.)

A couple minutes later, Mike reappeared, and this time Will was fixing a new string to his guitar. Mike threw his hands up in disgust, but he left without saying a word.

After three more minutes he loomed in the doorway and I knew we wouldn't be able to fob him off again. I don't think he really cared when we started, but by now he had an inkling that something was wrong, and he wasn't about to make it easy for us.

"You've got two minutes. No excuses. I don't care if you're missing strings or heaving all over the stage, you get your asses up there. Hear me?"

Ed tried calling Finn again, but there was no answer. I knew he'd be racing over, but we'd exhausted our quota of delaying tactics, and there could be no more excuses. I left Dumb warming up, and ran into the auditorium to search for Finn.

It was crammed full, everyone facing the empty stage in readiness for something magical to occur. I couldn't see over them to the entrance, so I began looking for a pathway through them, which is when I felt a hand on my shoulder. I spun around.

"Where's your fifth?" shouted Mike, wiggling his hands and fingers in a poor approximation of sign language. I pulled away, hurried back to the greenroom, but he stayed right behind me, trailing me like a bloodhound.

"Where's your fifth?" he bellowed as we entered the room.

"There are just four now," said Ed calmly.

"The contract says five. And I'm going to hold you to it."

"Then we won't perform," Tash sneered.

Mike's nostrils flared. "If you bail now, you're finished, and you know it. You'll be blacklisted on every TV and radio station across the country. This is an adult business. It's time you kids understood that."

Kallie stepped into the fray, thrust her guitar into my hands. "There. Now we've got five."

"What?" muttered Mike.

"Piper is our new guitarist."

"Her? But she's deaf. She can't even—"

Mike's appraisal of my qualifications came to an abrupt halt as Tash's guitar caught him squarely in the gut. "That's discrimination, and if you don't pay us, we'll let everyone know what you just said."

Mike wasn't impressed. "Don't screw with me. Discrimination or not, she's deaf. In case you've forgotten, I negotiated with her, and she can't even speak."

I'd heard enough. "Yes, I can. And I can read your lips too." Mike staggered back like he'd been Tasered. "So before you say anything else that will make me hate you even more, listen very carefully. I can feel music just as well as you can hear it. And if you want to debate that, go ahead—my mom's a lawyer."

Mike stared at me, weighing up his options. He wanted to win this showdown—he *had* to—but he also knew his head would be on the chopping block if we bailed. After all, he was the one who'd signed us up. Finally he shook his head and waved his arm toward the door. "Go ahead, then. The stage is through there. Have a great set."

No one moved. We'd never actually gotten around to discussing details like who should go on first, but even if we had, it would have been irrelevant. Because what Mike had realized—and we'd somehow overlooked in our quest to outwit him—was that we were about to face a manic crowd of over a thousand people with a guitarist who'd never touched a guitar in her life, and a lead singer who'd grown afraid of her own voice. I could already imagine Mike snapping souvenir photos as the crowd lynched us midway through our first song.

There was no other choice but to walk through that door, past Mike's self-congratulatory grin, away from the safety of the greenroom. And that was when panic truly set in. I couldn't move my feet—could barely *feel* them—and I was hyperventilating. I was sure I was about to hurl, but then Ed was next to me, holding my hand. Step by laborious step he guided me from the greenroom and along the corridor leading to the stage.

"I can't do it, Ed. Oh God Oh God Oh God I can't do it."

Ed squeezed my hand just once and looked at me, his eyes so wise and reassuring. "I'm going to unplug your amp. Just make sure you can see me. Watch my sticks."

"No, I can't."

"You *can*. You can do this. You can do anything. You're amazing."

Ed wrapped his hand behind my head and pulled me toward him, kissed me with a passion that bordered on madness. I kissed him back with interest, and it wasn't until I was standing beside his drum set onstage that I was again fully conscious of what was going on.

My heart was busting out of my chest. I felt like there wasn't enough air left in the building. And worst of all there was a guitar in my hands, and I couldn't even remember how it had gotten there.

In my borderline hallucinatory state, I even thought I saw Josh leap onto the stage and wrestle the microphone stand from Kallie.

CHAPTER 53

The crowd continued to cheer like this was part of the show—
a reenactment of Tuesday's meltdown, perhaps—but everyone
onstage had frozen. Kallie stared longingly at the microphone.

Josh turned toward us, careful to cover the microphone with
his hand. Spotlights gave him a demonic silhouette, and when he
opened his mouth I struggled to lip-read because his face was in
shadow. "Didn't really . . . gone . . . right?" I worked out the gist
of what he was saying, but no one responded. "Wait . . . what's
Kallie . . . vocals . . . kidding!"

Will stepped forward, and I just knew he was going to tell
Kallie to leave the stage, or to retrieve her guitar from me. I
hated feeling so completely unable to stop what was happening.
But in the glare of the spotlights I read his lips perfectly: "Leave
the stage, Josh. You're done."

Josh was undeterred. "I *am* . . . band."

As he pulled back his hair, the look on Will's face was one
I'd never seen before. It was the look of someone beginning to

discover his own power. "No, Josh. You *were* the band. And if you don't give Kallie that microphone, we'll tell the bouncers to remove you from the stage."

Josh just laughed. He removed his hand from the microphone, filling the air with the whine of feedback, then turned to the crowd. "Kallie . . . joke . . . unplugged . . . amp . . . useless," I heard over the loudspeakers, but it was even harder to follow him now than before. He paused to glance behind him, like he expected us to be applauding. And then he spotted me. "*Piper?*" He did a double take, whipped around to share the joke with the audience: ". . . manager . . . guitar . . . deaf!"

I felt the weight of a thousand pairs of eyes. I didn't need to hear his words to know what he'd just said. He was Josh, and I was an obstacle—there were no other variables in this equation.

I could have left the stage then and never looked back—no one would have blamed me—but I didn't. And it wasn't because I belonged there, or because I had pink hair. It was because I no longer carried the gene necessary to back down. In two months I'd faced more crap than Josh Cooke could begin to imagine, and someone as worthless as him was simply incapable of bringing me down. And because I needed him to know that, I told him in the only way I knew how.

I pity you, I signed, hoping that even if only two people understood me, the message would spread like wildfire.

Josh snorted contemptuously, but he was forcing it. He hated not knowing what I'd said, being out of the loop like that. He hadn't looked at the audience in ages, and it dawned on me this had nothing to do with reclaiming his former role anymore, or even stating his case to the crowd. It was about bringing us all down with him.

The crowd was booing now. I could feel the persistent hum growing more intense by the second. And I saw with frightening clarity the angry looks of a thousand-strong mob exposed to too many childish antics for one night.

"See!" Josh shouted at me with evident satisfaction. "No one . . . understands . . . saying!"

A stick flew across my field of vision and hit Josh squarely in the chest. The hum died down. I spun around and saw Ed towering over his drum set, a look of pure hatred in his eyes.

"She said she pities you!" he screamed. He shifted his attention to me, wanting to be sure I was okay with him standing up for me. But all I could think was that he had understood me when I needed it most.

I was on the verge of tears when I saw the stick making its return flight, but it crashed against a cymbal and clattered to the ground harmlessly. Ed picked it up and taunted Josh by spinning it around in his fingers.

The Showbox bouncers began sweeping toward the stage. They obviously knew about Dumb's reputation for in-group violence, and didn't seem eager to have our party piece reprised for the musically literate patrons of their historic venue. A burly guy in a black T-shirt almost knocked over a middle-aged couple clinging to each other for dear life—my parents. As our eyes met, I saw in their expressions the sad realization that their faith in me and in Dumb had yet again been misplaced. It was utterly soul-destroying, as crushing as the sight of Kallie and Josh wrestling for control of the microphone, or the bouncers launching themselves onto the stage at the very moment an ear-splitting shriek filled the air.

At first I assumed it was more feedback from the microphone, or maybe an alarm. It was high-pitched and piercing, and even though I didn't know where it was coming from, my immediate response was to press my hands against my ears to make it stop. Everyone else on stage was doing the same thing too—all except Kallie, whose body resembled a coiled spring, face twisted in anger. In her hand she clutched the microphone, shoved so far into her mouth it looked like she was making up for skipping dinner.

That sound was *Kallie*?

Beside her, Josh had frozen to the spot, but Kallie wasn't looking at him. She was looking at Tash, her eyes a blistering command to play, to stop the madness, to make music.

With steely determination, Tash thrashed out the opening riff of "Smells Like Teen Spirit." A moment later, Ed brought down his sticks like crashes of thunder, his face alive with maniacal delight.

It was all I needed. I began moving my right hand up and down with each of his cannon-like drum beats, even furrowed my brow and plucked a few strings deliberately like I knew what the heck I was doing. While Josh was being dragged from the stage, I looked up at the crowd, afforded myself a glimpse of what fame must feel like. But nobody was looking at me. Every eye was glued to Kallie, and it had nothing to do with the body or the face or the hair. It was all about the way she was singing, or shouting, or whatever her mouth was doing while her body contorted as if she were possessed by Kurt Cobain himself. She drove toward the chorus, moaning like she was in the final throes of death, and then suddenly her head was pounding and she was full-on screaming, and if I didn't know better, I'd have sworn that she was in need of a swift, sharp exorcism.

I glanced back at Ed, tried to stay cool when I saw the look of enchantment on his face. His sticks hammered away at the speed of light, but he smiled straight at me like this was *our* song—the one with the magical power to turn geeks into rock stars. And as I surveyed the chaos of a thousand thrashing bodies on the dance floor below, I knew that's exactly what we were.

With a final deep breath I leaped in the air and began throwing my body back and forth, my right hand yanking the strings of my silent guitar like I needed my fingers to bleed. And when I closed my eyes, it wasn't out of fear. It was because what I was feeling right there on that stage consumed me. I felt every part of that animal music, felt it eat me up and spit me out, and what emerged was a me a thousand times more powerful than Piper Vaughan. I was Piper Vaughan, guitar hero—spiritual descendant of Jimi Hendrix and proponent of pure anarchy.

And I ROCKED.

COOL·NESS [KOOL-NIS]

–noun

CATCHING your mom gazing at the crazy
crowd like she finally gets it

WATCHING your dad head-banging like he's
Finn's twin brother

LEARNING that your new friends Tash and
Kallie are a thousand times more complicated than you realized, and loving them
for it

FEELING every one of your boyfriend's pounding drumbeats, and thinking it's the most
romantic music ever written

REALIZING you're completely unique . . . even
in a crowd

CHAPTER 54

The roar that greeted us as we gave our instruments a well-earned break at the end of the song was as loud as the music had been. The crowd surged like a tidal wave, bodies crammed together, a single entity amped up on Dumb. And drawing them onward was the awesome magnetism of Kallie Sims, her soft-focus beauty suddenly transformed into something harder-edged, almost fearsome. As she stood at the front of the stage, her jaw set and eyes searing through the crowd, she radiated the otherworldly presence of a sorceress. And I swear that even if I'd never heard of rock music before that moment, I'd still have recognized its immensity.

Dumb had died. Dumb had been born again. Dumb was unstoppable, a force of nature. And the world had just turned on its axis.

I glanced over my shoulder and saw Ed sitting back, relaxed and confident, so in control, he could take my insanity and paranoia and melt them away. He smiled peacefully, lowered his drumsticks, and signed, *You rock my world.* I blew him a kiss, and for a few seconds we simply gazed at each other, until I felt a tap on my shoulder.

It was Finn, his face a mixture of unbridled enthusiasm and amazement. *Grace is with Mom and Dad in the greenroom,* he signed feverishly.

I pulled the guitar strap off my shoulder and handed the instrument to him, then clasped his head between my hands and kissed him. *Blow them away,* I told him, and I could tell he had every intention of doing just that.

As I left the stage, I felt a dozen hands grabbing my shirt like I had messianic powers. I wanted to ask them if they'd missed the bit about me being deaf, or the fact that I hadn't played a single note. Only I knew the answer to both questions, which is how I also knew that in some indefinable way I was partially responsible for what was happening. Maybe my moment of air guitar glory was over, but I was still the mover and shaker, the one who made it all happen. I was Dumb's manager, and I was freaking good at it too.

I passed ABH on the way to the greenroom, all four members standing in the doorway, as transfixed as the fans on the floor. They looked as unlikely to commit actual bodily harm as any quartet in history. Joby, the lead singer, stepped forward, but before I could apologize for what had happened with Josh he stretched out his arms and bowed down before me. I was speechless, although he probably wouldn't have been able to hear me even if I had known what to say. And then they were all grinning, thumbs raised in wholehearted approval of Dumb's performance. I had to take a deep breath to keep from crying.

I turned the corner and found Mom and Dad, looking much more comfortable in the gritty surroundings of the greenroom than I figured they would. They'd even let Grace sit on the floor beside them, where she played with a bottle of water, rolling it back and forth.

Is Kallie usually like that? asked Mom.

I shook my head. Mom looked somewhat reassured.

It's loud, signed Dad deliberately, and I could tell he approved of this particular quality of Dumb's performance.

I noticed Grace peering up, evidently less enamored by the Showbox than the rest of us. When she had our attention she cupped her right hand and drew it down her chest.

I guess she's hungry, I signed.

Mom laughed. *No. She just finished nursing. She just wants attention.*

I laughed too, admiring Grace's cunning. And then I felt my stomach flip. *She signed.* I watched Grace reprise her party trick. She signed "hungry."

Mom nodded. *Dad says she's a natural. Best in the class.*

Ed's words came back with the subtlety of a thunderclap. *You mean . . . she's been going to the classes as well?*

Dad was having trouble following the conversation, but he obviously got the gist of it because he turned away self-consciously. Mom wrapped an arm around his waist and pulled him close.

We thought it would be unfair if Grace was the only person in the family who couldn't sign. She leaned forward and wiped the tear from my eye. *No one should feel ignored, right?*

I was about to start bawling, and I think Dad knew it too. And whatever else had passed between us recently, that was something he didn't want to stick around for.

"Do you, uh, mind if we go watch Dumb?" he asked hopefully.

Although I couldn't hear a word, I read his lips just fine. "Actually, I'd like that very much!" I shouted. "That's my band out there."

Mom pushed her lips together in a thin smile and regarded me from the corner of her eye. I got the feeling she was deciding what she most wanted to say, like this was one of those moments when parents tell their kid they're proud, or disappointed, or confused. But Dad was pulling her away.

"You're one tough cookie, you know that?" she said as she was dragged through the door. Although I felt anything but tough at that moment, I knew exactly what she meant.

And then it was just Grace and me, the unstoppable Vaughan sisters, alone in a dark room with industrial carpet and vinyl furniture. It wasn't the right place to pull her close and rub noses and shower her in kisses and say over and over that I was sorry, but I did anyway, because I didn't want to waste another precious moment with my baby sister.

When I was done making up with her, Grace stared at me intently like she'd just noticed how different I was too. Maybe it was the pink hair, but as I held her close and we twirled in time with the *thump thump thump* of Ed's muffled drumbeats next door, I chose to believe that she was loving our shared gift of madness and movement.

I closed my eyes and felt time stand still, locked in the dizzying perfection of the moment.

Author's note

If you retrace Piper's steps across Seattle, you'll discover that one
of the landmarks she visits is missing. In the months between
the completion of this book and its publication, Jimi Hendrix's
boyhood home was demolished. The house was, admittedly, in
very bad shape when I visited—a far cry from his gaudy monu-
ment in the memorial park across the street—but it was a poi-
gnant reminder that the world's greatest rock guitarist grew
up in extreme poverty. For Tash the house was "a holy relic."
Thankfully, nothing can destroy Hendrix's music.

Acknowledgments

In roughly chronological order, I'd like to thank:

Stephen Carleston—my high school music teacher—for introducing me to Jimi Hendrix; and Nick Green—best man—for unleashing Kurt Cobain on me. You both have a lot to answer for. As does my brother, Mark John, who continues to view my rock music education as a personal crusade.

Gavin and Tamsin, who visited every Hendrix and Cobain site in Seattle without a word of complaint. And sometimes posed for pictures.

Before I started writing, I read the excellent biographies of Hendrix and Cobain written by Seattle native Charles R. Cross: *Heavier Than Heaven: A Biography of Kurt Cobain* and *Room Full of Mirrors: A Biography of Jimi Hendrix*. These books shaped *Five Flavors of Dumb* in countless ways. I highly recommend them.

The librarians at the St. Louis Public Library (especially the Schlafly Branch) for getting me everything I need, and for supporting YA in the best way; Louise Thommen, and the entire cast of the Coffee Crew, for allowing me to feature them in a cameo role; and the folks at Kayak's (especially Robin), for giving me a place to write.

The many professionals who volunteered to help out along the way (any textual inaccuracies are mine alone): Gabe Archer at Showbox at the Market (for the guided tour, and for answering numerous follow-up questions); Jacob McMurray at Experience Music Project (for info on Jimi Hendrix); Kara Simmons and Ella Eakins at Concordia Seminary (for allowing me to sit in on an ASL class); Kristina Shilts at the St. Louis Children's Hospital Department of Audiology (for the hearing aid tutorial); Steven Malawer (for an early critique of my accounts of deafness); Stephanie Zoller, Senior Producer for KSDK-TV (for the station tour); Heather Navarro (for legal advice on rock music contracts); Ouida Wymer at Lemon Spalon (for sharing hair dye swatches); the staff at the Chess Club and Scholastic Center of Saint Louis; and the Gallaudet University Financial Aid Office.

Tadd Simmons and Valerie Bu, who not only shared their experiences of growing up deaf, but read and critiqued the manuscript as well—I'm indebted to you both; my wife, Audrey, and sister-in-law, Clare, who read early, middle, and late drafts of the book, and always had insightful comments; and everyone at Emma's Book Club for taking me seriously when I said I wanted criticism.

The whole team at Dial Books: Kristin Smith (for the world's best cover); Jasmin Rubero (for the exquisite interior design); Heather Alexander (for the great comments and hair advice); Regina Castillo (for the spot-on copyediting); Kathy Dawson (for those last-minute improvements); and Lauri Hornik (for welcoming me to the Dial family in the first place).

Last, but not least, the two people who made it all happen: my agent, Ted Malawer, the most down-to-earth genius I know—you are practically perfect in every way; and my editor, Liz Waniewski, for loving the book when it was just an idea, and sharpening and polishing it until it was so much more—you've made every moment of this journey pure joy. I can't thank you enough.

BEHIND THE MUSIC

Of all the questions that readers ask, the most popular is: What songs were on your playlist while you were writing *Five Flavors of Dumb?* It makes sense, of course, because the book is filled with rock music; and yes, I listen to music as I write. But the truth is, there were over a hundred songs on my playlist, and it was a crazily eclectic mix. So, rather than fill pages and pages, I thought I'd keep the playlist to 20 songs that Piper might approve of:

PART 1: The ones that actually get played in the book:

"Smells Like Teen Spirit" – Nirvana

"Seasons in the Sun" – Nirvana

"Star Spangled Banner" – Jimi Hendrix
   (live at Woodstock, 1969)

"Purple Haze" – Jimi Hendrix (live at Woodstock, 1969)

PART 2: The three-chord rock classics that may have influenced *Dumb*:

"Twist and Shout" – Beatles

"Satisfaction" – The Rolling Stones

"Wild Thing" – The Troggs

"All Right Now" – Free

"My Generation" – The Who

(Yes, they're all British groups. Yes, I'm British, too. I might be biased.)

PART 3: The ones that sound like a synopsis for *Dumb*:

"Idioteque" – Radiohead

"Hot N Cold" – Katy Perry

"Paparazzi" – Lady Gaga

"It's the End of the World as We Know It" – R.E.M.

"We Will Rock You" – Queen

PART 4: The ones whose titles are like portraits of Dumb's band members:

Piper (manager): "Trouble" – Pink

Josh (lead vocals): "Cooler Than Me" – Mike Posner

Ed (drums): "Every Little Thing She Does is Magic"
– The Police

Tash (lead guitar): "Bad Reputation" – Joan Jett

Kallie (guitar): "You Know I'm No Good"
– Amy Winehouse

Will (bass guitar): "Zombie" – The Cranberries

Oh, and Ed gives bonus points to anyone who has heard "Ionisation" by his namesake, Edgard Varèse.

Turn the page to read a chapter from
Antony John's next book . . .

SATURDAY, JUNE 14

Lessons 15: 7–12

7. For there were two brothers. And yea, one was shorter than the other, and weaker. 8. And though he bestowed upon his big brother gifts of kindness and thoughtfulness and love, yet did the taller boy mock him, lamenting, "Why art thou so short? Art thou a leprechaun?" 9. And the shorter brother was too much afeared to speak. 10. So the stronger boy laughed, and cried, "What art thou good for? What can thou do that cannot be done far better by a boy of true stature, whose mind and body are strong?" 11. And though he was still afeared, yet the smaller boy recalled the events of the previous evening, and so girded his loins and spake thus: "Remember thee, 'tis easier for a short man to pass through the eye of a cat flap when he misseth curfew, and thereby to avoid parental detection and retribution." 12. And the taller brother knew that it was true, and shutteth up.

2:20 P.M.
Lambert–St. Louis International Airport, St. Louis, Missouri

Letitia is biting the inside of her mouth. Her left eyebrow is arched. I get the feeling she thinks my e-ticket is a fake, but I don't panic. After all, Pastor Mike—legendary host of TV's *The Pastor Mike Show*—called my journey a "pilgrimage." How can a *pilgrimage* go wrong before it has even started?

"Your bag's thirty-two pounds over the limit," says Letitia, smacking her gum.

"I'm sorry?"

"You can be as sorry as you like, honey. Don't change a thing. That'll be an extra seventy-five bucks."

I remove the case from the scale and open it carefully. Inside are dozens of hardback copies of my book—*Hallelujah: A Spiritual Chronicle of a Sixteen-Year-Old St. Louisan*. My editor complained that the title lacked "punch," so the cover just says *Hallelujah*.

I transfer ten copies to my second case, and return the original case to the scale.

"Still twenty-two pounds over," says Letitia.

The man next in line groans. He mutters to the lady beside him, but I don't hear what he says. I won't try to hear either, because eavesdropping is sinful, and I need to be good. Plus, I don't think he's being complimentary.

I move more books to the second case and the scale shows that it's now just under the maximum allowable weight. I smile at Letitia, who rolls her eyes and drums her fingers. I drag the second case onto the scale.

"Twenty-eight over."

Mental math tells me I won't be able to avoid going over the limit, so I pull out the credit card that my publicist, Colin, gave me for all book tour expenses.

Letitia studies it along with my ID. "Wait! Not *the* Luke Dorsey?"

I glance over my shoulder in case there's another sixteen-year-old Luke Dorsey beside me.

"I saw your interview on *The Pastor Mike Show*," she gushes. "The passage you read about the two brothers, that inspired me. I know you said it was written for kids and all, but my sister's taller than me and she thinks she's the big boss lady, so I said 'Just you wait 'til you need to get through the cat flap, sister.' And you know what, honey? She *shutteth up!*"

Letitia reaches under her desk and retrieves a copy

of my book. The cover is worn, as though she has read it several times. I guess I ought to be impressed, but instead I'm just uncomfortable. "Would you autograph it for me?" she asks, voice shaking.

"Uh, sure."

It's not the first book I've signed, not by a long shot, but I'm still not sure what to write. In the end I settle for: *To Letitia, who embraces the light.*

She nods like a bobblehead doll, and hands back the credit card without charging a fee. I'm about to accept it too, but stop myself just in time. "I have to pay," I tell her.

"Oh, forget about it."

"I can't. It'd be stealing. And stealing is—"

She gasps. "A sin, yes. It was evil of me to suggest it. Please pray for me." She runs my card through the machine and hands me the slip of paper to sign.

"I, uh, pray for everyone," I say—kind of a lame response, but she seems satisfied.

"Are you done yet, book boy?" asks the impatient guy behind me.

Letitia casts him a withering look. "Hey, mister, you shut your Goddamned mouth. This boy here's Luke Dorsey."

The heckler looks shell-shocked—his mouth flaps open and shut like he has been struck dumb. When he repeats my name, a silence descends upon the mass of travelers. Their lines part like the Red Sea.

As I shuffle between them, people reach out and touch my new blue blazer. I think Pastor Mike mentioned that something like this might happen, but that doesn't make it any less weird.

By the time I reach my parents at the security checkpoint, I've crossed myself ten times and signed three more copies. I'm sweating so badly, I take off my blazer and place it beside my backpack. All around me, people continue to stare, but now they're checking out my parents as well. Mom and Dad are almost sixty, but look even older. They're dressed in their Sunday best, even though it's Saturday. Most people probably figure they're my grandparents. Happens all the time.

Dad clamps a hand on my shoulder. "Are you sure you're all right with this, Luke?"

"Yeah," I say, though my voice betrays me. "I'm on a pilgrimage, right?"

"If you say so, son. But once you get to Los Angeles, it'll just be you and your brother. It's a great responsibility." He bites his lip. I can see he's having second thoughts about this. "I can take off work if you'd like me to come."

"Me too," interjects Mom. "Perhaps that would be

best," she adds, nodding at Dad. "After all, not every path is as straight and narrow as it might seem."

To be honest, I wish they would come. Pilgrimage or not, I feel like I'm caught in a whirlwind. Everywhere I go, people stop me. Every time I try to relax, there's something I need to do, to write, to say. How is my brother going to help with that?

Yet, as soon as these thoughts cross my mind, I feel ashamed for my lack of faith. Faith is what inspired me to start writing *Hallelujah* in the first place. Which means that faith has brought me here. Surely faith will see me through.

"I'll be fine. Honestly," I say. My parents still don't seem convinced. Since I have no idea how else to reassure them, I go with Default Setting Number One: a quotation from Psalms: " 'Yea, though I walk through the valley of the shadow of death, I will fear no evil.' Psalm twenty-three, verse four."

Mom frowns. "I wasn't suggesting you're going to get knocked off, sweetie. I just meant—"

I raise my hand to stop her. I know she cares about me, and she's worried, but she's really freaking me out. If I don't go now, I'm afraid I might not go at all.

I kiss each of them once on the cheek, grab my backpack, and stride toward the security checkpoint. I don't look back the whole time I'm in line. Finally, when I'm through security, I give my parents a single courageous nod. They're standing in the same spot, jumping up and down, waving madly. In Dad's right hand is my blazer.

5:50 P.M.
Los Angeles International Airport, Los Angeles, California

My brother, Matt, isn't waiting in the baggage claim area, which is surprising. It's not like him to flake out on me. As the minutes tick by, I'm not sure what to do first: call my parents for help, or get a taxi to my book signing.

Before I have to decide, Matt appears. He's wearing a tight black T-shirt that shows off his not-inconsiderable muscles. Curly light brown hair flops over the lenses of his aviator sunglasses.

"I told Mom and Dad I'd meet you at the curb," he says. "To save on parking."

"They didn't tell me."

"Evidently." He hugs me in a way that involves almost no body contact. "Another thing, just so I've said it: I never called you a freakin' leprechaun."

"I never said you did."

"What about that part in your book?"

Before I can tell him it had nothing to do with him, a family shuffles toward us. "Are you Luke Dorsey?" asks the father.

"Uh, yes. Yes, I am."

He nods for a second and then shakes his head. I'm not sure what this gesture means. "Is it true you wrote *Hallelujah* in two weeks?"

"Yeah. Well, more like two and a half. But, you know, Handel composed *Messiah* in two weeks, and that's a lot more work."

"Isn't it amazing how God inspires us?"

I nod because it's true—I had felt inspired when I started *Hallelujah* a year ago. School was out for the summer, and it was blisteringly hot, so I huddled beside the lone a/c vent in my bedroom and wrote. Over ten days and 150 pages the words just flooded out: an offering of thanks for my impossibly good fortune. No wonder that first part of the book was so humorous; what could I possibly have complained about? The momentum kept me writing through the church retreat, when words were harder to come by, and the jokes ran out—when I felt betrayed and alone. When everything changed.

"Modest too, see?" the guy tells his family.

I want to say thank you, only I don't want him to

think I agree. Instead I just glance at Matt. Behind the sunglasses, his brows are furrowed so hard he looks constipated.

"Well, I should let you get on with your good work," he continues. "I just wanted to tell you that you are one amazing human being. To have done so much already, had so many adventures . . ."

I'm not sure what he means by "adventures," but he doesn't seem to expect a response. So I shake his hand, and Matt and I head toward the exit, wheeling my cases behind us.

"Does that happen a lot?" he asks.

"Kind of."

"Wow." He makes a grunting sound. "That's seriously weird. I just can't imagine adults reading your book. Kids, sure. But *adults* . . . I guess it really is this big deal, huh?"

"Hmm. It's hard to believe."

"Sure is. I know the reviewers like that whole blend of humor and spiritual lessons and stuff, but . . . I don't know . . . it just feels kind of freaky to me. Like, one minute you're cracking one-liners, the next you sound like a suicidal version of Gandhi."

There's an explanation for that, but I'm not going to share it with Matt. Besides, once my editor mixed up the humorous and serious parts of the book, they balanced each other well. At least, that's what everyone said.